The Fighting Man

A 1066 Adventure

Walking across a ploughed hillside above the battlefield on an early autumn morning, turning ideas in my mind and turning clods with my boot, I picked up a fragment of iron, decayed by time and acid earth but heavy and alive.

I had found Ash.

Thomas Croft

The Fighting Man is an adventure story to be enjoyed by readers whether or not they are familiar with the events before, during and after the Battle of Hastings in 1066. Some names and terms, which I have italicised, might, however, need explanation and this can be found in the notes and glossary at the end of the book.

Cover illustrations by John Rabou (www.johnrabou.nl)

ISBN-13: 978-1978199262
ISBN-10: 1978199260

1. ASH

When, at last, he was old, Ash would try to tell his grandchildren about his adventures: the invasion, the battle, good times, hard times and, most important, the wonder of his friendship with Gam and how it changed everything.

Mostly, though, the grandchildren didn't listen. He was a village elder. They paid him respect and brought him little gifts of soft meat. They crushed nuts and mixed them with berries to be gummed and chewed with his stumpy, broken teeth then, gifts bestowed, duty done, the children would soon drift away between the huts, back into the fields and wood, back to their chores and games. Unlike Ash, they were busy and he missed and envied them their busy-ness, their chatter and purpose and quarrelling and gossip. He had his spot, a bench in the sun. He liked to drink in the warmth that came through the dappled leaves and which, for a time, relieved the ache in his limbs. He watched the children run and trip and climb and fall. They carried and pulled and heaved and shovelled and chopped. Never still. He looked at his hands, scarred by a lifetime's work, a missing finger, and remembered what, once, they could make; his legs which, once, ran for him all the day and he remembered when he had been young and busy, too. The wonder of it. The memory of it. The times before the great changes came into the world. Before the invaders from Normandy. Before the horses and armour and when he ran freely in the woods.

One boy listened. An odd boy who liked to sit on a log next to the bench making shapes with a stick in the dirt. He listened but, Ash knew, wasn't right in his mind. Didn't speak. They weren't sure he could hear at all. A small boy who took the knocks and kicks from the others but who always smiled and who seemed always ready to listen. Perhaps he found a refuge there knowing he was safe from the fists and stones and insults while he sat with the old man and Ash was reminded of himself as a boy when, so often, he had been alone and had no voice. The days before he met Gam.

He told the boy.

The land was quieter then. Not like now with this noise and bustle of coming and going. Not that we weren't busy. There was always the sound of chopping and trees falling in the woodland. Those trees: how they came down. It would take three long days for a gang of men to fell an oak, strip its limbs and chop out the boards. And the wood belonged to us all, it was free and it was our living. We chopped trees and cut great lengths of timber for building and fencing. The strength and smell of it. The undergrowth, the rapid grow back of briar and brush, this was the children's work: clearing the scrub. At the end of the day hands were torn and cut, knees and ankles bloodied, great piles of cuttings, briars and dead wood to burn. And the fires. Starting the fires and burning away the scrub. Always work to do.

I remember a day,

Ash told the boy,

I remember a day in the wood when it felt all wrong and that was the day I found Gam.

And, as if in answer to an unasked question,

Yes, Gam was a Norman, talked French of course but also talked English better than me. Always seemed half and half: half us and half them; half here and half somewhere else. But, mostly, Gam was just Gam.

I knew about them – the Normans. There was always talk. We all knew that the Duke, William, wanted to take our land. But our King had gathered his forces and was waiting to meet the invaders on the coast. These were days of expectation and false alarm. The old King – good King Edward - was dead. That happened in the hard winter, after Christmas. The news came to our village and we said prayers and held a fast – that's nothing to eat – until our stomachs shrieked and shrank. Then, just as we were used to being hungry, more news came of a coronation at the new church in London. Hurrah! we shouted for a new king: Harold who was chosen by the *Witan*. It was a special celebration because this was our own Lord Harold Godwinson the ruler of all of Wessex. And now we feasted until our stomachs were swollen and groaning.

With the start of spring there was more news. The traitor, William of Normandy was readying for war and was sailing from France. I was just a boy but I'd seen Normans. Plenty of them lived hereabouts and we met Norman travellers and traders from France and further off with strange clothes and speech who came back and fore across the sea, ready to buy and with their packs of stuff to sell. They came through our little hamlet, which was off the high ridge in the weald about a day's walk from the sea at Hastings. We lived just off the heights atop of three valleys where streams ran into rivers, rivers into lakes and the lakes into the sea. It was a spare living but we got by with the woodland, our meadows, our hens, geese, hogs and fish from the lakes. Near us was the Bodle Street, the ridge track that had been made and travelled by men and beasts over more years than anyone could remember. Parts of it ran straight and true, a good road made, we were told, by the Old People, dry and well drained on the high ground. Elsewhere it became wet and sticky with clay. Narrower tracks came off the ridge and into the forest and one of these, which we called Freckly Lane because of the way the light fell through the trees, came into our little hamlet which was mostly a muddle of huts. Travellers came through from the ports of Rye and Winchelsea mainly going west towards Lewes or north to London or further. Some found their way down the lane and stopped in the village to trade and to give us stories about what they had seen and heard and, they told us, there was no doubting it, great preparations were being made for war on the other side of the sea. The Normans were coming.

In those early days of spring the lackeys came – the servants of the *thanes*, our masters - with their orders, bossing us about. The *fyrd* was made ready. That was all the men of fighting age in our village. It was our duty to our *thane* and our honour to the King. The messages were sent from village to village. The men of the *fyrd* were to be readied to fight and to give the King two months of service.

All that spring the men, children too, kept busy. They didn't have much by way of weapons and most did what they could with the tools they had to hand. Scythes, woodaxes and *seaxes* were sharpened. Billhooks were mounted on long shafts and some made bows and arrows. Sling shots and catapults were got ready and old shields, in the family for years, were taken down from the rafters and repaired or made anew. We were an army of farm boys armed with farming implements which, we knew, could have little effect against the Normans with their chain mail and cruel cunning, their broadswords, their crossbows and, what we dreaded most, the galloping war horses.

Whenever I could I would go off to help Till. He could make and mend anything of metal. Till with his smoking, glowing forge, his charcoal-blackened skin and his big smile. Till, hammering and sweating. He was big, he was gentle and like a father to me. He could take a piece of iron and heat and shape it and sharpen it into a *seaxe*. That's a knife smaller than a sword but bigger than a dagger. When a boy began to be a man he was given his own *seaxe*. We used it for everything: clearing scrub, shaving wood, cutting our food. And, if needed, it could be good for fighting, too. Till made other weapons. Weapons for the bold men. He'd even made weapons for the *housecarls*: they were the King's special soldiers who guarded him with their lives. Great big men they were, like the Norsemen. They could be fun: they could pick you up swing you through the air and chuck you like a bag of grain and another would catch you. But you wouldn't want to cross them when they were in their fighting mood. A *housecarl* in a battle is a tempest, the fiercest of storms blazing thunder and lightning. A single *housecarl*, it was said, was worth four English footsoldiers and, they reckoned, better than six Normans.

My father was called to join the *fyrd*. He had no choice because, although he had once been a *freeman*, he had sold his land and labour at the time of the great hunger. That was a time before I could remember, when I was an infant and when I lost my mother and two sisters. Plenty, I was told, had been taken from the village in that time. There were too many mouths to feed and, sometimes, gangs of the slavers would come through looking for children to buy. They'd buy a child and make it work cruelly or take it down to the ships at Rye or Pevensey. They'd fatten them and pinch their cheeks to make them look healthy, like they were hogs, and sell them to serve the rich merchants. The villagers didn't like it but they shrugged it off. A hard life, they said, but better than starvation.

Although times were better now, Dad had lost everything – and much of that was his fault – and now he was in thrall to a *churl*. That's about as bad as it can get, like being a slave and having to work land which used to be yours for another's profit. So when the call-up came he was pleased to go with the *fyrd* even though he had next to nothing of his own to fight for. That was his duty to the King. In turn I had a son's duty to his father and I went with him carrying our spare clothes in a basket on my back. It was a great outing. We were away for weeks, mostly men and boys but some of the girls too and the younger women.

It was a mild spring. We slept out under blankets in the warm air on ground that was dry. We built fires and sang songs. We wrestled each other and practised moves with wooden swords and spears. We made shields from lime wood and leather and decorated them with dyes, coloured stones and any little scraps of iron we could find. Some of the men had battleaxes and, when the drink was in them, they danced and swung them in the air and whirled in circles round and round the fire. They were only farmers and woodmen but in the dancing firelight with the clapping of hands, beating of drums and the shrieking blasts of the horns they thought themselves the greatest *housecarls*. They'd have mock fights, wrestling each other, slapping and pretend hitting. Sometimes it got out of hand and became a real fight and then the children knew to get out of the way. We'd scarper and hide and next day we'd see them getting up, holding their heads from the drinking and beatings, examining their bruises and scars, laughing it off with each other, clasping hands, swearing eternal friendship and behaving more like children than us.

These were good times while they lasted. I remember the nights when we'd sit round a great fire with sparks like ladders climbing into the dark sky. That's when the sign came: *a big star* that moved across the heavens. It was there every night and it caused a deal of consternation. There were arguments and even blows exchanged about the sign. Most looked on the dark side: that it was a portent of bad things to come. Others that it was a vision from God, a finger written in the firmament, the rising star of the new King. We sat there at night listening to what was said. Most of the men were ignorant gossips and it got them going off on speculations and scary stories about strange shapes and moving figures in the heavens, hideous creatures coming out of the sea with eyes and mouths to gobble up children. Stories about goblins, pooks and spirits who lived in the misty marshes. They clawed the air with their hands as they described the cockatrice which is a creature half cockerel and half serpent waiting to attack lost travellers in the wood. We shivered and drew closer to the fire, afraid to leave the company and the light, trying not to look up at the star because, it was said, the sight of it would make you mad and blind if you looked too long and too hard.

But, whenever I was frightened, I always remembered what Till used to say. Good, kind, sensible Till who hadn't come with the *fyrd* because, he said, it was better for him to keep the forge and the metalwork going. We all knew though, it was because he had no appetite for a fight. In this he was without blame because, we also knew, this was not cowardice but kindness. Till was a puzzle: a big strong man but gentleness itself. He had two children: the elder a son, Lang, tall and strong like his father but headstrong, always in the front line of the *fyrd*; and the younger, a daughter, Elfhild, small and shy. We called her Elfin. Till had told me that talk of monsters was all nonsense. It was Till who gave me my first *seaxe*. It should have been Dad. That was the tradition: the *seaxe* gets given by father to son but, by that time, Dad had already got caught up in his fastness and meanness like something diseased in his mind. No matter that it wasn't from Dad. I knew this *seaxe* was special. I helped Till in the making, holding the blade with the tongs and beating it thin and flat and sharp. It was, Till swore, my very own *seaxe*. I held it up while it glowed red like a flame and I plunged it in the tub of water. I heard the water shriek and saw it boil and bubble. Till told me to watch the steam that came up, to breathe it in and to whisper a secret name for my blade which I did and I'll never tell that word to another living soul. The *seaxe*, he said solemnly, would cut true for me and be a tarnation to anyone who stole it or tried to use it without my say so. He told me that all the time I had the blade with me I need have no fear of spirits or bogarts. That, he said, was just the foolish talk of ignorant old men who were afraid of the dark, afraid of their own shadows. I remember how he looked at me when he gave me the blade. He had blue eyes which drew you in.

'Ash,' he said, 'you can go one of two ways. You can believe me when I tell you it's best to go true as the blade you're holding and true to yourself, finding the courage inside you. Or you can believe those stories which the wronguns will tell you and which will take you from the true path and get you tangled up in ignorance and cowardice.'

I believed him then and I always will.

Yet all that time while we marched on the country roads pretending we were a great army we knew that, back in the village, our hogs and hens and crops were being neglected and it would be hard for those we'd left behind to manage. Wherever we went we had great feasting – we were awash with food and drink and we didn't have to work - but our families at home would be scratching around for bits to eat and tearing their hair with worry wondering what might have happened to us. While we were loitering in the lanes, sleeping under hedges, building fires and looking at the stars, the families in our village would be worn down with toil and scraping around for food. They'd be thinking we'd been killed by the Normans, wondering if we'd ever come back.

To be honest we gave little thought to them so caught up were we in the spell of our success. It was like a charm was on us. We walked on the coast roads from village to village. Many of us, even the older men, had never been so far away from home. We went east along the cliffs to Rye, then along the coast to Romney and inland almost as far as Canterbury but the men of Kent were out saying they could look after themselves thanks very much and they sent us back. Then we worked back westwards across the downland beyond Lewes and into the country that was watery marshland towards Bosham. And there, one day, we saw the King go by with his soldiers and the noblemen on horses. What a sight they were and what a noise they made with the clattering of shields and weaponry. They flew the standards – that's the Dragon for England and then – the first time I saw it – the King's own standard, *The Fighting Man*. The dragon was big and golden, two clawed legs, a snarling head and another face on its tail. *The Wyvern*, that's what the men said when they saw it. *It's the Wyvern* and a cheer went up. The *wyvern*, the men said, was a dragon that could spit fire from its mouth and its tail. And then a louder cheer for *The Fighting Man*, a flag that glittered with gold and jewels in the light. On it a figure of a soldier with an axe raised high above his head. *It's the King*, we shouted. *That's the King. There he is*. And there, in the midst of his *housecarls* rode the King. He wasn't wearing his war armour. None of the nobles were. They had long green cloaks. And alongside each one, on a smaller horse and dressed in finery was a man with a hawk on his arm. The hawks had a hood on them and long coloured ribbons trailing with the silver *vervels*, that's the rings that bind the *jesses*, the leather laces, to the hawker's wrist, winking in the light. What a position that would be, I thought, to be the bearer of the King's falcon. We gave the King and his nobles such a cheer – a cheer so loud like, I should think, has never been heard. But they gave us hardly a glance. What a bunch of ragamuffins we must have seemed by comparison with those fine men with their painted shields, their flying standards and clanking weapons riding horses with gold cloths under the saddles and coloured trinkets hanging from the reins. Then there were the marching men: foot soldiers with great long spears, men with swords, archers with long bows on their backs and quivers of arrows bristling, all laughing and chatting to each other as they walked along like they were on holiday. Onlookers came running out to give them little gifts of flowers or some fruit wrapped up in green leaves or a horn cup of drink. Then the camp followers came tagging along after. There were tumblers, jugglers, dancers, all sorts of strange folk. There was music, drums and horns, which got caught up with the dust and smell of horses, sweat, leather and the stink of grease which they use to keep the wet out of their armour and weapons. What a glorious procession and what a wonderful racket.

Yet, what were we? Not real soldiers. Not much better than a troupe of camp followers ourselves. Ragged, dirty, dancing and shouting, our dogs yapping and running. Watching the rabble following the army was like looking at ourselves and we felt a bit ashamed, seeing ourselves for what we were, a bunch of bumpkins trying to behave like fighting men. We did a good job, certainly, of frightening the country people. We could show off and talk a lot of big talk about what we could do. They seemed as frightened of us as they were of the Normans. And yet, as the days wore on and, every night, the star was back in its place, there was great fear in the countryside. The men of the *fyrd* liked to tell stories to

11

the gaping villagers and herders they met about the terror of the Normans, so we were looked to as protectors. The people we met were happy to give us all they had in return for our promise to protect their pathetic little huts, their tiny meadows, their patches of vegetables and plots where a few hens scratched and squabbled and a hog or two was fattening for the winter pot. They joined us in our shouts: *The King! The King!* and, mostly, *Out! Out!* And for that they were happy to give and we were greedy and ready to take.

But seeing the King's soldiers had disheartened us. Our men were strong but they knew more about farming and tree-felling than fighting. We boys knew, for all the bragging and bravado, we were weak up against real soldiers. Looking round at our rag tag army we knew that most would show a dirty pair of heels if ever they saw a Norman soldier. All our talk now was of the great army of King Harold and his *housecarls* who were like giants and gods to us. We knew in our hearts we would be happy for them to be at the front of the fighting. We felt secure, too, confident that they could never be overcome.

We walked to the edge of the land, stood on the cliffs and looked out to sea. Sometimes there were boats and, thinking it might be the Norman fleet, we'd hide in the bracken until we saw the dragon on the sails and knew they were the King's boats. Then we'd be up and cheering and hallooing and waving. The men on the boats would whistle and shout and wave back.

2. ARI

Working our way back along the coast we arrived again in the port of Rye where we saw the men with their falcons and, for the first time, I saw Gam. He looked to me just like a boy dressed in a strange bird costume, one of the merry troupe of performers who were drumming up business and who were especially pleased to see our army of gawpers with coins to chink in their purses. Gam, the birdboy, wore a long brown linen tunic sewn all over with coloured rags which were meant to be feathers. His arms were covered in long ribbons to make them look like wings which he flapped up and down as he ran around hopping like a bird about to fly. He had yellow leggings and funny green shoes. I couldn't see his face properly, only his eyes which peeped out anxiously from a sort of bird mask with a long yellow beak and a red coxcomb on the top of his head both made from stiff straw. Sometimes he'd run up to children in the crowd and pretend to peck them and they would squeal and run away. There was the playing of horns and drums; there were tumblers and jugglers who skipped and danced but, up close, they looked ragged, thin and shabby. Some were dressed as animals: a unicorn, a dragon, a bear; some were dressed as soldiers. There were fools in outlandish Norman armour, their cloaks coloured and made to look like chain mail which they kept tripping over. Some had small shields and weapons of wood and straw which they poked at each other and at people in the crowd. Everyone laughed at them, and booed and jeered. The falconers were the best. There were three of them - and the birdboy. Two of them, one thin, one fat, walked proudly with an arm outstretched and each with a beautiful hawk on their leather gauntlets. Behind them came a big man, like a giant, carrying a perch on which crouched a huge, hooded bird, the biggest any of us had ever seen. It made us gasp in wonder.

We, the men of the *fyrd*, formed a corridor to keep the crowd back as the merry troupe marched to the top of the town. There we had the best places as, together with the townsfolk, we sat in a circle on the green to watch the show. The tumblers rolled, jumped and leaped over each other. A strong man lifted a boy from the crowd and held him above his head, the sweat running down his face. A tiny man, a fool with a painted face, a costume of rags and ribbons and feathers in his hair, ran around hitting people with a bladder on a stick and pinching the women. Sometimes he'd sit in their laps, cuddling up to them pretending to be a baby to make them scream. One of the men piddled in a pot then looked around as though he didn't know where to empty it. Then the fool tiptoed up behind him and grabbed the pot. The man chased him and the fool kept running at the crowd with the big pot as if to throw all the piddle over the people making them shriek and laugh and scatter but, each time, pulling back at the last minute until finally he ran, tripped and emptied the pot over a group of frightened children huddling together. But all that came out were wood shavings. It was a really good trick and I couldn't see how he did it.

Jugglers threw leather balls high into the air and caught them cleverly. One man juggled with two wooden stools and then with a real sword. We knew it was sharp because he asked someone from the audience to come forward and to hold up a turnip. He swung the sword round and sliced through the turnip with a clean swipe. He threw the sword in the air making us gasp as he grabbed it each time by the hilt as we knew if he took it by the blade he'd have his hand cut off. We stamped and shouted our appreciation smacking our hands together, whooping and waving our sticks and spears. Those who could do it wagged their tongues and made that warbling sound in their throats so that your skin prickles. I did some of my bird noises.

Next there was a mock battle. The men dressed as foolish Normans ran around the circle shouting their battle cries and all the time bumping into each other and tripping over. Two men dressed as English soldiers with real weapons pushed their way through the crowd and, as we cheered, they chased the Normans round and round hitting them and kicking their backsides until they ended up in a heap of bodies in the middle. A man came in, walking slowly, dressed in a fine glittery cloak and wearing a gold crown which, we knew, represented King Harold. He climbed on top of the heap of Normans holding a flag with the *wyvern* on it and the crowd shouted, stamped and warbled with delight.

The two English soldiers then gave a fighting display, whirling their swords around their heads, jumping and whooping. They slashed at each other with the broadswords giving a grunt and a shout with each blow, the other leaping back just in time from the tip of the sharp, singing blade. After fighting for a short while they handed their swords to the fool who took them with a bow, staggering under their weight. He carried them round the circle for the crowd to see and cheer. He then collected two stout sticks and gave them to the men who fought with them making a loud clatter, parrying the blows and pushing against each other. By the time they had finished they were both wet with sweat and panting from the exertion. The soldiers, jugglers and tumblers all got together and did a jolly dance, leaping and capering with music from the drums and horns. It was wonderful and I have to say this show had a great effect on me. Growing up on the edge of our quiet little hamlet I'd seen nothing like it before.

After the show there was food and drink and a good deal of merriment. There was wrestling and dancing and games of *hazard* with the dice. Amongst all this activity the master of the birdmen and his assistants set up a table on which there was a pile of shining bracelets. The birdboy banged a drum and danced around to attract a crowd and the master made a speech. I was pushed to the back and couldn't see or hear easily. The crowd was dense and jostling and I didn't like the stink so I kept to the edge. From what I could hear the master was talking about the star in the heaven. He was quite honest with us and confessed the truth that he didn't know rightly if it was a good sign or a bad. All he could say was that he'd travelled far and wide and the star wasn't only here, it was in other parts too. The wisest people he'd spoken to believed, he said, that it was an eye watching our conduct from the heavens. It might, he said, bring fortune or it might bring misery. We all knew we were living in troubled times which, he believed, had disturbed the mysterious star. How should we best protect ourselves in these difficult times? By trusting in God and living rightly, he said, being honest and hard-working. However, and here he winked his eye and tapped a finger against the side of his long sharp nose, a little magic from the cunning folk might do no harm. He himself, he said, wore a special charm, a bracelet made from a mysterious metal taken from deep in the ground in a secret place on the far side of the land. He wasn't sure it would give him protection against the evil of the eye in the sky but wiser folk than he, and especially those in the east, wore these and he held up a glittering handful of the bracelets. The wise folk, he said, told how the metal had a charm which was a powerful shield. Such folk swore by it, said the master and, surely, they couldn't all be wrong. Since wearing the bracelet, he himself had felt younger and stronger than ever before. And here he said something which made the women in the crowd, especially, shriek and laugh. It made him feel safer, too, as he travelled the seas and the roads and easier as he slept at night with the strange star travelling overhead in the heaven. Once he used to be troubled by a damp cough and a pain in the gut but these had eased. He no longer had bad dreams, only the sweetest of visitations in the night and, again, he said something which made the crowd shriek and laugh. He had brought some of these bracelets with him, only a few were left and wherever he went folk demanded them. Could you think, he asked, of a nicer gift for a wife or child or sweetheart? He could, he declared holding his hand on his heart, be a rich man if he had taken all that had been offered for the charmed bracelets but it was not in his nature to do this. He wanted everyone to share and, because he liked the look of the people here, he asked for very little in return: a silver penny was all, or if there were people with no coin, a brooch or buckle might do. There was a clamour of people pushing forward to buy the charms and the master and the birdboy were soon doing brisk business. So many people were trying to buy that there was scuffling and the big falconer and the strongman had to stand at the front of the table to stop it being pushed over.

Later in the afternoon there was more banging of drums and blowing of horns for the falconry show. One of the falconers stood in the centre of the circle twirling a long leather leash with some meat on the end and first one then the other of the small hawks flew round and above our heads before landing on his gauntlet. Each time the birdboy ran round and round in a dance like a hawk, urging us to clap our hands and shout. One man strode to one side of the circle and one to the other and the two hawks flew back and forth trailing their long, coloured ribbons from gauntlet to gauntlet. The men then walked stiffly round the circle holding their arms out so that we could all look closely at the beautiful falcons. The drums began to beat and there was a gasp as the big hawk was brought into the circle on its perch. The master spoke to the crowd, pointing to the bird and telling us where it was from. He said this was a special bird, not a hawk but an eagle, the biggest of its kind in the whole world. He said that they were taking it to Winchester to show it to his majesty in his court. He said the bird had come from a distant mountainous country and had been brought through danger and difficulty over land and sea to England. We, he said, would be the first in the country to see it fly and, with a flourish, he removed the hood. The bird blinked in the light and turned its great head to look at the crowd. I felt it looking at me and I saw sadness in its eyes.

The three birdmen and the boy now grouped themselves together next to the eagle.

'Before we display this majestic bird,' the master said, 'we must introduce ourselves and I will tell you a story.'

I immediately sat up straight. I loved nothing better than a story. I'd heard stories from travellers by the fire in the village and sometimes a *gleeman* brought songs and sounds.

'We all have our shadows in the animal kingdom,' the master declared. 'Whoever you are, wherever you are you have a friend in nature, a secret shadow. You might have heard it talked of, a *familiar* the Old People called it, in the sky or in the wood looking out for you.' He spoke so eloquently and made the most wonderful gestures as he spoke, making shapes with his hands in the air. I listened intently but there was an annoying family behind me, chattering and fidgeting and eating. They kept making unkind comments, too. For a moment I missed what was said then saw the master looking slowly and steadily around the encircled audience, pointing his finger. 'Take a close look at your friends and neighbours, especially when they don't know they are being watched,' he said. 'Is there something in the way that man sits,' and he pointed at a man in the crowd, causing laughter, 'or that woman laughs,' more pointing, 'or that lad stares with his wide eyes,' pointing at me, I think, 'that shows you what their familiar might be? They might do this,' and he threw himself down on all fours and moved his jaw cleverly as though chewing the cud and we all laughed because he imitated a cow so well and someone in the audience mooed and others took it up. The master raised a hand to silence them, 'Do theaeeaaaay,' his voice bleating , 'sound like a goat when they taaaaaalk? Do they…?'

'Stink like a hog,' shouted someone from the crowd and there was laughter which the master simply ignored.

'Do they sing as sweet as a linnet when they're stirring the pot and think no-one can hear them?' and he did an imitation of a woman cooking and swinging her hips to make us laugh. 'Do they sniff around into other people's business and steal like a fox?'

'Lot of old rubbish talk,' said the man behind me with his mouth full of food and his children joined in with their own rough comments so, again, I missed what was said but saw the master had suddenly changed his tone as if letting us in on a secret.

'My familiar is....you can see.' He held his head up, his black bristly hair sticking upright, his thin curved nose took on the form of a beak and he lifted his black cloak with his elbows so that it stuck out like wings. 'It is....?' he looked round at the crowd. There were some jeers and rude words which he ignored.

'Crow,' I said it quietly to myself at the same time someone called it clearly, *Crow*.

The master lifted his head and gave three distinctive life-like, crow-like caws. 'Yes,' he said, 'I am Crow.' He pointed to the big man who had carried the eagle, 'And this man?' and the man stooped and stepped forward stolidly as though pulling a heavy load making horns on his head with his hands.

'Ox,' I said to myself. I heard one of the family behind me mutter, *'Orse*, in a know-all tone and was pleased to hear my quiet voice given a loud echo from the crowd.

'Yes,' said the master, Crow, 'he is as big and as strong. He is Ox. And here?' he gestured comically to the fat man. 'Well?'

Again some shouts and rude comments from the crowd but then the fat man squatted down on his haunches and sprang forward, stopped, looked round, opened his mouth to give a grotesque croak before hopping forward again.

'Frog,' I said quietly. I was enjoying this. The name was shouted and I was pleased by the confirmation. 'Yes,' said Crow, 'he is Frog. So, there,' with a flourish, 'you have us. We are the falconers, the birdmen from France: Frog, Ox and....,' he gave a theatrical bow...., 'Crow.'

'What about 'im?' shouted a man from the crowd, pointing at the birdboy.

'Ah,' said Crow as if he'd forgotten, as if taken by surprise, 'ah....the child, our little bird, our little eagle,' and he stroked the feathers on the breast of the big bird beckoning to the boy who ran and sat cross-legged at his feet. 'And our story....'

I found myself adopting the same cross-legged pose, listening alertly.

'A child, like this one, had a mother.....'

'Well we've all 'ad mothers,' shouted someone rudely.

'Looking at your ugly face, my fellow,' said Crow turning to stare hard at the heckler, 'I think we can all guess what kind of mother you had!' and there was loud laughter and derision. 'Had a mother,' Crow repeated and the audience hushed as he continued the story, 'who was a noble lady in the land across the sea to the north. Her lord had gone on campaign. The warriors in those parts are drawn to war in distant lands and the lady was left alone...'

There were loud *Aaaaahs* from the crowd and I joined in quietly.

'The days passed. She watched, she waited. His lordship did not return. Every day she stood in the cold bitter wind at her door, always watching. But nothing.' He suddenly struck a pose, standing with hands on hips like a woman, peering this way and that – a perfect imitation - and we laughed. 'Except….except,' he hushed us, 'one thing did she see, each day, circling high above the mountains which grow tall in those lands. A bird. At first a mere speck in the sky but,' he shielded his eyes with his hands, looked up at the sky and pointed and I found myself looking up, too. 'As each day it came lower and closer she could see……she saw it was a huge golden bird circling lower and lower.'

The birdboy stood up and ran, gliding, he seemed to fly in circles coming closer and closer to Crow the storyteller.

'Coming closer and closer until one day it alighted on the branch of a tree almost within touching distance of this noble lady. What a magnificent creature. An eagle. It stood tall and proud, golden in the light of day, its eyes flashing like sparkling jewels.'

The birdboy stood tall, putting his head on one side then the other in perfect imitation. Crow had us now. He held us. Even the family behind me had started to listen.

'And the woman told the bird, the eagle, of her sadness and loneliness. She told him how she longed for a child whom she could love and who would keep her company and the bird put its head to one side and listened.'

The birdboy cocked his head as though listening.

'Every day the eagle visited and every day came a little closer until, soon, it was feeding out of her hand.'

The birdboy hopped up to Crow and pretended to peck from his outstretched hand making us laugh at his near-perfect imitation.

'Each evening the woman would prepare something, a tasty morsel, something the bird would enjoy. And this noblewoman and the eagle became closer and closer.'

A woman in the crowd sniggered explosively. Crow stopped, turned towards her and gave her a look which made everybody laugh. The woman's friends prodded and pushed her and she went red in the face and covered her head with her hands. 'Yes, madam, they became close. True friends. The lady poured out her heart to the bird until….one day….her lord returned from his travels. He was weary, tired, dirty, cold, beaten by the wind and weather but oh so pleased to be home. There were celebrations, a feast and much joy. In her excitement the lady, now reunited with her *handfast* lord, forgot her friend the eagle. Time passed and, in time, a child was born, just as the woman had wished.' He gestured at the birdboy who stood up and gave a short bow. 'A boy like this child, here. The boy took the father's name as is the custom there but the lady also whispered a secret name, a pet name. When she was alone with the child she called it *Ari* which, in those parts, is the name they give to the eagle.'

'What did 'e say?' the child behind asked his mother. He dropped the food he was eating and the woman cuffed him and he started howling and I couldn't hear what was being said. Why had they come here if they didn't want to listen?

'And all was well in the household,' Crow was saying, 'until, one day, the lady heard a terrible cry and, rushing to the room where her child lay sleeping she saw her lord standing by the child's bed with her old friend, the eagle, hanging…dead…from his hand. He had wrung its neck and its lifeblood ran dripping on to the rushes on the floor. 'What have you done?' she cried and the man, her lord, shouted back in anger, 'I saw this terrible bird come in through the door. It perched on the end of the bed looking at our child. A moment later and it would have carried the baby off in its great claws. I seized it by the neck and dashed it to the ground…..'

There was muttering in the crowd. 'Nonsense,' I heard someone say.

'The lady cried aloud. The lord was puzzled. Why was she distressed? Why didn't she seem pleased that he'd saved her child from the talons of this cruel bird? The lady grieved because, she knew, the bird had come only to pay homage to her child, to give its blessing to the baby she had wished for and talked so much about. In those northern lands the eagle is sacred and she knew that the killing of the bird would bring misfortune. So, weeping, asking for forgiveness she made a place for the eagle in the cold, hard ground. First, though, she cut the talons from the bird and buried them under the hearth. She took the feathers, too, and when she had laid the bird in a secret place she made a little feather cap for her child which, when her lord was away, she would put on the child's head.'

'A what?' said the child behind me.

'An 'at,' snapped his mother, 'an 'at of fevers.'

The master gestured at the birdboy who waggled his head. 'But the child was strange with an eye always on the open doorway and the sky. His only words the high mewing noise made by an eagle calling to its young.' Crow made a mewing noise which was so good that the great eagle on its perch turned to look at him. 'The child hopped….like a bird. Hopped and jumped like a bird….,' and the birdboy jumped and hopped, '…sometimes, the woman thought her child was flying.' Ox stepped forward, lifted the birdboy and whirled him round, threw him into the air and caught him. 'The child grew. One day, her lord away, the lady put the hat of feathers on the child's head and allowed him out of their hall to play in the sweet cold air. She turned back to fetch a warm cloak for his little shoulders, away only for a moment but, when she returned, the child had gone. She searched everywhere but the child was nowhere to be found. Then, a clatter of wings in a nearby tree. A young eagle looked at her from the bough then flew away, soaring high into the sky…..' The birdboy ran, flapping his ribbon wings, away from Crow's outstretched hand.

'This is all make believe, all nonsense,' repeated someone else behind me and I turned and gave a look because hadn't Crow said this story was true?

'They called the wise woman to help in the search for the child but she told them it was her belief the child was…..a shape shifter…and had gone.'

A shape shifter! This was interesting. I knew about shape-shifters.

'This isn't right,' said someone loudly and a woman stood up and shouted, 'I don't like to hear of these things.'

'Some people believe in shape shifting,' said Crow and raised his hands in a baffled gesture, 'others don't. It's hard to know what to believe.'

'This is all wrong,' said the woman. 'This is ungodly.' She made a great show of walking away. 'You shouldn't be preaching these things. These are things of the dark, the ways of the Old People. I shall tell of you to the holy fathers,' and she marched off.

Crow pulled a puzzled face, 'I am not preaching,' he called after her, 'I am a simple falconer and am only telling the things that I have heard on my journeys.'

'I shall tell,' the woman shouted again. I noticed she was wearing one of the charmed bracelets.

When she was out of earshot, Crow hunched his shoulders, spread his hands and pulled a comical face. 'Well,' he said, 'I suppose you can't please everyone,' and there was some laughter. But it was clear he had lost his way. 'These are strange times,' he said and seemed to have forgotten to end his story. I had expected more and my head was muddled. Was the boy, Ari, indeed a shape-shifter and was that the same boy now running around the circle in a costume?

As I was thinking this over the big bird was released and flew low to the ground then high over our heads to land on a perch that had been set up behind us where one of the falconers now stood on the far side of the green. A whistle from Ox in the circle and the bird came back to its perch in the centre. It did this three or four times. The birdboy now ran and hopped then stood in the middle of the circle. Crow gave him a leather glove to put on and a piece of meat to hold. He made an announcement to say how dangerous this pass would be. Again, the eagle flew out of the circle and landed on the far perch. Now the boy held the piece of meat aloft in his gloved hand. Ox whistled and the bird flew low and fast and snatched the morsel of meat from the glove. It sat on the perch devouring it while, again, we clapped and cheered.

Crow was talking again and pointing at the crowd saying he wanted someone with a brave heart to come forward to feed the bird. Before I knew what was happening the man behind me who had been eating with his mouth open grasped my arm and held it up. I turned on him angrily and shook my head at Crow who was now pointing at me. The people near me were shouting encouragement and a woman behind me was pushing me with her foot but I wouldn't budge. Then the birdboy and the little fool with the bladder came and grabbed my arms and pulled me up and into the centre of the circle where it was all a blur of noise and laughter. They put a glove on my hand. It was much too big and went up nearly to my armpit and all the crowd laughed. 'This lad,' shouted Crow above the noise, 'has a familiar and his name must be Sparrow.' There was more laughter. Ox came forward and gave me a piece of stinking meat and showed me how to hold it with the glove. The big bird on the perch flapped its wings and looked at me with its great sad eyes. The birdboy was showing me how to hold my arm aloft with the meat. He spoke to me quietly, 'Not too tight,' he said. 'Hold it loose and don't be scared.'

The crowd went quiet as the bird flew off again. The birdboy was next to me. He gestured at me and I stretched my arm into the air. I saw the bird flying directly at me faster than I thought possible: a great dark low swift shadow. I couldn't help myself. I ducked down and the bird missed the pass. The crowd hooted with laughter. The bird flew off again and circled. This time the boy stood closer to me. I couldn't take my eyes off him. He came closer and held my shoulder, telling me to just stand still. I shut my eyes as the bird came at me a second time. It hit my arm hard, sending me on to my backside and snatching not just the meat but the glove too and flying with it to the perch. The crowd shouted and laughed some more. I sat on the ground, my hand stinging from the blow, looking at the bird on the perch hungrily eating the meat. The boy pulled me up and the audience whooped and stamped. He took off the hood he was wearing and I saw his face for the first time. It was round and freckly and pretty, red from the heat of the mask and the running. I stared open-mouthed because the birdboy was a girl. She stared back, frowned, rudely stuck out her tongue. Suddenly, she was magnificent and my heart was full.

Crow silenced the crowd with a wave of his hand pointing at me. They whooped again. He held up the golden crown the King had been wearing and which, close to, I could see was just straw and fakery. He said something about a reward for my bravery: did they think I deserved a golden crown? The crowd shouted a loud *Yes!* and they were laughing because they had seen the fool with the bladder creeping up behind me making faces and holding a goose egg. As I turned to see why people were laughing and pointing the fool smashed the egg on my head so that the yellow yolk ran down over my face. There was more laughter, shouts, Crow was saying something about the lad wanted a golden crown and what could be more golden than the yolk from an egg. Oh, how they laughed at that. The little man with the bladder danced around me and Crow shouted out that now he had not one but two fools. The birdboy who was a girl ran towards me with some straw to wipe the egg away but I'd had enough. I ran back into the crowd, through them and away, their laughter and hoots of derision following me as I ran through the deserted town.

I ran down to the harbour and, retching from the smell, washed the stinking mess from my head and hair in the shallows of the sea.

That was just about the end of my adventures with the *fyrd*. Of course the others had to spin the joke out for as long as possible. They mocked me and called me *birdboy* and *Sparrow*, *egghead* and *fool*, laughing and slapping each other on the back. It drove me more into myself and further and further away from others. I thought a lot about the show in Rye the antics of the girl dressed as a birdboy and, especially, Crow's story about Ari. I wondered a great deal about shape shifting. But I heard the men in the *fyrd* scoffing at it all, saying what nonsense it was, just stories for children and old women. They talked more about their games and betting, what they'd had to eat and drink, the coins they'd lost on the throw of the dice in hazard. The master with the birdmen, they said, was a rogue and out to rob fools of what was in their purses. I noticed, though, that they were all wearing the charmed bracelets that Crow had sold them in exchange for their silver pennies.

Our little army began to break up. The call of the land and of our families at home was too strong. The *fyrd* had an obligation to the King. We would serve for two months. We couldn't spare more. Soon we knew that time had gone. The villagers, too, were less friendly when they saw how we wasted food and drink, costing so much to feed and doing so little practical work. There had been too much drinking, some bad behaviour, some thieving, squabbles: it couldn't go on. The villagers wanted to see the back of us. They'd expected the Normans. The Normans hadn't come. The season was moving to more warmth and the country folk, always

29

busy, now had more than ever to do. What was growing needed to be nurtured before the time came for reaping, harvesting and storing. It was the march of the seasons towards winter that the villagers feared more than the march of a supposed Norman army. The food, the hospitality for our ragged army soon dried up. We were sent on our way.

We came back to our homes and picked up the pieces where we'd left off. It wasn't that we didn't think the Normans would ever come but we felt secure knowing the King was on the coast. *No need to fear an invasion,* said the wise heads, *while the King stands ready.* But others: *he's cunning that William.* And now, whenever the woodland went quiet or felt wrong we lifted our heads from our work and wondered.

3. AXEFACE

It was then I saw Gam again. She was lost in the wood and I found her and I hid her. Well, it was Misty who found her. She's a good dog with a sharp nose on her, especially if food is about. And, that day, we were both hungry.

It was a black day. Since the *fyrd* I'd kept away from others, tired of the jokes and taunts and bullying and I was in one of my black moods. I'd had another clout from Ern because of the hogs. I was tired from running. So much of my time spent running. Running to fetch and carry, running after the hogs. The worst is the hogs belonged not to us but to Ern. It was Dad's responsibility to look after them but he got no reward from it. And so often I'd find myself running from him, his bad temper and harsh words. Sometimes he'd hit out at me but not like Ern and the older boys. Always they were quarrelling and they were rough and heavy handed, too ready to give a clout or throw a punch. I think they took pleasure in it. Dad was less harsh but since we'd come back from the *fyrd* he'd not seemed right. He made his living, mostly, from the woodland: stakes, pegs, ash handles for tools, willow for baskets, good hornbeam for charcoal, oak for building. He was a good woodman, could pick up a piece of wood and look at it and sniff it and tell you what it was ready for, if it was seasoned and ripe for building or too wet and sappy. But, more and more, he was in a muddle of confusion, sleeping badly and late, not able to fix himself on anything, leaving more and more for me to do so our little bit of land, the hut and tiny barn, were mostly in a mess.

That day we were weeding and clearing in the fields and it was slow, hard work. Since we'd been away the crops had withered, the weeds and vermin had got in amongst them. We knew it would be a hard winter and we needed to get our grain and root vegetables into dry storage. The animals, too, needed fattening. Then there was a shout. The hogs were out. They'd rooted out the stakes and got out through the fence. A hog can make the difference between life and starvation in the winter and, in the summer, they need to breed and grow which means constant watching and tending. They were contrary beasts and, any chance they got, and they'd be off like they knew what was in store for them. I was the one, of course, who got the blame. It wasn't my fault. Fact is I didn't like the hogs. They were a nuisance: messy and noisy. The hogs would go for you, too, if you gave them half a chance and if you had a bite from those teeth – that was poison. People died from a hog bite. I didn't want to spend my life looking after hogs. I wanted to work with Till, making things. I was, I knew even then, good at making. Till always said – and he was right – you've got to find what you're good at and follow it.

When he heard the hogs were out Dad came shouting for me. He would have clouted me had I not kept my distance. I'm not big but I'm quick on my feet. I don't have much to say but I've got a mean side and I showed it to him on my face. He shouted for all to hear that he reckoned I was getting above myself, that I was a troublesome child and we'd never be free of our debts to Ern. Anyway, the upshot was he told me to round up the hogs, fix the fence then clear off. I could be a wild boy of the woods for all he cared, he said, using bad words which I won't say here. So I whistled up Misty and took off.

We ran up to the street then down the track into the wood. A lot of that has been cleared now but, back then, the wood ran thick and wide down from the ridge. Few people went far in there because it was a dark maze of paths, sudden falls and bogs. It was easy to get lost but it was home for me. I'd been born in the wood and had lived in it for as long as I could remember. I knew the tracks, the shortcuts, the secret paths, the safe ground, the sticky unsafe marsh and where there were deep ponds which had no bottom and could swallow you up. Some of these were filled with black stinking water. Others were red which ignorant souls think is blood but is actually, as Till told me, the colour which comes from the heart of iron. And, he said, you can know this by looking at the way the iron rusts in the rain bleeding the same colour.

Being chased off into the wood was nothing to me. I'd been there at all times of year and in all weathers. But I was hungry and, if I'm honest, I felt my aloneness. Our hut was way off on the edge of the village – the poorest part. We didn't see people much as Dad's work in the early summer was mainly in the woodland, clearing, felling and coppicing – that's cutting branches from chestnut trees and using them for stakes. One of my jobs was taking wood up to Till's forge and this was something I liked. The forge was near the top of Freckly Lane close to the Bodle Street, well placed to catch the trade that went back and forth. People gathered there. Till was in the iron business and everyone wanted metal and something made or mended. Other boys would be there, bringing wood and charcoal, their hands and faces black from the smoke and burning. It was warm and bright.

The sparks would fly as Till and Lang hammered out their songs on the big oak block. Walking in the wood I often day-dreamed about being Till's son, like Lang, having a sister like Elfin and working in the warmth of the forge with always some company and chatter. But working for Dad in the wood, I was out in all weathers and mostly on my own. Dad would have had good business if he had stuck at it but, until the debt was paid, what we earned from the wood went to Ern. We had to tend and fatten Ern's hogs although we'd be allowed to take one or perhaps two – usually the smallest and meanest – to keep us going through the winter.

This Ern was what was known in the village as a close body – that is he kept everything close to himself. Ern didn't miss a thing. He'd come along and lean on the fence like he was passing the time of day but all the while his eyes would be wandering over the hogs, counting them – there were thirteen at the time – checking them over. He was a big man in our village and hog breeding and rearing was his pride and joy.

'Is that sow maybe a bit lame youngun?' he'd ask. Or, 'What's she got on her side there – is that a sore?' Always fussing and interfering. And the hogs, I found, were a bit like their master, Ern, a bit like a lot of people: never happy. All a hog wants is to run off further and further into the woods where there are boars and bears and wolves and wild dogs and thieves and all kinds of mischief and where it will get itself eaten. A good hogboy can give a shout and his hogs will come running back home to him like puppies. But I wasn't any good with hogs. I didn't like them and they didn't like me. If they could cause me bother then they'd do it.

I knew, that day, I was in danger of going hungry. I was a growing boy and thought often of my stomach. I was hoping I might run a hare down, or a wild fowl. But I'd run off in haste and I didn't have my sling shot with me. I could usually bring a bird down with a sling shot and there's nothing more comfy than finding a snug hollow in the wood and slowly roasting a plump bird, although fishing in the lake comes a close second: catching a fine trout or a nice bream or perch, gutting it and turning it on a spit over the fire. With my mind turning on food I knew there was nothing for it but, as Till would have told me, to stop fretting and make myself useful. My anger towards Dad and Ern was gnawing at me. I was tempted to let the hogs run off, even chase them further into the wood but that was just my temper and the sensible part of my mind told me it would be best to round them up and to take them back to our compound. I'd be eating humble pie but there's nothing wrong with that if, like Till says, you have a little bit of drink to help it go down.

I was thinking so much about this and feeling so sorry for myself that I nearly ran into the travellers. Luckily I was alerted by the birds. A woodpecker's sharp hammering drummed me out of the thoughts I was wrapped up in. Then a jay lighted on a bough just ahead and called in its fast, sharp voice telling me to look out. But I heard the men coming before I saw them and had plenty of time to pick a spot to hide. I can run through the wood like a mouse over the leaves and I can hide so you'd think me invisible. Misty, too. We've learned to be still and silent. We could do that so well that travellers could pass inches away from us, animals too, while we stand quietly in the scrub or behind a tree. Or sometimes

I'll climb a tree and Misty will hide and we'll watch them go by. We've watched all sorts like that: people, wild hogs, deer. I've seen foxes and otters, wolves even. Once a man came through with a bear on a leash walking behind him just inches from where I was hiding. The bear looked at me, poor thing: a terrible look in its eye. I think it saw me. But the man didn't. He just walked on caught up in his cruelty.

These travellers were well out of their way, far from the path, lost and caught up and cursing in the briars. They were thrashing through the undergrowth and shouting at each other. I didn't understand what they were saying and I knew straightaway they were Normans. They had some fancy gear on: hats with feathers and long woollen cloaks which Norman travellers liked to wear and which are the last thing you want in a wood because they keep getting caught up on the thorns. Their necks were shaved which was the way the Normans wore their hair and their faces were smooth. The most curious thing was the baggage they were carrying. Two of them had tall packs on their backs, bigger than any I'd seen before and all covered over in fancy coloured cloths. I wondered how they could carry them so easily without them toppling over. I guessed they were some sort of peddlers and traders.

Now, instead of hiding, I might have been tempted to show them the road out. There could have been a penny or two in it for me. But the jay's repeated screeching call told me to be cautious and I slipped behind a tree and watched them struggle out of the bushes and on to the path: three men who I quickly recognised. They weren't wearing their fancy show clothes but I could tell these were the French falconers from the show in Rye. The two carrying the tall packs, Frog and Ox, were sweating from the struggle of walking on the muddy and uneven ground. They looked different – grubby and ordinary – away from the crowds, the applause and the show. I guessed what was in their packs. It would be the birds in cages and all their fancy trinkets and dressing up gear. I soon saw what all the noise and commotion was about. The fat packman, Frog, was ill. He kept stopping and emptying his stomach into the bushes, holding his head, groaning and making an awful croaking sound every time he was sick. And, as he bent, the pack on his back swayed forward precariously nearly toppling him over. I guessed what the trouble was. I reckoned he'd been drinking bad water. There's good springs here and bad springs. If you drink from a bad spring you'll be sick. The other two were getting impatient. The master, Crow, who carried a much smaller and smarter bag across his shoulders, was easily recognisable as the thin man who had run the show in Rye. He kept looking round like he knew he was being watched. I didn't like the look of him then any more than I did when I saw him at close quarters before the egg was cracked on my head and he called me *Fool*. There was something in his face that had the feel of ice-cold metal on a winter morning and which cut a fear into me. If you looked at him head on his crow-like face was a thin wedge and, from the side, it was shaped like an axe, smooth like polished iron. An axe can get lodged in a log of wet wood and, do what you will, you can't shift it and it was like that with this man. I had him stuck now in my thoughts and the shape of his name shifted. He became, for me, *Axeface*. He was sharp like an axe, always on edge, a fidget like he had fleas up his tunic, shifting all the time from one foot to the other, talking and, I guessed, cursing impatiently. He and the other packman, the giant, Ox, started to walk on shouting at Frog who, yet again, was bent over retching and feeding the briars and bushes with the contents of his guts. I didn't understand what they were saying but I had the gist of it: they were lost and they were impatient to move on. Then Frog, threw off his pack and dumped his bundle of stuff down, hoiked up his cloak and dropped his breeches, disappearing behind a bush. I reckoned his sickness had got to the runs stage.

While he was making a horrible noise and a stink the other two moved off, shouting over their shoulders, I guessed, that they weren't waiting around for him. At last he came out of the bushes looking a bit thinner, very white in the face and wiping his hands on the grass. He started shouting after the other two – *wait for me*, I guess - and they hollered back – something like, *well hurry up then*. He picked up his gear, struggling to get that ridiculously tall pack on to his shoulders and stumbled on after them. As he went off out of sight I saw he'd left something behind. I nipped out from where I was hiding, Misty a silent shadow beside me, and there, chucked down in the briars was a broadsword. It was dirty but, even at a glance I could see it was a good one. Then I was back in my hiding place as I heard them padding back with more shouting and a heck of a racket as Frog came panting and thrashing through the undergrowth looking for the sword. He stumbled, still moaning and groaning straight up to the bushes where he'd done his business. He stared in disbelief at the ground where the sword had been. Then he got a stick and started whacking and probing in the briars muttering to himself what, I guessed, meant something like: *I know I left it just here.*

Now I knew he could search all day and not find it because the sword wasn't there anymore. I had it, holding it across my thighs as I squatted just a few blade lengths away, Misty next to me, both of us chuckling at the show.

There was more shouting as the other two – Axeface and Ox – came back. Frog was waving his arms, pointing at the ground, pointing at the bushes. The other two didn't want to come near because of the horrible stink that was still in the air. They waited a little way off while he smashed the bushes with his stick, almost sobbing with anger. He kept shouting a word which I think would have been *Thieves, Thieves*. Ox was sniggering but I had my eye on Axeface because, I knew, he was the danger and I quickly noticed the way he worked. He pretended to be watching the hunt for the sword but all the time his eyes were darting round like small birds in a bush and I knew he was watching the wood and I knew he was suspicious. I think he knew someone was there, that they were being watched. And all the time I could feel the weight of the sword – it was a big one – across my thighs, cold but taking up the warmth from my body. I knew it was wrong to steal but I explained it to myself by saying that I doubted the sword came honestly to those men. It was my weapon now.

Suddenly Axeface spoke – sharp and hard. You could tell it was an order. Although he kept muttering and complaining Frog jumped to it and the three of them set off again through the wood, Frog staggering at the rear and turning to look back still unable to believe the sword was lost.

I crept out, rubbed Misty's head in reassurance, and we set off again, deeper into the wood in the opposite direction taken by the falconers. I knew what I had to do now and that was to whistle up the hogs. But, as I walked, an idea like a baby bird was hatching in my mind, chipping away at the inside of a shell trying to get out. Catching sight of the man's sharp face had reminded me of my humiliation at the show in Rye and, slowly, I was thinking of how I might take my revenge. I retraced my steps and crept through the undergrowth and across the thick boggy ground that separated the two sides of the valley we were in. I moved quickly and could soon hear the falconers walking on the other narrow path. I gave a shout, 'Hoi,' muffling my voice with my hand.

'Can you help us?,' came back Axeface's response, 'we're travellers out of our way. Where's the wretched road?'

'Here,' I shouted.

'But it's thick with briars,' he complained, 'there's no way through.'

I tried to deepen my voice, 'Here,' I shouted again.

I could hear them thrashing and cutting. 'Where are you?' shouted Axeface, 'we can't see you.'

'Here.'

'Where?' I heard some splashing and cursing. 'It's wet and muddy,' shouted Axeface, 'this can't be right.'

But by now I'd moved further along the valley, 'Here,' I shouted again.

'Where now?' came the exasperated reply. 'You seem somewhere else now.'

'Here.'

'Where are you?' shouted Axeface. 'We're armed and you'll regret it if you mislead us.'

'Here,' I shouted but now from a different place.

And so it went on. I dodged from tree to tree and led them on a dance. I chuckled as I heard them going deeper into the trickiness of the marsh. I could hear the splash and slurping pull of the bog as it sucked them down to their knees in mud. I heard one of them, Ox I think, falling and roaring, Frog croaking with fear and, always, Axeface shouting curses. I kept calling but they soon knew they were being tricked and sent a volley of obscenities and threats at me. I responded with a string of bird calls, mainly the chattering laughter of the woodpecker. When I was comfortably sure they were stuck and lost in the middle of the marsh I whistled for Misty and headed off on my mission for the hogs.

That wasn't so difficult. There was a sheltered dip and clearing further down near the marsh where the earth was soft with years of damp mulch and where the hogs rooted around with their snouts for buried beech nuts, acorns, worms and grubs. I knew they'd still be there because a hog will eat all day, anything and everything, making discontented hog noises. I've often thought it must be easy to be a hog. All it has to do is to eat, sing to itself in its hoggy voice, scratch against a tree or rub itself against other hogs and sleep. They don't have to work and worry like us and I sometimes think we'd be better off as hogs. I was thinking this as I followed the stream down to the clearing where, I knew, the hogs would be. When we got closer I'd send Misty round the back to stop them running further into the woods.

As I walked I started swinging the sword over my shoulder like a soldier. I tried to imagine myself about four times the size, a *housecarl*, a warrior dressed in fine clothes with a shining helmet and a decorated shield in a battle. I took some swings at the bushes, whipping the top off a small tree with a single lop imagining it was Ern's head. I tried to use the sword with one hand but it was too heavy. I practised swinging it above my head where, as I whirled it harder and faster, it whistled and hummed to itself until Misty gave me a look to say, 'You'd better be more careful'.

Yet I didn't feel big and I didn't feel proud. The truth was that, as much as I was dreaming, at one moment, of chasing Normans with my sword, then the next wondering what it must be like to be a hog, Axeface's hard stare and voice were in my head and frightened me a bit. I was also beginning to feel bad about the sword. I knew that stealing was a sin and I'd heard terrible stories about what happens to thieves. A thief could have his hand cut off and we all know that no good ever comes from stealing. I tried to play it in my mind to make it all right, that I'd just found a sword and I rehearsed what I'd say if I got caught. I'd say I found it in the woods and thought it was an old one and that I was taking it up to the forge to hand it in. But in my head all this got mixed up with the morning's argument with Dad and what I knew would likely be coming from Ern – a clout if the blame had been put on me as it usually was – for the hogs getting out.

Strange. I knew my way easily through these woods but I could get lost in my thoughts. They crowded in like the briars and I quickly got tangled up thinking one moment that I was all the horrible words Dad threw at me, that I was a wastrel who would come to no good, that I deserved all the blows I got from Ern and the best thing I could do would be to behave like they wanted and to try hard to become a hogboy. Then I thought about Till and being true to myself but that got me thinking I was cruelly used by Dad and wishing that something better would come along to improve my lot. I started dreaming – what Till calls *crying for the moon* – about finding lost treasure or some great lord and lady making me their servant and dressing me up in finery and how I'd serve them. Perhaps I could learn to be a falconer and live in the *mews* looking after the falcons or perhaps I'd work in the kitchen helping to prepare feasts and banquets and I could eat the leftovers, have a full belly all day and a soft bed to sleep on at night.

There, once again lost in my thoughts I could have run into trouble. Again, my friend the jay which, like its cunning cousin the magpie, knows everyone's business, shrieked at me and I should have listened. Instead, for the second time that day, I nearly stumbled. Luckily Misty was ahead of me, growling and running. There, in a clearing just ahead, was a boy. He had been squatting over a dead hog but was now up, jumping and dancing trying to keep his heels away from a snapping Misty. He had a knife in his hands and I could see he had been trying to cut up the hog. There was blood everywhere and my first thoughts were of the mess he was making. Then I recognised something about that hopping and dancing. She wasn't wearing the bird costume but this was, I knew, not a boy but the mysterious girl from the falconry show in Rye.

I felt a surge of anger as the memory of the broken egg on my head, my humiliation, the baying laughter of the crowd came sharply back. Worse, I quickly saw that this was one of Ern's hogs. Now, I don't like Ern and I don't like his hogs but then I don't like a stranger stealing them either and, already, I could feel Ern's heavy hand on my neck as I tried to explain that one of his hogs had been killed, a young one, too, with lots of growing still in it. Misty ran for cover as I lifted the broadsword up above my head in a fighting pose yelling at the top of my voice. I won't tell you the words I used but they were ones Dad had thrown at me that morning.

'That's my hog,' I was trying to shout. 'You've killed my hog,' but I was so angry and breathless the only word to come out was 'Hog!'

The girl backed off quickly, putting herself against a tree which is a pretty good defensive move. I came at her in a fury, swinging the heavy sword around my head. My hunger, my dark mood seemed to be her fault. All my troubles took the shape of this startled stranger, the stupid, hopping girl with her silly tricks, pretending to be a boy and who now looked surprised but not particularly scared up against the tree.

I was angry. I'm not sure I wanted to hurt her but I did want to make her look as frightened as I felt. I was, though, soon in trouble. I was panting from the effort of swinging the heavy sword, which was no longer singing in the wind and flashing as it had done earlier in my imagination, but wobbling clumsily. By contrast the girl seemed calm and steady. 'Be careful with that sword,' she called as I advanced. 'You can do some damage with that.'

But all I could manage was that breathless, 'Hog!' as I raged and ran. Then it was all a mess and muddle. You can't do too many things at once: shouting, swearing, running and waving a heavy broadsword made for a warrior. The weapon slipped out of my hands. I tried to adjust my grip but it tipped forward with a mind and weight of its own. It stuck in the ground turfing me head forward like a tumbler vaulting with a stick over a hedge. I don't think the girl meant to hit me. Rather, I crashed into her and, instinctively, she struck out, hitting me in the face with the protective flat of her hand. Then she had me by the shoulders pushing me over so that I fell heavily on the hard ground banging the side of my head.

The trees and sky whirled around above me and the girl whirled too, standing with her fists raised. I squeezed my eyes shut and when I opened them they were full of tears. The girl squatted next to me, looking anxious but with a grin on her face. Worst of all Misty was sitting beside her wagging her tail and she also had a grin on her hungry face as the girl stroked her head. The sword was still stuck and twitching in the ground.

The girl looked different now that she wasn't wearing the bird costume and she seemed more friendly. But when she spoke I remembered how she had stuck her tongue out at me and had grinned when they smashed the egg on my head.

'I know you,' she said, 'you're the little sparrow who kept staring at me. We made a fool of you with the egg.'

Fool! I was furious and hit out at her but she laughed, easily dodging the punch and pushing me back on the ground.

'Sit up,' said the girl. 'Your nose. There's blood.'

My nose was bleeding and my ear was ringing like I'd had a giant clout from Ern. My shin was skinned and bleeding where I'd tripped on the sword.

'You're not a fool,' said the girl, realising she had offended me, 'and you're not a sparrow. I think you were brave.' She helped me up. 'Anyway,' she went on, 'that's an old trick with the egg. They did it to me until I said I'd run away if they did it again so they started to get someone to come up from the crowd. And I didn't mean to hit you,' said the girl. 'You tripped. You tripped when you were running. You mustn't run like that with a sword. It's one of the first things a warrior learns: how to handle a weapon. Look,' she pulled the weapon out of the ground holding the hilt in her right hand and resting the blade across her shoulder. She was bigger than me but even she was having trouble holding it. She gave a thin whistle of appreciation. 'Nice broadsword,' she said, examining it like an expert. 'It's a Norman sword. The work of a craftsman.' She looked along the line of it critically and also, I thought, familiarly and I wondered if she recognised it as Frog's sword but if she did, she didn't show it. 'You should take better care of it you know. A sword like this could make your fortune. Where did you get it? This is a sword for a man not a hogboy.'

That word again. *Fool* and now *hogboy*! I felt the anger rush up into my face and I retorted with the best I could manage, a spluttered '*Birdboy*!' and more bad words.

She shrugged, laughed and gave a funny sort of bow. She handed the sword to me holding it delicately by the blade and offering it hilt forward. 'Here you are then. Take it back.' I stood up and took the sword. Blood from my nose dripped, a red rivulet running down the grooved centre of the tarnished blade and dripping from the tip.

'I'm just saying you need to take more care of it and you need to learn how to use it. And, I tell you what,' she pointed at my bleeding shin, 'you tripped over the hilt – that's the handle, the bit you're holding,' she added annoyingly as though talking to someone who'd never seen a sword before. 'If you'd tripped on the blade it would have taken your leg off. You're lucky. Where's the scabbard?'

'Eh?'

'The scabbard, the sheath…the…the long pocket to put the sword in?'

I shrugged.

'It's dangerous to carry a sharp sword unsheathed,' she said solemnly, 'and also the blade will rust, will lose its edge if it's not protected.'

I was never much of a talker and I was fascinated to listen to her. She talked like some of the better travellers I'd heard. Like she knew what she was saying. She talked like a Somebody. When I talked, if I talked at all, I'd just lower my head and mutter like a Nobody. This girl stood confidently, arms folded looking me in the eye, speaking clearly but with an odd accent that marked her as foreign. It calmed me and I forgot my anger for a moment but, as I took the sword in my hand again and felt its weight, my temper came back choking me as I tried to speak, breathless and tearful so all that came out was another trembling, 'Hog!'

She looked dismayed. 'I'm sorry. Was it yours?' She laughed uneasily, 'I thought it was a wild beast in the wood. Does it matter? I was in the tree.' She looked round anxiously as though we were being watched. 'I was in that tree hiding because I'd heard a noise and these hogs came through – a whole lot of them – a family do you call it of hogs….a herd? – and I had my crossbow. Do you want to see it?'

A crossbow? So, she is a Norman, I thought. I knew about crossbows but hadn't seen one. I could see the strange machine lying next to the dead hog. I was itching to get my hands on it and to see how it worked. I'd heard it said that a crossbow will send an arrow – but they call it a bolt it's short and stubby – straight through a shield. But I shook my head as though I wasn't interested.

'I shot the smallest one,' she said. 'I thought I could, you know, roast it on a fire and eat it.'

I started to find my voice. 'You're in right trouble,' I said. 'We both are.'

'Trouble? Why? Who with?'

'Ern.'

'Hern? Who's Hern?' She put an *H* in and I wondered if she was making fun of the way I spoke. 'I can speak to him. I could explain.'

'Ern,' I corrected her. 'It ain't Hern, it's Ern and, no you can't speak to him. He wouldn't give you the time of day.'

'I've got money.' The girl dug in her bag and produced some coins. 'Can I buy the hog?'

'You can do what you like,' I said and I used more rude words. 'Right trouble.' I whistled for Misty.

She offered me the coins. 'How much for a hog? Surely you sell them? What's the price for a hog? Aren't you the hogboy?'

If only she knew how I hated that word, *Hogboy*. I sprang up, startling her, and knocked the coins rudely out of her open hand. They scattered on the ground.

'I got to be going.'

'Please stay? How old are you? I think we're about the same age.'

I started to walk away.

'At least let's roast the hog together. Now it's dead, why waste it? You look hungry, too – and the dog.'

'Eat it yourself,' I said. 'You killed it, you eat it.'

'But I don't know....,' the girl gestured at the hog. 'I need a fire. How can I make a fire?'

I realised she hadn't got a clue where to start. And that pleased me, knowing that I knew something she didn't know. 'You need fire,' I said, 'to start a fire. And I've got no fire with me.' I began to walk away. 'You best enjoy your meal. I'm off to tell Ern and,' I sneered, 'you'll be in right bother.'

I walked off whistling again for Misty to follow. She had been sniffing at the dead hog appreciatively. Now she put her head down and growled her disapproval that we were about to walk away from a free meal.

'Wait,' said the girl. 'How do I get out of here?'

'Where you going?'

'Well I don't really know. I just need to get away from this place.'

I shrugged. 'If you don't know where you're going I can't help.'

'Well, London perhaps.'

'I never been there.'

'Is there a road?'

'Bodle Street's up that way,' and I nodded my head vaguely.

She didn't seem to understand.

'Just keep climbing up,' I said. 'Up the bank. Follow the hill. Keep going. You'll find the street.'

'Is it far?'

'Fair way,' I said. I wasn't being helpful.

'Well...,' she paused. She looked dejected and for a moment I thought she was going to cry. That pleased me. She'd seen my tears now I might see hers. 'I don't even know the direction. Which way do you think I should go?'

'London's north,' I said and I pointed, 'over that way. Sea's down there so north would be that way.'

I walked off.

The girl stood there with the bloodied hog at her feet. It started to rain.

'Wait,' she said. 'What's your name?'

'Ash.'

She waited for me to ask me hers but I didn't.

'Thanks…,' she struggled with the name.

'Ash,' I said again. 'They call me Ash.'

'Thanks for helping, Ash.' I thought she was being sarcastic but she wasn't. 'I'm Guillaume. And I'm sorry about the hog.'

'What?' I couldn't understand the name and, anyway, 'I thought you were Ari.'

'Eh?'

'In the show. The man said you were Ari. Said you were a shape-shifter'

She laughed, 'Ah, that nonsense. That's not my name and the shape-shifting is just a stupid story. Don't believe anything that man says.'

'And,' I challenged her, 'you're not a boy.'

'Am,' she snapped sticking out her chin the way Elfin does when she's cross because she's being teased. 'My name's Guillaume.' She repeated it, 'Guillaume, Guillaume. It's a boy's name.'

But the best I could do with it was the way it sounded: Gee…ham…Geeam…*Gam*. And Gam is what she became. I walked off with the miserable Misty leaving the lost girl in the rain.

4. DAD

The rain came on as I walked. And now my head was full of Gam. I reckoned she was nobility. Foreign nobility. But what was she doing in the wood? She was dressed for travel rather than for show but she looked like the better off people who passed through on Bodle Street from time to time but always in groups, usually with horses and never alone. She had a leather jerkin and, amazing to me, leather boots. My sandals were thin. Not bad in the dry spring but leaking in the wet weather and no good in the mud. But she was equipped for proper walking. Her feet would be dry and warm. How I envied those boots.

And, now, I had another thing to feel bad about. My heart was full when I thought about the girl so why had I been so rude and unfriendly? I shouldn't have left her like that and, at least, I should have given her proper directions for the road. She would be easily lost in the wood and hungry without a fire. I thought of her alone and cold in the dark. I wanted her as a friend but something, the shadow of my black mood, had got in the way. I blamed myself – my anger and stupidity – for behaving so badly. I could, at least, make a fire for her. But then she'd probably feed it with green wood which would make smoke and attract unwelcome attention. Goodness knows what rogues and tricky travellers there were in the wood now that the times were becoming so unsettled. She had the crossbow but that might not do her much good unless she was quick. Even if she got to the road she wouldn't be out of trouble. Dressed in the leather jerkin, a child alone, she'd quickly stand out. And the wrong sort would soon sniff the money, too. And why wasn't she with the falconers anyway? I guessed she was a runaway.

Lost in these thoughts I found my feet taking me another way, walking me away from where the hogs would be and, instead, back up towards the ridge and the iron workers. This was well out of my way and an unwelcome journey. Up there, though, there were charcoal burners and this was the nearest place that fire was easily found. Three or four big charcoal pits were smouldering. I couldn't see Cola who was the master here or any of the charcoal boys who, I knew, would want a favour in return for any bit of fire. I loitered behind a tree to make sure no-one was about then nipped out to the nearest pit. I rooted round with a stick at the base of one of the fires and quickly had what I wanted – a brand of smouldering charcoal. I put it in a little horn cup I had and fed it with some other charcoal bits and some ash burrs, blowing on them gently to keep the seed of the fire alive. I put this in my bag and also found some dry tinder. I carried this precious commodity as quickly as I could, before the seed of the fire died, jogging back down the lane to where I'd left Gam. Even at my steady pace, this was a long journey. I thought all the way of her face and voice and what I'd say to her. I'd show her how to make the fire, how to clean and cut the hog and how to roast it on a spit of wood without burning and ruining it. I didn't mind any more that it was Ern's hog and I was thinking of where I could get some herbs and watercress to go with the roast food. I'd ask her about Axeface and the falconers and, if she was running away, I'd find ways to help her escape. I imagined myself protecting her against all sorts of dangers with the broadsword and how she'd smile and thank me.

But, when I got to the clearing, she'd gone. The dead hog was where she'd left it but no sign of Gam. I gave some quiet whistles and called her name more boldly. Nothing. I put the tinder on the ground out of the rain under the shelter of the tree and fed it with the charcoal, making it glow with my breath until I had the miracle of flames. I'm good with fires. I fed the small yellow and orange tongues with dry twigs like a mother bird feeding her young, then bigger pieces of wood so I soon had a good dry fire of strong red flames and little smoke going. I kept a lookout for Gam but saw nobody. I gathered small dry firewood and left it in a pile beside the fire. The trouble is once you have a fire underway all you want to do is stretch out and doze beside it. But the hogs were on my mind, the light was dipping and I knew there was work to do. I called out for Gam again. I tried whistling and made some owl hoots. No answer. I waited a bit more then walked away. At least, if she came back, the fire would be ready for her.

Still feeling unsettled in my thoughts I got on with the routine of what was left of the day. I found the hogs just where I thought they'd be. I counted them up. One short. Ern was sharp, would be quick to notice and then, I knew, there'd be more trouble. He'd take it out on Dad. There'd be more debt. But I got on with it, whistling, calling, coaxing and with Misty snapping hungrily round and round behind them I drove them through the wood back up towards the compound. On the way I stopped in a secret place, I had: a cleft tree. I slid the broadsword in where I knew it would be safe although, if I were to keep it there longer, I knew I'd need to wrap it in cloth soaked in grease to keep the wet out.

There's another curious and contrary thing about hogs. Just as, earlier, they'd made up their minds to escape, now they seemed to want to do nothing more than hurry back home in a long line, bigguns at the front, littluns at the back, as if they'd never meant to get out in the first place. But it was still a long haul and the day was coming to a close as I got them to the pound and shut them in, lashing up the fence so they'd be safe for the night, at least. The last of the daylight flickered like the end of a candle now and the village huts looked grey, damp and gloomy. Rainwater dripped from the thatched roofs making muddy puddles on the ground. I was tired out and famished with hunger. I went to our hut but it was cold and empty. I guessed Dad had gone up to the village. There was some sour ale in a wooden bowl and I had a drink which refreshed me a little. I went outside to the hen coops and rooted around. No eggs. Even the hens looked half starved. I stood shivering in the gloom, the side of my head hurting from Gam's blow, wondering what to do. My mind went back again and again to the fire and the hog that could be turning and roasting to a crispy golden colour on a spit. I went down to the spring and washed the blood from my face. I looked at Misty who looked at me with her face all pinched. We both needed a meal. The best thing would be to go up to the village and scrounge some food. There were families there who knew me and would share. But they'd want something back, a favour, some fuss and gossip and conversation and I had no time for that. If it was quiet, though, I could sneak round the back of the Big Hall which still had food from the winter's store and I could fill my bag. Anyway, I needed to let Dad and Ern know the hogs were back. So, I went on to the village.

I walked in my quiet way, hoping not to meet anyone and I was surprised to see the lights of torches burning. I could hear talking and laughter and the sound of Lang's little flute playing its melancholy tunes. There was a good fire going outside the Big Hall and a group of men sitting round it, drinking, eating and talking, their beards and faces reddened by the flames. I paused in the shadows.

There was Ern, Dad, Lang and six or seven of the other men. I knew they were drinking and I could smell the rich roast of cooking food. And there, on the other side of the fire, sitting comfy and elevated on benches covered by warm rugs were two of the travellers I'd mischievously lured into the boggy marsh: Axeface and Ox. A little way off, on a pile of skins, Frog lay snoring. Their wet clothes which, I supposed, had been washed clean of mud, were drying and steaming on poles near the fire. I could hear, straightaway, our men – Ern, especially – bragging, making themselves big by telling tall tales, using bad words, laughing at funny and rude stories. I bided my time, thinking over what to say about the hogs and trying to work out what was going on with the strangers. Our men were talking about the *fyrd*, boasting about the fighting they would do, about seeing the King with his army and, they said, the king getting down from his horse and speaking to them and thanking them which I knew was a lie because I'd been there and the King had ridden by without as much as a glance at us as we stood there with our mouths open catching flies. And the two travellers were, I could tell, just pretending to listen and pretending to be impressed. And I was thinking these were Normans and they were being told too much.

But what, mainly, had stopped me in my tracks was seeing the big bird again. Between Axeface and Ox a stake had been driven into the ground with a crosspiece at the top. Perched on it was the eagle, bigger in the firelight than I remembered. It had a leather hood over its head and was drooped and sleeping. Its huge talons, decorated with coloured leather *jesses* and silver *vervels*, gripped the wood. I couldn't take my eyes from it. Then, as though he could hear me thinking, Axeface spoke suddenly and sharply.

'Who's that? Is someone spying on us?'

He was staring straight into the shadows where I stood with Misty and, again, I thought, *He's a sharp one*. And I stepped forward.

'That's just my boy,' said Dad. 'Come here Ash.'

I hesitated.

'It's the bird,' said Dad to the others. 'Come on Ash. No need to be afraid of the bird.'

But it wasn't so much the bird I was wary of. It was Ern. I walked forward slowly and cautiously, Misty at my heels, and nodded to the men. Ern looked up and I expected a cross word if not a blow but he gave a tipsy smile showing his broken and dirty teeth.

'Hogs in?' he asked.

I nodded but didn't look at him. I kept my eyes on the bird.

'They all right?'

Again I nodded.

'Fence?'

I nodded.

'He doesn't have a lot to say,' said Axeface, looking at me hard.

'No. He's not a talker,' said Dad.

'Not like his old man,' said one of the other men and they all spluttered and laughed.

'Food, boy?' Said Dad.

I nodded hungrily.

Dad looked across at Ern. It was something I hated. We were in thrall to Ern and had to ask his permission to take something from the pot. It made me realise why Dad behaved like he did: bragging and boastful. It gave him a chance, even for just a moment, to imagine he was like the others: free, a churl with *hides* of land of his own. Ern smiled and waved his hand as though he were some great lord granting permission for others to eat. I would have liked to kick the pot of food over and march off but my stomach was doing the thinking now and I lowered my head in a gesture of ingratiation.

'Yes,' said Axeface. 'Give him food. By heaven he needs feeding. He's a little one.'

'He's on the small side,' admitted Dad as though acknowledging it was his fault I'd been half-starved most of my life.

'A boy like that needs feeding,' said Axeface. He reached forward and filled a bowl generously with the stew – delicious meat and vegetables from the cooking pot - and then a hunk of heavy dark bread and passed it over to me. But then, as I reached for it, showing my face in the firelight, he grabbed my arm and squeezed it hard, his thin fingers biting painfully into my muscles like a pair of the tongs Till uses for gripping the hot metal. I wouldn't, though, show him the pain. I looked up into his face until his cold eyes drove into me and I looked down.

'Frightened of the bird, boy?'

I shook my head.

'Well, you should be. She'd eat up a little morsel like you.'

The men laughed but I heard Dad say, 'Don't worry Ash. It's fast asleep.'

'I've seen you before boy, haven't I?'

I didn't respond.

'You're my little sparrow. Do you remember me?'

I shook my head.

'But you remember her,' he nodded his thin head towards the eagle. 'You wouldn't forget her, would you boy?'

Again I shook my head as the men laughed.

'You were a good little sparrow,' he said.

'A good fool,' a man called out.

'No,' said Axeface. 'He was brave, a showman. He stood his ground. I like that. We took good money from the show that day.'

'He didn't like your golden crown,' laughed one of the men.

'It was for the show,' snapped Axeface. 'A silly piece of trickery to make fools laugh. I meant no harm.'

He squeezed my arm harder. 'Where have you been all day?'

I didn't answer.

'He'll have been in the woods,' said Ern. 'He's always in the woods skipping his work. Or down at that lake, fishing. He'd rather run in the wild like a beast than do proper work.'

'And wouldn't we all,' said Dad, trying to lighten the mood. 'If a child can't leave his work from time to time what chance do the rest of us have?'

But Axeface ignored him, his eyes piercing into me.

'You've got blood on your face, boy. Have you been fighting?'

I shook my head.

'He probably fell out of a tree,' said one of the men. 'Nesting, I expect.'

'Climbs trees does he?' said Axeface.

'He's my hogboy,' said Ern, 'but it seems he has time to fool around in trees. Serve him right if he's had a fall. Might knock some sense into him.'

Dad looked across at me. 'You all right, Ash?'

I nodded.

'Seen anything in the woods boy?' said Axeface.

I shook my head.

'Found anything boy?'

I shook my head.

'Sure you haven't found something that shouldn't be yours?' squeezing hard.

Again I shook my head.

'Haven't been up to tricks, boy, have you? Misleading lost travellers.'

Another shake of my head.

'By heaven he doesn't have much to say,' said Axeface again.

'He's a good boy,' said Dad. 'He might not be a talker but he's a goodun.'

'Well, I'll make him talk,' said Axeface, 'I want to hear his voice.'

'You'll leave him alone,' said Dad thickly and I was grateful to him for standing up for me.

Axeface let me go and handed me the bowl of food. 'Perhaps some stew will loosen his tongue,' he said with a smile.

One of the other men grabbed some strips of meat from the pot and threw them over to Misty who snatched them and devoured them greedily.

'These men have been lost. They're looking for a boy,' Dad nodded at the strangers. 'Did you see a boy in the woods, Ash?'

I shook my head, eating.

'He's a runaway,' said Dad. He looked at me hard. 'You sure you didn't see nothing in the wood? They're after a boy who has run away. He was in service to these gentlemen who treated him kindly. And now he's rewarded them by running off. And, worse, they've been led astray in the wood. You sure now?'

I told a lie with a shake of my head.

Dad looked at Axeface. 'That's the truth. My boy wouldn't lie.'

Axeface looked hard at me. 'There's a punishment for liars in our country,' he said. 'A liar will have the tongue cut out from his throat. You wouldn't want that boy?' He looked at Dad and laughed, 'Perhaps that's why he doesn't speak. He told lies and now he's lost his tongue.'

He looked round for appreciation and, all round the fire, they laughed, showing him their tongues as they did so.

Except Dad. He looked at Axeface. 'I told you. My boy doesn't tell lies.'

I kept my head down and continued eating. An awkward pause. Their eyes were on me and they weren't yet ready to pick up their earlier conversation. I knew they were trying to see what was in my head but, I thought to myself, I hadn't told a lie because I hadn't seen a *boy* in the wood.

'And the hogs are all in nice and snug?' said Ern again.

Another nod of my head. Another lie. And a piece of the hot meat burnt my tongue.

'You keep your eyes open will you?' said Dad

I nodded.

'There's a reward if you find our runaway,' said Axeface, 'and more if you can find the rogue who led us astray. Real gold, not eggs,' and he chinked a purse up and down in his hand.

'These gentlemen,' said Dad solemnly, as I ate, 'have been kind enough to pay for this feast. They're on their journey to Winchester. They've got themselves lost in the wood, separated from their travelling companions. The ones we saw in Rye. Some fool led them into the marsh where there's danger. It brings shame on us that travellers should be treated in this way.'

'The others will wait for us on the road,' said Axeface arrogantly. 'Their show – just tumbling and foolery – is nothing without us, without our falcons and our stories. But we have wasted our time on these wretched tracks and lanes, taken into a quagmire by a rogue who will regret his foolery when we meet him. All because of a stupid boy who decided to run away and who, I hope, has come to grief in the wood.'

There was a silence. We stared into the crackling fire all busy with our thoughts. I chewed and swallowed my food hungrily but thought of the lonely Gam, hungry in the woods. Owls hooted. Foxes bayed.

Suddenly Axeface spoke. He spoke into the fire, not looking at any of us and saying his words like a splashing stream in the rocks as if this were something he said over and over again. These were words I'd heard before. Words he had spoken while Gam hopped and jumped around the circle of gawping townsfolk.

'We,' said Axeface, 'are the birdmen. She,' he gestured at the enormous bird, 'is a great lady we will show to your king. A gift from Normandy. Have you ever seen a bird like it?'

Nobody responded or looked at him. He spoke to the fire, a showman addressing a crowd. 'You think, perhaps, she is a great hawk but, no, she is an eagle from Byzantium, the mountains on the eastern edge of the world.'

He drew his gaze away from the flames and looked at me. 'Do you know where that is boy?' I shook my head, eating.

'Of course you don't. For you the world ends at the English coast.'

Some of the men laughed knowingly as though they were great travellers. Such hypocrites. Few of them had been more than a few miles from home.

'Still no words, eh? You're lucky she is asleep,' he gestured at the bird, 'she might want your tongue. Or your liver. A boy of your size would make a tasty morsel. Or the dog perhaps.'

'That's enough of that,' said Dad. 'No need to frighten the boy.'

'If he's a good boy and tells only the truth,' he need fear nothing, said Axeface.

He picked up the conversation started before my arrival. Yet, all the time, I felt his eyes on me.

'If you would wish it we will fly our birds for you as we did in Rye. Tell your friends and neighbours. Bring them to our falconry show. These birds have been seen in the great towns of France – Rouen, St Valery, Bayeux,

Fecamp and now we have brought them to show you. We will ask no money of you poor country people. We get rich rewards in the towns. Of course, if you enjoy the show and wish to offer something we would be grateful for any little hospitality you might show to strangers. We ask only what you can give.'

He paused, drank deeply, spoke in his French tongue to Ox now dozing beside him, then continued to address the credulous faces reddened by the food, drink and flickering firelight turned up to him.

'We ask little because, I guess, there is little wealth here. This seems a wild and backward place for travellers like ourselves,' he said. He took a piece of cloth, crumpled it into a ball then lay it on the ground pointing to the way it was twisted and folded. 'To me,' he said critically, 'your land looks like this: ridges and rivers, thick forest and wet marsh. Our land in Normandy,' he made a gentle motion with his hand, 'is smooth and rolling. We were easily lost today. The tracks here are poor.' He lent forward as if making a proposition. 'If you had better tracks you would have more trade. This is rich country, close to the wood and close to the sea. Traders would come for skins, wood, metalwork but would need carts. I could bring you trade but you need better routes to the sea.'

One of the men laughed. 'It's the wild weald,' he said, 'all wood and marsh and clay in these parts. As you've found out you don't want to lose your way here. You're lucky. There's folks gone into those woods have never come out.'

Axeface suddenly swung his gaze, just like a hawk, lighting on me. 'Was it you tried to deceive us, boy? Revenge, perhaps, for the egg trick?'

I kept my head down and chewed my food. My cheeks were burning. It was as though the man could read my mind.

'He's a good boy,' said Dad. 'He'd do nothing like that.'

Axeface ignored him, still staring intently at me. 'Do you know the woods boy?'

I pretended to be absorbed in my eating which, I can tell you, wasn't difficult.

'He knows his way better than anyone,' said Dad proudly. 'He can pick his way through the woods better than most.' He rubbed my head affectionately, took my bowl and filled it to the brim again.

The food was good. The sort we get on high days and holidays. I ate steadily and, with a nod of approval from Ern, Dad filled my bowl twice again, each time grabbing more strips of meat which Misty gulped down. I found a fatty bone for her and she was soon gnawing and making contented dog noises. Funny, I was thinking, how animals let you know when they're happy. Hogs with their wheezing and grunting, Misty sort of purring like an overgrown cat, birds singing in the bushes in the spring. And, thinking this, full to the brim, I was soon asleep.

I woke up once when there were raised voices. An argument was going on. It was about Duke William and the King. The rights and wrongs of it all. Who should rule. One of the men who'd had too much beer was shouting about let em come. Had they seen the King's army? Let em send as many Normans as they wanted we'd soon send em packing. Loud talk about the line of English kings. *Athelstan*, good old *King Edward* and, even, how God had chosen King Harold. Some shouting about the star in the heavens and what it foretold. It could have got out of hand and come to blows, the men arguing amongst themselves, but then I heard Axeface. He used a different voice, no longer the braying showman but confidential, soft and sweet as honey to calm them. It was all just politics, he was saying, and why talk of politics when they could be friends together and eat and drink. He spoke with a quiet authority. He was sure there would be no fighting. Talking but no fighting. But while there was talking there would be preparations for war and, for us – he swept his hand around the fire – that could bring only profit. Armies needed weapons and the smiths who made the weapons needed iron. Soldiers needed shields and armour. They needed shoes for marching and food for their stomachs. 'Here,' he chuckled, 'you are well placed to supply the needs of the fighting men. You are near the street to London. There is timber and good hunting in the forest, fish in the lakes. And birds to be found. This is good hawking country. Find me a nobleman who doesn't love his falcon more than his wealth and more than his wife. Your *thanes* will pay highly for a well-trained falcon. There is labour and craftsmanship here. Falcons need their perches and hoods and *jesses*. The serving men who carry the birds need their gauntlets. There are fortunes to be made. Leave the politics,' he said soothingly 'to those in the court. Leave the wars to the warriors. Enjoy the good things in life. Here, a little more to drink, perhaps.' It was a voice which calmed the men and which easily lulled me back into sleep.

Much later, something made me wake again. I heard my name. Ern's voice. Then Axeface. *The boy*. I heard it again and again. Something told me to lie still. I opened my eyes a fraction. It was so deep in the night that the first glimpse of dawn was lightening the sky. I peeped cautiously. The fire was smouldering on the last of its embers. Men, Dad too, lay around it sprawled on rugs and all fast in a drunken sleep except for Ern and Axeface, two bodies as tight and close as each other talking conspiratorially. Ern was talking quietly and so quickly that, at first, I couldn't understand what he was saying. Then I heard names and numbers and places. I realised he was giving Axeface information about the villages and hamlets: how many families, whether they were steady and loyal or easily bought, where the farms were, the good tracks, the grain stores, the ironsmiths. He told about the *fyrd*, the number of men from the area, their fighting qualities and weapons. Then, again, my name used: *the boy*.

'If he knows the wood,' said Axeface.

'Like no other,' said Ern. 'He might play the fool but he's clever. He's a boy who could show you the way. Nobody knows the wood and the tracks like him.'

'And climbs trees?'

'Like a pinemartin,' said Ern. 'But no good to me. I want a boy for the hogs and this one's too sharp. Always wants to be off doing something else. I'm happy to let him go.'

'And I'm happy to buy,' said Axeface, 'if we can agree a price. I want a boy who knows the tracks and can show the way, who can climb trees and pluck young hawks from their nests or take the eggs. We raise falcons for the noblemen and collect songbirds for their ladies.'

'Dangerous work,' muttered Ern. 'The hunting birds in these parts nest high.'

'If a boy falls, then we'll get another. A boy runs away and we replace him.'

I could feel his eyes measuring me. 'A little alteration and he will fit the bird costume. He can be made to dance and hop like the other. But, this time, I will keep a tighter rein.'

'Then we can agree a price,' said Ern. 'Remember, I have to find another boy for the hogs.'

'I will pay but I will not pay much,' Axeface bargained. 'If the boy is, as you say, difficult and wilful, he will need to be trained up for our life and that is an expense. I would be prepared to pay a little on account and if the boy is a success then I will give more when we return this way.'

Their voices lowered to a whisper as they bartered. I found it hard to lie still, fear and outrage almost shaking my body. I was being sold like an animal or a sack of grain or a pile of goods.

'And the father?' asked Axeface. 'Will the father be trouble?'

'He's in my purse,' said Ern. 'He has no say until he buys his freedom. He's got no say in what I buy or sell.'

For a moment Axeface seemed puzzled. 'How can you do this? How is it that one man can own another?'

'It's *wergild*,' explained Ern. 'Revenge money. That man,' he pointed his foot at Dad's sleeping form, 'killed my brother. They were partners and had a good business. They were carpenters. They built our great hall,' he gestured at the hall and I was amazed and suddenly proud of Dad. I never knew that he was such an important maker. I had known him only as someone always on the scrounge. 'But they argued,' continued Ern. 'There was a falling out. It was the time of hardship. We'd had a bad summer. Poor crops and a hard winter.

There was little to go round, many here died, tempers were short. He,' again he pointed at Dad with his foot, 'always had a short temper. It might be something to watch in the boy. Anyway there was a fight and the partner, my brother, was killed. The boy's father ran off for a while but came crawling back hoping it would be forgotten. But I claimed revenge. That's our strong law and none can gainsay it. A sum of money was agreed and demanded. But,' he spoke contemptuously, 'the man had nothing and so he works for me. He stays with me until I choose to release him or until the money is paid.'

'It seems harsh,' said Axeface.

'It's our law,' repeated Ern stolidly. 'It's an ancient law. Our tradition. Our honour. It's a good law.'

'And this purse?' I heard the clink of coins. 'The money for the boy?'

'It's mine,' said Ern. 'The father is mine and so is the boy. If I choose to sell him then the profit is mine. Leave him to me. I'll make it right with his father.'

They were walking towards me. I closed my eyes tight shut. They were standing over me and I heard them spit on the palms of their hands and shake in agreement over me. Then the chink of coins, laughter and chuckling. Something about, 'He's not likely to go with you easy,' and Axeface brushing it aside with a harsh word.

'He won't disobey me. When I buy a pup it quickly learns who is master.'

A pup? I was no better than the man's dog. Misty stirred and growled as though she'd heard it too and I knew she was awake.

I heard their footsteps moving a little way off. They were on the other side of the fire now, talking more quietly. I tried to gather my thoughts. I lay still, but with my heart thumping, trying to think of the best thing to do. I waited, hearing the men talking on and on as Axeface squeezed Ern for information. I thought their plotting would never end. Finally it was quiet. I lifted my head. All the men seemed asleep. Two or three were snoring loudly. I got up carefully, Misty beside me, and crept away into the dark shadow of the surrounding huts.

I should have run straight for the woods but I was thinking of Gam, the hungry runaway and so I circled round to the Big Hall. Here there were some sacks of oats, some bread, cheese, eggs and dried fruit. I'd taken from here before and I think, in the village, they knew. I was, as always, careful with what I took, stowing it carefully in my bag, a little at a time. Often, too, I put back: mushrooms, eggs, trout, perch and eels from the lake, sometimes a hare. I didn't think of it as stealing. I crept from the hall, my bag a comfortable weight across my shoulder. I quietly shut the door and put the peg back in the latch, turned......and there was Axeface looking at me grimly.

As he lunged to grab me by the shoulder, Misty flew at him and he backed off enough to give me the chance of a headstart. It was all I needed and, quickly, I was away, dodging in and out of the shadows.

A shout went up. 'There he is!'

Then another: 'Thief!'

I ran for the wood. I knew the way better than anyone and I knew that I could run faster than anyone. For a moment there was quiet and I was sure I'd be away and clear. Then a commotion behind me: men shouting, dogs barking, geese honking. It was half light, the dawn coming up but still night around the edges of the huts.

More shouts and the cry again, 'Thief!'

The word seemed to trip me and, by some magic, Axeface seemed to be in my head muddling my thinking and, for a moment, I lost my bearings. Why it happened, I can't explain but instead of running straight and clear I ran hither and thither in and around and between the huts, the bag of food banging against my back as if encouraging me onwards. I vaulted over fences, tripped over a small hog and brought a stack of iron and pottery cooking vessels crashing to the ground. Heavy footsteps and shouts behind me but I then knew where I was heading: across the village to the gate and the safety of the wood. They couldn't catch me there.

Ahead, as if to encourage me further, an elderly cockerel flapped in the air to stand proud and tall like a sentry, high on the gatepost, his neck and head stretched upwards ready to announce the new day as though the miracle of it was his own doing. Beyond him there was a stretch of meadow growing light in the dawn and, a little further, the concealing shadow cover of the wood. The sight spurred me and I ran faster but there was a sudden change to the feel of the air above me as a shadow far faster than me swooped low overhead, black and straight and silent. Just in front of me the cockerel exploded in a burst of blood and feathers, its morning song turning into a gargled cry of surprise as the eagle smashed into it at high speed, knocking it to the ground and pinning it with savage claws. The wings of the huge dark bird were mantled over the cockerel as it hacked into it with its cruel, curved beak. As the eagle pulled at and ravenously swallowed the soft, still living flesh it lifted and turned its head in a silent challenge to anything that might dare to steal or share its meal.

I had skidded to a halt in surprise, afraid I have to admit, of the giant bird, squatting, between me and the freedom beyond the gate. Then a sharp command: 'Stay there boy.'

Axeface. Where was he? I stepped back as he slid out of the shadows by the fence, leaning against the gate, commanding and relaxed. How did he get there? 'Stay!' As if speaking to a dog. 'Keep still and she'll not hurt you. If you move she'll have the eyes out of your head and the tongue from your throat.'

Ox, the big falconer, came panting up planting himself wordlessly and protectively between me and the eagle. He watched it feast with the kind of loving admiration a mother gives to her child as she watches it enjoying a breakfast she has prepared. Axeface strolled forward from the shadows and joined him. Neither gave any attention to me as they watched the eagle gorging itself. Others began to arrive. Ern, panting and already perspiring even in the cold dawning, some of the other men, shaking and wiping sleep dust from their eyes and all of them in awe of the eagle feeding hungrily on its prey. For what seemed a long while, as the dawn sunlight slowly illuminated the scene, we stood in a circle watching the bird in wonder. One or two of the men whispered to each other in admiration. At one point there was a chuckle: 'That cock reckoned he was top of the heap but he's found his match now.' And, 'Bet that came as a surprise to the old bird.'

I mingled with the gathering crowd of early risers, more and more villagers awoken by the commotion, and began, once again, to think about my chances of a dash for the wood. My feet edged me towards the fringe of the crowd but, just then, Ox gave a low whistle, holding out his arm and the huge eagle, sated, lifted itself and flapped lazily on to his thick leather gauntlet. The big and muscular man staggered and bent a little – the stout bough of a tree rocked in a strong wind – as the heavy bird settled. At the same time I felt myself similarly pinioned in as Ern's heavy hand settled on my shoulder.

'Thought you'd run off, eh?'

He shook me harshly. Too harshly because I squirmed out of his sweaty grasp and leapt back into the crowd. He was powerful and fast but I was used to his moves and dodged him with moves of my own. He bent forward to grab me again but he'd overlooked Misty who threw herself at his fat backside, a flying bundle of angry energy scattering the crowd around us. She must have taken lessons from the eagle, I thought, as she sank her teeth into his fleshy buttock, tearing at the flesh and drawing blood. He howled in pain and anger, turning and knocking the little dog from him with a blow from his fist. Misty fell awkwardly at his big feet and, seizing his chance, the furious Ern drew a *seaxe* from his belt. 'No!' I hurled myself at him but he easily cuffed me aside, swearing violently and obscenely. I fell but was up and at him again on sprung heels, hanging on to his arm, desperate to protect Misty.

'No! You leave her be. Misty, run!'

The little dog was winded and dazed. Ern's blade flashed as he knocked me aside again and it would have been the end of her had the bird not reacted. Startled by the noise and waving arms, perhaps because she thought she was being attacked, the eagle screamed and bated in a panic of flapping feathers. Her eyes beaconed with hatred and she flew at Ern. Had she been free she would have torn his face off with her talons. Held by the leather *jesses* she did no more than turn upside down, screaming and beating her wings in a frightening tantrum of anger. Yet, seeing her coming, anticipating the trajectory of her flight, Ern had fallen backwards into the mud with a sobbing cry, covering his face with his huge hands. It could have been terrible but it was comic. Part of the crowd burst into laughter and others clapped as though they'd watched the antics of a tumbler performing an elaborate trick.

The fury of the flapping eagle had forced Ox on to his knees as he struggled to calm her, whining and whispering until he placated her, coaxing her back on to his arm. The shaken Ern struggled to his feet. He looked ridiculous. His normally florid face was ashen. He turned to the crowd now growing around the scene. 'It's that blasted boy's fault,' he shouted. He ran at me again. 'You'll get the hiding you deserve.' He raised a fat hand. Then, everything froze as his arm was gripped by a stronger hand and a stern voice.

'You'll let him be.'

It was Dad.

For a moment the two men faced each other, their arms and eyes locked in anger and hatred until Dad released Ern from his grip. The big man stepped back spluttering in anger and pain, trying to keep his dignity while holding the torn tunic around his bruised and bleeding backside. The eagle which seemed, like everyone else, to have taken a dislike to him, screamed again, stood tall and flapped its wings. Ern leapt back again in fear, stumbled, almost fell and there was more laughter.

Dad looked at Ern. 'What's this I hear about my Ash? Eager to sell him. Is that it?'

No answer from Ern.

'The days of selling children like hogs are gone,' said Dad.

'That's right,' shouted a voice from the crowd.

'There'll be no selling of children here,' called another.

Ern looked around uneasily. He didn't know whether to speak to Dad or the crowd.

'That boy's a thief,' he shouted.

'You take that back,' said Dad. 'That's a lie.'

'He's a thief,' repeated Ern defiantly. He snatched my bag from me and held it up. 'Take a look in this. Food. Our food from the hall.'

'You leave him be,' shouted a woman. 'He has a right to take if he's hungry, the poor mite.'

'It's stealing,' said Ern.

'Not the little he takes,' the woman argued. 'What's he got in there? A few morsels.'

'I should think you could spare a bit of food from your table you fat fool,' shouted another woman.

'Can't see you going short,' shouted another. 'And the boy gives back. Fresh fish he brings. Food from the wood.'

There was a murmur of agreement from the gathering crowd.

'So, there,' said Dad. 'I'd call that bartering, not theft. You best leave him alone I think.' He took back the bag and handed it to me.

'That boy is to go with these masters,' Ern said lamely. 'It's been settled. All fair and square. Hands shaken and legally done.'

'Is to go?' said Dad. 'Has he been asked?' He looked at me. 'You been asked about this, Ash?'

I shook my head.

'He don't go if he don't want to,' shouted one of the women.

Ern paused, looked for support. But there was none. 'He's bound,' he said. 'And,' he repeated, 'it's all done by the law. To this master.'

'Leave him alone,' shouted another voice.

Ern looked round desperately for allies, turning to Axeface who spoke quietly in that honey voice he had and which, for a moment, silenced the crowd.

'We have merely offered the boy service,' he said, 'an opportunity to learn and travel. His life here,' he gestured at the compound, 'is a life of hardship and poverty. He could travel with us and make himself useful. Why, as we've told you, we are off to the court, to see your king. Think of the favours that might be bestowed on the boy. Think of the honour it does for your village.'

'Honour my backside,' shouted another voice. 'You're here for what you can get and no mistake. You don't care about the boy, or us. And I don't think you care for our king neither.'

There was more shouting and agreement. The word *Normans* was called out with derision.

There were chants of *Out! Out!*

Dad stood firm and quiet. 'Ash is my boy.'

Then Ern turned on him. 'You are bound to me,' he spat the words at Dad. 'And until you are a free man you have no tongue.'

It was the wrong thing to say. The crowd turned on him.

'Leave them alone you fat rascal. You oaf. He's the boy's father. Let the boy choose.'

'We have paid money for the boy...for the boy's services,' said Axeface, 'but, if he would rather stay here.....' He turned to his companions, 'I think we are not welcome. We are not liked here. We will go elsewhere.'

He nodded at Ox who walked off slowly and carefully with the eagle. Then he turned to Ern, 'If you will return the coins we gave you. There are other boys in other villages with more ambition.'

He lifted his head and spoke haughtily to the crowd, 'I am sorry for the....chicken,' nodding contemptuously at the remains of the blood and feathers on the ground. He threw some coins into the mud. 'For your chicken.'

Nobody touched the coins. A man spat. The mood was turning ugly.

Axeface gave a thin laugh. He looked at Dad and said spitefully, 'I said I could make the boy talk,' and strode off.

Ern, alone, looked dejected and confused. He spoke slowly and carefully, weighing his words. 'You forget I am a free man here.' He spoke not just to Dad. 'I am the master to many of you. The law is with me and, before this day is out, I will have my satisfaction.'

Someone blew a farting noise and there was laughter and jeering.

'Perhaps because you fear an invasion some of you think we need no longer fear the law. You will learn differently very soon.'

'We don't sell our children,' said Dad firmly. 'The boy will choose his own path.'

He looked down at me. 'Do you want to go with the men Ash?'

I shook my head. 'And what about Ern? Do you want to be a hogboy for Ern?'

Again I shook my head.

'Hogboy?' Ern said with contempt. 'He can't even do that right. He's good for nothing like his father.' He turned and limped away followed by the jeers of the crowd.

Then the villagers were round us. There were pats on the back, praise and reassurance for Dad. 'Good man. You showed him. You stood up for your boy. We'll stick together.' Then, slowly, as it grew more light, the dawning of anxiety and words of caution. 'Ern's not a man you want to cross. You were in the right but, trouble is, he's the master and has the law with him. Best clear out for a bit.'

Dad looked at me. 'You best stay scarce too, Ash. Stay away. You'll be all right won't you?'

I nodded.

'Go up to Till's perhaps,' he suggested lamely. 'This will soon blow over.'

I must have looked anxious because he put a hand on my shoulder. 'You'll be better on your own, boy. You don't need to worry about Ern,' and there was a determination in his voice which chilled me.

One of the village women put her arm round me like a mother. 'Ash, you can stay with us. There'll always be shelter and a bit of something for you to eat here. There's no need to go hungry.'

I shook my head, picked up my bag and whistled for Misty but there was no sign of her. I walked away. I wanted to shout to Dad, to thank him for standing up for me. I wanted to say I'd save the *wergild*. I'd pay off Ern and make us free men. I shouted these things in my mind but said nothing. I wish I had.

I reached the tree line beyond the village, looked back, saw them looking at me, then turned deep into the woods taking the same track I had laboured up with the hogs yesterday. The trees and undergrowth were full of the sounds of early morning as the woodland creatures busied themselves for the day ahead. Above me a buzzard, out early to take what chance the new day might bring was being chased and harried by crows. The bigger bird turned and flicked them away making sudden kinks in its flight to avoid them. But the crows maintained a steady pursuit until the buzzard tired of the game and flew off.

5. GAM

As I hurried through the wood, my head was filled with thoughts and worries. I wondered what had happened to Misty and I thought about Dad who, for the first time, I saw in a different light. He had stood up to the bullying Ern. He had done the right thing. And he seemed to have opened a door for me. *The boy will choose his own path*, he had said and I knew I could. What that path was I wasn't yet sure. I knew one thing though, I wouldn't be a hogboy and I wouldn't serve Ern. I thought this as I came to the secret tree where, yesterday evening, I had left the sword. *The boy is a child. He's free*, someone had shouted and I thought *yes, I could be free*. I sat under the tree and, suddenly, a warm snuffly nose and a wagging tail. Misty was there beside me, panting. She had tracked and chased along my trail. I pretended to rub her coat but my fingers felt her body tenderly, searching her spine and ribs, checking for damage. She's a tough one, I thought. She'd taken a blow from Ern but had rolled with it and away from harm. She was shaken and a bit whiny when I felt her back leg but I found her some meat from the bag and she was soon licking her lips contentedly. I chuckled as I thought of the damage she'd done to Ern's fat backside. 'We won't be trodden down by anyone,' I whispered to her. As the day grew warm and light, I felt stronger and more cheerful. I stood up and drew the sword from the tree. Something told me it was going to be needed.

I followed the tracks and paths I knew so well. I could hear the stream roaring, the whispered conversation of trees rubbing together in the wind, the chatter of small birds, the screech of hunting birds, the caw, caw, caw of crows and the drum of woodpeckers. And then I was in the clearing where, yesterday, I had left Gam in the rain. She was nowhere to be seen. There was a faint glow of life in the smouldering ashes from the fire I'd made and I could tell that she'd been back because the firewood I'd left had now gone. Ern's dead hog was still there. Gam obviously hadn't enjoyed a meal from it but other things had. There wasn't much left on the carcass which had been pulled about and eaten by foxes, I guessed, ravens, crows and kites. It was a mess. Misty went up for an exploratory sniff and backed off in disgust.

I looked around for signs. Nothing except, ah, there were the coins I'd knocked from her hand yesterday. I gathered them up and stowed them in the bag with the food. I managed to find my voice and ventured a soft shout: 'Gam…Gam. It's Ash.'

Nothing. I searched the grass and quickly found a trail. I was good at tracking and this was easy. The ground was damp clearly showing the unsteady steps of her well made boots. I followed her tracks as they meandered uphill, as I'd expected, towards the ridge. But then the footsteps stopped and I could see, more heavily, evidence of where the runaway had turned and run back downhill, deeper into the wood and towards the lake. From time to time I ventured sometimes a whistle and sometimes a shout: 'Gam….Gam….It's Ash.'

I began to think she was far away, off on her travels, and with it I felt bitter disappointment. I'd wanted so much to see her again.

And I did when, later that morning, Misty found her. A miserable little girl, lost and cold in the wood, smaller and dirtier than I remembered. She seemed to have shrunk in the night.

Misty had started barking excitedly, paws scrabbling as if trying to climb up the trunk of a big oak tree and, looking up, I saw a figure perched like a nervous bird on a bough, half hidden in the leaves, just above my head.

'Gam!'

But she made no answer. Just sat, looking dejected.

'Gam! It's me. Remember. It's Ash. The hogboy. Come down.'

Again, no answer.

I opened the bag and brought out some bread and cheese.

'Gam! I've brought you some food. Come down.'

There was a long pause as we looked at each other until, with a sigh, she spoke wearily in her strange accented voice sounding alone and miserable.

'You're singing a different song.'

'What?'

'You weren't like this yesterday. You didn't want to help me yesterday. And you didn't want to be called a hogboy.'

'I know and I'm sorry. I wanted to help but I was angry.....because you'd killed the hog. Why didn't you eat it? Didn't you find my fire? I came back and made a fire for you.'

She raised her hands hopelessly, panting out a list of complaints. 'I didn't know how. How do you cook a hog? I couldn't keep the fire in. It kept raining. I couldn't cut the thing up. It was disgusting. It stank.' She was wailing with despair. 'I hate this place. This wood. I'm cold. I'm wet. I'm starving. I couldn't sleep. It was so

81

dark. I was hoping you'd come back. I sat by the fire. But there were noises. The wood's full of noises. I heard wolves. Are there wolves here?'

'Reckon so,' I said trying to suppress a grin at the miserable way she was carrying on.

'I thought things, wild animals, might see the fire and attack me. Then, anyway, it went out so I looked for a good tree to hide in. Then I got more lost. And I dropped my crossbow. This is an awful place.' She paused for breath. 'How did you find me?'

'I tracked you. I thought you were heading up that way,' I jerked my head, 'for the road but you've been round and round in a big circle.'

'I tried, but I was scared,' she confessed miserably, tears splashing her cheeks. 'That's where I was going. The road. I thought I was brave but then I thought I was being watched and followed. There were men. Strange men, all dirty, sitting around a fire. I approached them but they shouted at me and drove me away.'

I laughed. 'They're the burners,' I said, 'the charcoal burners. They won't hurt you. I know them. That's where I get my fire.'

'Look,' I waved the bag, 'I've got some food. You must be starving.'

The sight of the food was too much for her. She slid clumsily down from the tree. Then she hesitated.

'I don't trust you. Who've you brought with you?'

'Eh?'

'Have you brought anyone with you? The men?'

'The sooty men, the charcoal burners?'

'No the other men. Normans. The falconers from the show. Scur.'

'Scur?'

'The thin man. The master of the birdmen.'

'Axeface!'

'Who?'

'Axeface. You know, Crow, but I call him Axeface because of the shape of his face. No! No, I'm on my own. I swear.'

'What'll you swear on?'

'I swear on my life.' I pulled out my *seaxe* and held it up like a cross. 'Look, on my life, on my knife and on the cross.'

'Well then,' said Gam irritably. 'You'll be damned to hell if you're lying.'

'I'm not. Here, eat.'

I opened the bag, found her a comfortable fallen tree limb to sit on and watched her eat.

I left her for a while and went back to the remains of her fire and brought some fire seeds in the charcoal. I built another fire below the tree and, while she watched, I soon got a good warm blaze going. We sat crossed legged on the tree roots, away from the smoke. Gam warmed and fed herself greedily.

'I know about the birdmen,' I said, 'Axeface and the other two. I know they're looking for you and now they're after me.'

'Go on.'

And I told her everything. The talk tumbled out of me and that was the way it was with Gam. I could talk to her as I'd never talked to anyone before. She chuckled as I told her about watching the men, finding the sword and misleading them into the marsh. I told her about their behaviour in the village, the boasting and tall tales around the fire. I told her about what they'd said about the runaway boy in the wood, Ern's treachery and their attempts to buy me and to take me with them. I told her about my narrow escape, the flight of the eagle, about Dad and that, I knew, Ern would be humiliated and would be wanting a terrible revenge.

When she'd finally finished eating, Gam told me something of her story. 'The men are tricksters,' she said. 'They go from town to town with the birds. The eagle is, indeed, a wonder. The big man, Ox, is a proper falconer. He's not a bad man and he loves the birds and looks after them well. But Scur – but I like your name better; let's call him that, Axeface – has him in thrall and I don't understand why. His companion, Frog, is slow-witted and easily led but he's also quite gentle and kind. You can deal with both of them. Scur – the Axeface – has some hold over both of them. I'm not sure how he does it. I feel his power.'

'Me too,' I interrupted. 'When I was trying to run it was as if he was in my mind. And he popped up in front of me out of nowhere.'

'He's tricky,' said Gam. 'He's a twisted piece of work and I'll tell you more of him later. The falconers, they make money as showmen: they show off the birds and collect coins. They train birds, too. They buy and sell them. And then there is this nonsense. They meet credulous villagers and tell them they are taking the great eagle to show to some nobleman or to the duke or, like they said in Rye, to the King. It's a lie.'

She paused and stared into the fire before continuing. 'When we were in France we fell in with the troupe of showmen. We would provide entertainment on village greens. We have given shows in Normandy and now here in your country.'

'How did you get mixed up with them?'

She hung her head, tears in her eyes, 'My own foolishness. It's a tangle. I'm headstrong. I was a...a servant for a big family in the town of Fecamp in Normandy. Perhaps you've been there.'

'Me? No, I haven't been hardly anywhere,' I said. 'The day in Rye, I was coming back with the *fyrd* and being out with them was the first time I'd been away from the wood.' I joined her stare into the flames adding wistfully, 'I would like to see other places though.'

'You will, Ash,' she said, 'I'm sure you will.'

'What was it like with this big family?' I asked enviously. 'Did you have brothers and sisters, uncles and cousins?' I'd always wanted to be in a big family.

'No, I mean big, important. They are an important family in Normandy. A noble family.'

'Were they rich?'

She nodded and I gave a little whistle of appreciation. It would be so wonderful, I thought, to work for a rich family and perhaps to sleep in the dry in the kitchen by the warm fire.

'Why did you leave?' I asked. 'Was it better with the birdmen, with the falcons?'

'No,' she said angrily. 'Those men, that Axeface, they made me....they made me look foolish. I would have to stand with a glove...but, then, of course...you've seen me do it. A piece of meat in my hand, whistle and the bird would fly and take the meat. Then they wanted me to wear a leather cap. To make the show better.' She gestured, 'A piece of meat on top of the leather cap. The bird.....not the big bird, that would be too dangerous....they wanted the falcon to chase me, to fly and snatch it. But I wouldn't do it.' She spoke softly and almost bitterly to herself. 'How dare they!'

I passed her a horn cup of water and watched her drink hoping it would calm her a little. She drank and wiped her mouth delicately before continuing. 'And I would go round and collect pennies. But you've seen the show, you know how it works. The dancing. I didn't mind the dancing in the bird clothes. Making the children laugh. You must be careful. That's why they want you. A small boy like you. Like me. For the bird clothes. They will dress you in the bird clothes and make you dance. At first I thought it would be fun but I quickly tired of it.'

'Is that why you ran away from them?'

'I ran away from them as soon as I could,' she said. 'It wasn't easy. Axeface watches all the time.'

'But I still don't understand. Why did you go with them in the first place?' I was beginning to guess that she must have been kidnapped.

Again she spoke softly as though speaking to herself. 'I ran away from my home….my work. I saw the falconers doing their show and decided to join them.'

'Ran away?' I was incredulous. Why would anyone run away from such a position with a rich family? 'Did they, your master in that place, did they treat you cruelly?'

She waved her hand. 'No. It's hard to explain. I was stupid. I don't like to be told what to do and how to behave. I thought as a birdboy I would be free, there would be adventure.'

I wasn't sure she was telling me everything and I couldn't understand why she was still pretending to be a boy but I could see that my questions troubled her so I let her change the subject.

'It wasn't all bad, I suppose,' she said. 'Sometimes in the shows, the people shouting and cheering and wanting to give you presents. And I was learning things: how to work with the hawks and I'm good with the eagle. They were teaching me to use the crossbow so I could shoot at a target. That's how I shot your...the hog. With the crossbow. And now I've lost it,' she said bitterly.

'Don't worry. We'll find it easily,' I reassured her.

'Anyway, I only had one bolt left,' she said, 'and now it's in the hog. I couldn't bring myself to pull it out.'

I laughed at her squeamishness, 'I'll get it for you and I'll wash it clean in the spring.'

'But after,' she continued, 'at the end of the show they would treat me like a common beggar. They would send me round to gull the villagers wheedling money out of them. The superstitious nonsense with those charmed bracelets. It's a lie. The showmen secretly laugh at the foolishness of the country folk.'

'So you ran away from them?'

'Yes,' she said through her tears. 'Not easy. Always, Axeface watched me. And threats. He made threats, especially we are here now in England. He said the English would kill me if they found me because I was a Norman. He said they would think I am a spy. Once I tried to run away in the night but they caught me.' She thumped her hand on the ground. 'I will be even with him.'

I let her pause and gather her thoughts. She watched the flames in the fire then continued, 'I bided my time. Axeface had a disagreement with the others: the tumblers and players. They often fell out. We left them on the road. We were travelling from the coast and we came into a clearing in the wood to make a camp and exercise the birds. I was practising with the crossbow. I missed the target and they sent me off to find the bolt.

The bolts have iron tips and are expensive. I kept running. I ran from them in the wood. Axeface shouted and sent the other two after me. But the one is stout,' she giggled, 'and the other is slow. And I don't think their hearts were in it. I got away easily.'

She paused, still staring into the fire, 'But Axeface will try to find me.'

'Why don't they just let you go?' I said. 'I heard them say that boys like us are cheap. Why would he bother trying to find you?'

'Because I am worth something to him,' said Gam bitterly.

Again I thought it better not to question her. 'And Axeface bartered for me,' I said, 'because they'd lost you.'

'Yes. A small boy is good,' she said. 'We're both small. For the costume and they can train us to do tricks. People give more when you go round with the cap if you are small and look pleading,' she pulled a mournful, pitiful face which made me laugh. I tried myself, turning my mouth down, sucking in my cheeks to make myself look even thinner and making Gam laugh in turn.

We sat quietly for a while.

'What will you do now?' I asked.

'I don't know. Push on, I suppose. I thought I could try my luck in London or your city of Canterbury. But then Axeface is right. As a Norman, with the trouble coming, this is not a good place to be. I don't know what to do. I think it's best to go back to the coast, find a place on a boat and travel back to Fecamp if I can find my way.'

'You'd best to go back to Rye or Pevensey or Winchelsea,' I said, 'that's where most of the boats come in and out. You must, though, be careful travelling. Axeface will look for you and there are rogues on the highway and in the wood. Also, with the talk of the invasion, you're right, people here think the Normans are not trusted.'

'And you must be careful, too,' she said. 'This man Hern you talk about. I don't think it's safe for you in your village. Also, there is certainly trouble coming. It's all we heard in France and now, on the roads, here. A fight between your people and my people.'

'We....you and me...we don't need to fight, do we,' I asked cautiously. I rubbed my ear, still sore from where she hit me yesterday and thought I'd had enough of fighting.

'Of course not,' she said decisively. 'I think we should be friends. We should help each other.'

She looked at me, smiled and raised a hand. I grasped it.

'Friends,' I said, 'and Misty too.'

She laughed, 'Yes, the little dog. But we must think carefully about where to go.'

'Perhaps I could come to France with you,' I suggested.

She nodded, 'I'd like that. But is it safe to travel?'

'It's probably safer here in the wood for a bit,' I said.

'Here?' she was surprised. 'But how can you live here?'

'Easy,' I said, 'if you know how. There's fish and you can hunt. There's nuts, berries, eggs. You can live here like a lord.' I looked up at the trees. The wind was getting up. 'We should find some shelter now,' I said.

'Perhaps but…oh, I don't know….perhaps I should push on.' She was in an agony of indecision. 'Staying for a bit might be safer, but where?'

I said nothing.

'Where could we go?'

'I know a place,' I said.

'Is it safe?'

'Trust me.'

'Where is it? Is it far?'

'It's a secret. Not too far away.'

'Is it a good place to stay?'

'Yes.'

'What's there?'

'Shapes,' I said.

6. SHAPES

And this is where our good days began. Around us a storm was gathering. A storm that would shake the world. But Gam and I were going to its quiet centre. The quiet in the middle of the storm and the best time I can remember.

Ash wants to talk about the Old Place but struggles to describe it. He draws a shape in the dust with his stick: a steep, sudden hill, some short, straight lines for trees, a wiggle, the stream at the bottom. How to describe it? A hollow deep in the wood as if a giant hand, years ago, took a scoop out of the earth. Well away from the tracks beaten by the feet of travellers, the ground suddenly becomes steep, a valley overgrown with briars and birch trees, dropping sharply, almost a cliff, and a good way down to a stream where there's a circle of old trees – yew trees which, we're told, live for ever and which, some say, are sacred. No woodman would ever take his axe to a yew tree. This is a quiet, sheltered, secret place just right for a small friendless boy and his dog. And it was the dog that found it.

Chasing a hare, Misty had disappeared into the bushes at the top of the steep drop. I called her and tried to follow but it seemed hopeless: a thick barrier of gorse and briars and that long steep slope down to the water. Where had she gone? I was worried that she'd got stuck so I didn't give up. I used the *seaxe* to cut my way through the briars. It was hard going until I found a tricky but manageable way of working back and forward, clinging on to roots and branches to let myself slowly

91

down to the level of the stream. I was soon mucky, scratched, sore and bleeding. Misty, below, barked encouragement. I shouted to her to come up but she kept running in and out of a gap in the sandstone rocks as if trying to tell me that she'd found something.

I was covered in clay, grime and blood from where my hands and legs had snagged on the briars. Where was Misty? I could hear her barking: an echoing sound. I peered cautiously through the gap in the rocks where I'd seen her disappear. It was a tunnel, dark but with a glimmer of light ahead. I was reluctant to enter but Misty kept running in and out as if to show me there was nothing to worry about. It was a squeeze on all fours to get through but, once in, I found I could stand easily. A few steps and I was in a large chamber. The ground beneath me was smooth, dry and firm. A greenish light was coming through the end wall and I realised I was in a building of some kind made not with wood but with stone. At the far end the wall had fallen partly away leaving an opening curtained by ivy and foliage giving the room a soft green tinge. Climbing to the top of the wall I could part the leaves and I found myself looking down to the stream. This, I knew immediately, would be a good place to hide. The entrance was a narrow tunnel, easily concealed and, importantly, the collapsed wall offered an escape route.

As I explored I realised the room I was in was big: bigger and grander even than the Big Hall in our village. Who, I wondered, had made it and why? Looking up I could see the remains of a roof which would have been built not with thatch but with red tiles, now mainly a tangle of thick tree roots and bits of vegetation growing through from above. On one side there was a hole in the roof: a chimney and, below it, a fireplace. So, people had been here before me because there was evidence of a fire: charcoal and sticks, some broken and blackened clay pot abandoned long ago. I was in a hall, hidden under the hill.

I crawled outside through the tunnel, gathered wood, dragged it in and soon had a fire going. We sat there, Misty and I, snug, warm and dry. I began to realise that this could be a perfect camp. There was a stream for fresh water and there would be fish. I could hunt in the wood where there would also be fruit and berries. I patted Misty. We could live safely here.

And then as the fire built and flared, I looked round sleepily and sprang up in terror. In the firelight illuminating the walls I saw shapes which seemed to dance and move. Shapes were moving along the wall: plants and animals – boars, bears, wolves, dogs, dragons and birds. Birds that I'd never seen before with strange heads and mouths instead of beaks, with paws instead of claws and the tails of beasts. I began to think I was in a magic place of some kind. Was this the home of some sorcerer or *shaman*? A dragon's lair? I couldn't take my eyes off the walls. The figures moved mysteriously in the firelight but, looking closer, they stayed where they were. I looked at Misty, scratching and grooming herself by the fire. She had a sharp nose for mischief and, if the figures were spirits or bogarts, she would have been spooked. I was unsure what to do. Outside it was dark, cold and damp; in here I was warm and dry but there were strange things on the wall. Comfort won: I reckoned if I let them be they would do me no harm and so I stayed. Now, when I came to the wood, the hall with the shapes became my home. Dryer, warmer and safer than the woodland shelters I'd built. Where the stonework had fallen and where the roots had got in were natural alcoves and shelves. Now, when I collected stuff, I could bring it here. I had a larder for food, bits and pieces of clothes, some furs for warmth, odds and ends of wood and metal that might, at sometime, come in useful. Nothing wasted.

I took Gam there.

I took her on a winding trail through the wood and, as we walked, I realised how familiar these paths were to me. I could find paths where others would see only a tangle of roots and briars. I knew almost every snag and dip, when to avoid a mud patch and when to hop or leap over a stream or pick my way across a near-invisible sucking bog. Misty was sometimes behind me, sometimes in front then falling back to push at and encourage Gam who stumbled and panted and muttered complaints behind me. *Where are you taking me Ash? Are we nearly there?* I could have taken her on a straighter journey but I wanted to make it hard for her to remember the trail in case, ever, she betrayed me and tried to bring someone else there.

When we reached the top of the bank she whistled in disbelief as she looked down over the precipitous drop of trees and scrub. 'I'm not going down there,' she said nervously.

'Just follow me. Put your feet in my tracks. It's not hard once you've done it a couple of times.'

'Can't we wait until we get our breath back?'

'No,' I shook my head. I was keen to show her the place. 'Let's go now. There'll be a fire and food. We can wash in the stream.'

And so I coaxed her down the steep gorge. Misty, who knew the way, ran up and down confidently giving little barks and yelps of encouragement. It wasn't easy but when at last we got to the bottom, Gam sank down breathless by the stream staring at her torn hands and muddy feet. Her fine leather tunic, which hadn't been looking its best when I first saw her, was now a mucky mess.

'Look at my clothes,' she wailed.

'Just wait here. Rest up a bit. We can clean ourselves later. Don't follow me.' I wanted to surprise her. 'Misty, wait here with Gam.'

The rain was holding off and I left the two of them, Gam sitting in a daze of exhaustion, Misty trying to sit still next to her but quivering with excitement and waggling her tail. I crept in between the two rocks and into the chamber. I soon had a fire going and, from it, I lit a torch I'd made from dried rushes. I laid out a platter of food scraps – some bread, fruit and fish, some beer from a jug – on a large flat tile I'd found. Then I crept out. The sun was shining weakly on the bank. There was still a chill in the air but Gam looked happier. 'Come and see,' I said.

Gam, curious, followed me, squeezing through on hands and knees into the chamber. Once inside she stood up cautiously, not knowing what to expect. She was dumbstruck as she stared around. 'What is this place? Is it yours?'

'I found it,' I said. 'It's a secret. I call it the Old Place.'

'What's all this?' She looked round at the bits and pieces of wood, iron, pottery, cloth, I'd found and stored.

'It's my stuff,' I said.

'Where did you get it?'

'I found it.'

She looked at me dubiously, 'Did you steal it Ash?'

I shrugged, 'Not really. It's just things I found.'

'But what is this place?'

'I dunno. Look,' I made a torch of dry rushes and held it close to the wall, 'shapes.'

Gam, fascinated, followed the light along the wall. 'These are pictures. Old pictures.'

'Pictures?'

'Yes. Haven't you ever seen pictures?'

I shook my head. 'I think they're shapes,' I said, 'shapes from shape-shifters.'

'You've been listening to too many stories,' said Gam, 'these aren't real.'

'I know. I'm not stupid,' I retorted.

'They can't move,' she said.

'They do.'

'What do you mean?'

'They do move. I'll show you.'

I took the torch and passed it quickly back and fore along the wall. It was a trick I'd learned. The images of the animals and beasts flickered in the light.

'See.'

But then she laughed, enjoying the scene as much as me. 'It's a hunt,' she said. 'Look, the dogs are chasing the animals.' She was delighted. 'Look at the birds.'

We began to look at the pictures more closely: faded pastel colours, sometimes rubbed away or blackened with damp and moss but still, mostly, clear and sharp. We began to name and count the animals we could see, the dogs chasing tusked boar, antlered deer, wolves, hares and bears. There were borders decorated with intertwining plants, leaves, grapes, berries and trees. All sorts of strange animals we'd never seen: a bird with its beak in a monster's mouth.

'Look,' I could make them move faster or slower by angling the burning torch.

'But they're not moving, Ash,' Gam said again. 'They just look like they're moving because of the torchlight.'

'Please yourself,' I said.

And we did please ourselves. We had the fire; we had food and drink; we were dry and warm. We explored the building we were in: the knotted roots in the roof, the window looking out over the stream. We talked about the food we would need, where we should store it and where we would sleep. We had fish, we had meat and eggs. There were berries and nuts and fruit not far from our door. We were snug birds in the hollow; the Old Place our nest.

'Tell me again about this stuff,' insisted Gam.

'It's only things I've found that might come in useful.'

'But where did you find it?'

She wouldn't let go, like Misty with a bone, and I was becoming impatient with her questions. 'Just here and there. You don't have to go on about it.'

'Ash, are you a thief?' she asked solemnly.

'No,' but I was lying, 'it's just stuff that nobody wanted.' Then, to change the subject, 'I think we ought to get cleaned up. We're both pretty dirty.'

'You go first,' said Gam. 'I'll wait until you're done.'

'Well, let me show you.'

I took her outside and we followed the stream a little way up the hill to where it cascaded over into a shallow pool. A clear waterfall of cold water.

'This is where I wash,' I slid out of my clothes, chucked them on the bank and leapt into the pool of water with a shriek. It was cold. I splashed around then stood under the waterfall rubbing myself clean.

Gam walked off. 'Come on,' I shouted, 'don't be scared. It's only a bit of cold water.'

But Gam was walking further away with her back turned on me.

'Come on Gam. We can't go around dirty. We'll stink if we don't wash.'

She shook her head.

'What's wrong?' I shouted from the water but she'd trudged further downstream.

I climbed on to the bank, rubbed myself dry, dressed and wandered down to where she was sitting.

'Nice and clean,' I said. 'Go on Gam. You've got to have a wash.'

She nodded, 'I'll go up there now.' She looked miserable.

'What's wrong?'

'Ash,' she said, 'you've told me your secret. I'll tell you mine.'

'What?'

'It's what you said. You're right. I'm not a boy.'

'I know. But you can still have a wash.'

'Yes, I will. But not together. Where I come from we don't do that.'

'Why not?' I was puzzled.

'We just don't.'

That night we had a blazing fire and we treated ourselves to a good meal. We still had some food from the bag but I'd caught a fat pigeon which we roasted. Gam, I quickly realised, knew nothing about cooking. But it was something I could do well. I'd cooked for Dad and sometimes I'd helped Elfin, cooking for Till. I'd learned to use herbs -wild garlic, nettles, dandelions – for the flavours and I could make tasty stews with fish and vegetables. After we'd eaten we lay back, warming our toes and watching the light flicker on the shapes on the wall, bringing them to life as, outside, the night grew black. Nothing more had been said but I knew we were both turning things over in our minds.

'It doesn't make any difference,' I whispered.

'What?'

'You being a girl.'

'That's good,' she said sarcastically, 'and it doesn't make any difference to me.'

'What?'

'You being a boy.'

I chuckled, and gave her leg a playful kick. Then I had a sudden thought, 'It's like shape-shifting,' I said. 'First you were the birdboy, then I thought you were Ari from Crow's story, then you were Gui…Gui…you know, Gam and now you're a girl.'

'That's rubbish, Ash. There isn't any shape-shifting and I'm just me.'

'Well, boys are best,' and I gave her another playful kick.

She kicked back, 'At what?'

I paused as if I was thinking, 'Cooking,' I said.

'That's true. You cook well,' she patted her stomach.

'Running in the wood. And finding places like this.'

'That's true, too.' Then, 'What about the crossbow?' she asked.

'Yes,' I conceded. 'You're good with that.'

'And fighting?'

'You were just lucky because I tripped on the sword.'

'And the eagle? I think you're scared of the bird.'

'A bit,' I agreed.

'Well, I'm not. And Scur, I mean Axeface, as you call him?'

'I think we're both scared of him.'

A pause then I said, 'Gam. That's a name for a boy. If you're a girl do you have another name?'

'Yes, it's Guiane.'

'Gee…I don't get it,' I said, 'it sounds just the same. It's still Gam.'

'It's similar,' she explained. 'The proper name is Guianette but I've always shortened it to Guiane. The boy's name I chose was Guillaume. Try saying it.'

'Gee…Gee….It's no good,' I rolled the name around on my tongue but tripped every time I tried it. 'Can we just keep it as Gam?'

She laughed, 'Yes. I like it and I've got used to it. Guillaume is the same as William in England.'

'Like the bad Duke in Normandy?'

'Yes, you call him Duke William.'

He gets called other names round here, I chuckled.

7. EAGLE EYE

Gam hates to see anything tied or tethered. She thinks often and with pity of the eagle strapped to a rough perch, the mighty, secretive bird paraded as a tawdry thing, hawked around the country greens, ogled by bumpkins.

The eagle is too noble to feel pity for itself but, nonetheless, dreams of the open skies, the high thermals on which she once soared and glimpses, from time to time, a soaring cousin, a buzzard or kite, and her heart contracts with envy. Hooded, tricked into a life of dozing darkness, she takes wing in the ether of her mind, no longer a hunched figure of dull feathers on a perch but high-rising to a speck in the sky.

And what would a speck of eagle see?

She would see this little patch of this little island on the great spinning globe: the south-east corner of Britain. Territories come and go but at this moment, in September 1066, Ash and Gam are in Sussex within the Anglo-Saxon kingdom of Wessex, about 50 miles from London and 40 miles from France. They are separated only by a capricious barrier of stormy water from a disgruntled and ruthless Norman duke preparing his forces for invasion. While the children in the hollow warm their toes by the fire and doze, trees in Normandy are being felled, weapons and armour are being prepared, soldiers are being recruited and trained with the promise of rich rewards.

Looking closer the eagle's eye would trace the coast road from Hastings winding uneasily along the high ground, following the ridge northwards and westwards before turning inland towards London. On either side there are a few fields, sparse hamlets and thick woodland.

Ash and Gam are about two miles away from the road where the wood is at its thickest as it runs down towards the marsh. From the ridge you follow tracks made by the woodcutters and charcoal burners and occasional travellers. Then the tracks thin down to smaller runs made by the habitual routes of woodland animals. When these give out you must pick your way through and round thickets of thorn, gorse, scrub and briar which work to mislead you into sucking wet clay and gurgling black bogs. Here and there small springs bubble to the surface and from some of these, but by no means all, you are able to drink. Then there are dips and hollows which, mysteriously, are sometimes dry and sometimes ponds – shallow or deep, you don't know – of sinister red water, evidence of the ancient iron workings.

Others, many others, have been here before. Long ago the Romans, the Old People, greedy for metal. This spot, close to the coast, was rich in iron ore and all that is needed to smelt it: good hard wood for the charcoal, clay for the kilns, ample running water to turn the water wheels which pump the bellows which blow the air to feed the fire and cheap, sometimes free, slave, labour.

Back then the woods were alive with noise and work, the flaring of the fires and kilns, the shouts of men. The makers and smelters of iron, those who dug the pits, gathered the ore, made the charcoal, watched the kilns where red hot temperature must be maintained night and day, moved the heavy iron bars – sows - using oxen, to haul them slowly through the clinging mud of the woodland - all, they all had a hard time of it. They lived in makeshift camps in the wood. Did they laugh, sing, gossip, complain and crack jokes like us? How can we know? Their names and faces, feeble hopes and plans are lost in the tangle of undergrowth, whispered in the leaves and echoed in the groaning of the trees. Their masters, the engineers and artificers, the planners and cruel overseers and officers had more comfort. A smooth road leading from their fort at Richborough in the east brought them along Kent Street to a bathhouse, tiled and heated, where they could have rest and refreshment. They could wash themselves in hot and cold waters in the Roman way, rub their skins with olive oil, scrape themselves clean with the sharp metal blades called strigils and treat themselves to delicacies sent from the continent. Here, for precious moments, they could immerse themselves in warmth, gossip, music, food and pleasure while the outside of the bath house was beaten with cold rain, wind and frost. Here they could briefly imagine themselves back in the warmth and sunshine of home which, foolishly, they had left so long ago and to which, probably, they knew they would never return.

The bathhouse was tiled and artists were brought in to decorate the building with mosaic floors, fountains and frescoes. The pictures they made were a sentimental tribute to the warm climes, the grapes and fruits, familiar animals of the lands from which many of these men had been reluctantly exiled to a small damp island at the northern end of the empire. The artists also added fanciful beasts from their own imaginations or as reminders of the fables the men resting in the bathhouse would know by heart. These men worshipped here, too. They had shrines protected by yew trees, sacred springs *and rocks. Now, like the lost voices of the men who had been here before, the old gods also, sometimes, whispered and beckoned.*

Times changed for the Romans: politics changed; the economy pinched as their empire corroded. First in a slow trickle, then in a faster moving stream of panic the iron kilns were neglected and abandoned. Finally the Romans left and the bathhouse stood empty. The skills of iron making were lost. Time passed. The bathhouse became overgrown. Animals got in. Travellers squatted there for a time but, finding no reason to settle, moved on. New masters came and went, Vikings mainly: the Norsemen – that's Northmen, Normans. But, by then, the weather had weakened the building. A period of torrential rain, drought, more rain and the cycle of soaking and drying went on year in, year out so that the bank of clay and iron waste, the slagheap behind the bathhouse, began to move, slowly at first, then more quickly, finally settling and covering the bathhouse like a heavy blanket. Seeds dropped, weeds and vegetation quickly spread: moss, ferns and grasses. Then, more slowly, trees grew on top, their roots reaching down through the earth and rubble to entangle themselves in the broken biscuits of the old tiled roof.

The building simply became part of the landscape: a hill concealing a magical cave; a vertiginous drop to a secret doorway. Who knows what is under our feet?

And Ash found it.

'How,' asked Gam, lying back in the warmth of the firelight, 'how ever did you find it?'

Ash was proud of his knowledge of the wood. There wasn't a part or path he didn't know in detail. But it was a melancholy knowledge which he'd acquired the hard way driven, so often, from the village by hard knocks and threats when Dad was drinking or hungry or, as often the case, hungry because he was drinking. Then, he would roam the tracks and woods. It was hard at first, especially when he was very young and especially before he found Misty. Now, lying on his back, close to the crackling fire, the warmth of food in his stomach, the pictures on the wall flickering and dancing, he could talk about it. He realised, too, this was something he'd held, contained tight in himself; why, in the village, he was considered a mute, an oddity, an outsider. It was a knot which, as he spoke to Gam, seemed, magically, to spring undone.

Ash talked aloud as he'd never talked before. The words impressed themselves on Gam who, sitting listening, looked spellbound at her young companion lying on the floor by the fire. Ash was little. There was nothing to him, almost a pile of tangled rags on the ground, his long hair a nest of flaxen curls surrounding a face usually pale and streaked with dirt but now red from the warmth of the wood fire. And Gam felt a burst of warmth greater than that from the fire. Ash was talking like this because he had her trust. It was friendship and this was something neither child had ever properly known. And now, Gam resolved, they would always be friends. The twisting tracks of the wood had brought them together. As she listened she realised how rough things must have been for Ash, how lonely he must have been, how hungry and miserable. And yet, as he spoke, there was not a trace of self pity or recrimination. Ash told his story just as it was, in that matter of fact way he had about him. She marvelled, too, at the clarity of his voice which, when they first met, had been flat, slurred, hesitant, unsure of itself like a fledgling about to leave the nest. Now his words took wing.

8. WORDS

Ash loves the chatter of things: small brown birds chirruping in the scrub, the mew of buzzards, small rivers burbling, goats bleating, hens grousing, hogs complaining; nothing dramatic by way of alarm or scream, just the gentle sound of something thinking aloud to itself. And now he can do this with Gam. Before, he used to think. Now, what he thinks he can say. On his back, by the warm fire, looking up at the tile and tangled root roof of this magical hideaway he can speak his thoughts and, as is the way when we are in easy company, he sometimes doesn't know what he is thinking until it is said.

He tells Gam.

I knew they didn't like me. It wasn't their fault. I just came along at a hard time. There wasn't much in the village. It was the bad weather but also bad husbandry because you didn't need to look far at other places and they were doing all right: trading, sowing, harvesting. The main problem was Dad. He always thought he'd been overlooked; thought he was cut out for better things. He thought he was something of a warrior, was always telling us what he'd done in the past, fighting with the *fyrd*. But others said different, that he'd done more skiving and running away than fighting. And when things went wrong, he took it out on me. So I got to going off. The first time I remember, I was only small.

'Why are you laughing?'

'Well, you're not exactly big now,' chuckled Gam.

There was such a row in the hut, Dad roaring, stuff being chucked about. So I went out and sat in the bushes. Then I could hear them looking for me and calling so I went further into the wood. People from the village brought rush torches and dogs to look for me so I went further until I was lost. I found a place under some tree roots. It was damp and cold, I nearly froze and I was hungry. Crikey, I was hungry. I still remember that night. It went on for ever and I was scared. I tell you I've seen stuff since but nothing scared me like that first night. The noises: badgers, foxes and owls mostly but I thought they were wolves and monsters. I thought the wood spirits were coming for me. When it got light I crept back to the village and the hut. Funny thing nothing was said. Dad let me sleep. I hadn't slept all night. But then when I did wake up I started eating and then the rows started again. And so it went on. All right for a bit then the arguments again and so I'd take off again. After a while I got wise to it and I kept an extra shirt and a bag with some food hidden in a secret place. It was still bad but not so bad. And I took my knife – the *seaxe* - and I knew that whatever came at me in the night would have a fight.

Gam suppressed a snigger.

'What's wrong?'

'Nothing,' she said, 'just thinking of you fighting off a pack of wolves with your knife.'

Then I got to planning things in my head. I'd guess when something bad was up so every time I went out I took something into the wood. Made myself a camp and put a store of things there. And I learned to build a dry shelter and make a good fire. But I was awful lonely until Misty came along.

'Tell me about Misty,' said Gam and she stroked the head of the little dog who shifted and whimpered in her sleep.

One day Till came to our hut. He and Dad used to sit and talk. They'd pretty much grown up together. Till knew what was going on and he always had a soft spot for me, would look out for me. One day he came and he had a parcel of cloth in his arms and he said, 'Here you are youngun,' and gave me the cloth and it was wriggling and there was Misty. A little pup. 'She's only a little one,' said Till. 'She's not had it easy and she's not very trustful. She'll need a bit of nursing but, once she's right, I think she'll be a goodun.'

That was the best day ever because I now had something to look after and something to look after me. And we've always been like that. We look out for each other. She was like a little runt. There was nothing to her. Could hardly eat at first. They were going to put her down, Till said.

'What is she?' said Dad.

'She's a hunting dog,' said Till. 'Get her right and, with a dog like that, the boy will never be hungry.'

We were quiet for a while. Misty muttered in her sleep as though she knew she was being talked about. We watched the twisting flames of the crackling fire. The sparks, fairy folk, flying up the chimney.

'Then, what about you, Gam?' I asked cautiously.

'What about me?'

'Did you have a dog?'

'No,' said Gam, 'although there were dogs there, where I lived. But I didn't have a dog like a friend as Misty is to you.'

'And….?'

'And what…?'

'Well, I don't know anything about you. Except you ran away and then the birdmen. Tell me about you.'

A long pause.

'It's difficult,' said Gam. 'What do you want to know?'

'I don't think we should have secrets,' I said. 'What are you?'

'What do you mean?'

'Well, what are you? You speak funny.'

Gam laughed. 'I speak two languages. That's why.'

'So you're a Norman?'

'I suppose I am but, perhaps, half. I never saw my mother but my father said she was from Kent.'

'Can I ask you something?' I said. It had been bothering me. 'If you were a servant, like you said, why don't you know how to cook or make a fire or cut up a hog?'

Gam hesitated. 'There are different kinds of servants,' she said. 'My job was to help in the chambers where the family slept. I hardly ever went into the kitchens.'

'I think,' I said tentatively, 'I think you're not like us.'

'How?'

'Well, like Till says. He says there's stations in life. We've all got a station. Some are bound like me and Dad and have to work for others. Some are *freemen*, some are *churls* then there's *thanes* and knights all the way up to the top.'

'The top? To where?'

'Well, the King, I suppose. Where are you, Gam? I'm not much, I can tell you. I'm at the bottom.'

Gam kicked me affectionately. 'No you're not.'

'But where are you?'

A pause. 'Well, I'm….I mean the family where I worked…as a servant….the man, the father of the family is a knight.'

'Crikey,' I gave a whistle of surprise, 'then is he with, you know, the bad Duke?'

'Yes, but there, you have to understand, there they don't think he's bad.'

'They say, here in the village, he wants to steal the crown of England.'

'And there, in Normandy, they say the crown of England has been stolen by your king, Harold.'

I lowered my voice. 'Be careful Gam. You can't say that.'

'I'm not saying anything about what is right or what is wrong. I'm just saying what is.'

Their chatter has hit a bump but like a running stream drifts easily around and away.

They talk about hiding in the wood.

Trees, said Ash. That's what he liked. He reckons you could live in trees. You can hide in a tree and who knows you're there? You can look down and watch people going past and they don't know. The things you see. And he tells Gam about the things he's seen when hiding in the trees. Strange animals that, normally, would run in shyness away from humans. An owl that popped out from its nest next to where he was sitting, looked at him, blinked and stared in annoyance. It flew off and, shortly, came back with a vole in its beak, looked at him again and popped into the nest. People who, thinking

111

they were alone, behaved oddly: talking to themselves, making speeches to invisible audiences, singing, shouting. And courting couples kissing and frolicking in the grass not realising they were being watched from the tree. He made Gam roll with laughter as he described the antics he'd seen.

But, said Ash, he hid in the trees less these days because it wasn't fair on Misty who couldn't climb.

What if dogs could climb trees like cats?

They laughed at the thought of Misty sitting in a tree and she complained in her sleep as if she knew she were being teased. They talked about animals and their differences. Why could cats climb upwards but find it hard to come down? What if cats grew as big as dogs? Which animals were clever? The crow family they reckoned were the sharpest: crows, rooks, daws, pies, jays and, most of all, the ravens, whereas waterfowl and hens were the stupidest. Which animals in the wood were the most dangerous? Wild hogs they reckoned because they were unpredictable.

They talked about the birdmen.

'You know what they're doing,' said Gam, 'they're spying. They're what we call Anybodies. They know a battle is coming up. They'll be on any side, wherever there's treasure or profit, something to gain.'

'What will they do if they find you?'

'Probably give me a whipping but not a lot more they can do. They need me because I can write.'

'Write?'

'Yes. I can do letters,' and she drew a shape with her hand. 'I can make maps and drawings – the roads, the villages, the good places to hide, the open places where a fight can take place. These are the things those men trade in. They buy and sell birds but they also trade in secrets. They steal secrets and sell them. It's information. It's knowledge that will help Guillaume, William of Normandy with his attack.'

I was puzzled by the letters. 'Is that magic?' I asked suspiciously.

'No,' she laughed, 'it's words. You speak words but then they're gone in the air…'

'No,' I interrupted, 'they stay in your mind because you remember them.'

'True,' she conceded, 'but some things like names – places, numbers - are hard to remember for long. I can fix those words on a piece of skin – vellum, it's called, it's very precious – and they stay there for ever.'

'Not for ever.'

'Well, for a long time and longer than you could remember if you only heard the words but couldn't see them.'

'But how can you see words? Where are they?' I was puzzled.

'I make marks with a pointer,' she explained, 'that's the sharp end of a bone and the mark comes from ink which is like colour in water – like the dye that's used to give linen its colour and how they make and decorate the flags for soldiers. Look, I'll show you.' She took a burnt stick from the fire and drew on the wall.

This was a great wonder to me.

They talked of God and heaven and the beliefs the older people had. Could you see God in the night sky? What about the star everyone had seen and which, they said, was a sign? What about the old gods which, some said, were more powerful? They talked of the secret places in the wood where there were spirits and how to tell if these things were good or ill. 'Here,' said Ash, 'they believe more in the old gods. A holy father came to our village but they drove him away with sticks.'

They talked of sickness and death and why it was that some people lived long and healthy and others became unwell. Did you bring sickness on yourself or was it visited on you? What will happen after this life? 'I'd like to be in a picture,' said Ash, 'quiet and still until someone comes with a light to make me dance.'

They talked of what had gone before. Who were the Old People who built this hall? Where had they gone? Were there ghosts? Ash talked about the ghosts he had seen. At night, hiding in the trees he saw men marching through the wood but they made no sound.
'Dreams,' said Gam.
'No,' said Ash, 'I saw them marching but they were walking on the air.'

They talked about the pictures on the wall and wondered who had made them, what their names were, their stories and adventures. Had others, children perhaps, hidden in this place before?

I was fascinated by the magic of the letters and the pictures and I came back to them time after time.

'Show me again,' I said.

Gam collected some sticks of burnt wood from the fire and, while Misty and I sat patiently watching, she drew two figures on the wall. When, at last, she had finished, she stepped back, 'That's you and me,' she said.

'Which is you and which is me?' I asked.

'Can't you see?' Gam took my hand and coaxed me to trace the figures she'd drawn with my finger. 'Look, this is me and this one is you,' but although she said it so confidently I couldn't see the difference. Then she worked some more. A different figure: an animal, 'and here's Misty.'

To me it was a kind of conjuration and I marvelled at it. 'Do some more.'

She drew birds and fish. She drew dogs, hogs, deer and wolves. Then she made letters.

'What's that?'

'It's Ash. It's your name,' she traced the letters and spoke them slowly, 'A-S-C. And here's mine, G-A-M.'

I put my finger on the letters wondering at the magic of it all. The nearest I could come to it was that the shapes were like the twisty hazel sticks that are cut and laid to make a hedge. 'And Misty?'

'I'm not sure how to write it,' she said. 'It's not a familiar name to me. Look,' and, slowly, she wrote D-O-G. 'It says dog because Misty is a dog.'

'Can't you write her name?'

'Well, I'll try.' She wrote a long, mysterious string of letters.

'Is that it? Why is it longer?'

'Eh?'

'Why is Misty, longer? She's not bigger than us.'

'It's just her name, Ash.'

'But why is her name bigger?'

'That's just how it is. Some names are short and some are long.'

'Ours are the same,' I said, measuring *ASC* and *GAM* with my fingers.

'But Gam is short for Guillaume or Guianette,' she said, 'look,' and slowly she wrote *GUILLAUME*.

I was indignant, 'It's longer than Ash. It's longer than me.' I stood tall as I could up against her. 'Yet we're the same height. Well, you're a bit taller.'

'It's only names, Ash,' she explained. It's nothing to do with how big you are.'

'If Gam is short for Guil....,' I tried to say Guillaume but always stumbled, 'what's Ash short for?'

'Nothing,' she said. 'Ash isn't short for anything. Ash is just Ash.'

'That doesn't seem fair.'

'It's nothing to do with how big you are,' she explained again then, suddenly, 'what about Ox? The big man, the falconer, was called Ox,' and she wrote the two letters on the wall. 'It's a tiny name but he's a big man,' she explained.

I had to agree that it seemed right but I couldn't leave it alone. 'I still don't get it,' I said. 'I'm not a tree and he's not an ox.

Gam banged the palm of her hand on her forehead in exasperation. 'Ox is just a name that was made up for that stupid story you heard in the show. Axeface just called him that,' she protested, 'and your mother and father called you Ash because....'

'Because I was born in an ash tree,' I shouted.

'Not *in* a tree, Ash. Perhaps you were born *under* a tree or *next* to a tree. You couldn't be born *in* a tree.'

'Could,' I said. 'Dad told me they called me Ash because I was born *in* an ash tree.'

Gam pulled one of her faces. 'Here,' she handed me a stick. 'You try.'

'No,' but she was persuasive and I picked up a blackened stick and dabbed it on the wall. Nothing but silly marks. Gam kept encouraging me, sometimes guiding my hand so that slowly, tentatively, I drew shapes.

I was a bit disheartened. Even after several attempts I could manage little more than clumsy marks. It was hard to control the black stick. But I persevered and went over to the other side of the room and found a bare, smooth piece of wall to work on.

After a while Gam came over to watch. 'What pictures are you making?'

'This,' I said proudly, 'this is the wood where I live,' and I pointed to some upright marks I'd made. 'These are trees and,' a squiggle, 'a bird and this,' some wavy lines, 'the stream and this,' I'd made a circle, 'is the sun.'

'And this?' Gam pointed to two clumsy circles.

'That's us,' I said proudly.

'But what are these?' she pointed to some sticks which looked like twigs sticking out of the circles.

'That's our arms,' I said and I realised I'd forgotten the legs.

'How many fingers have you got, Ash?'

'I can count,' I said defensively. 'Five fingers on each hand.'

'Well your pictures,' said Gam, 'have got…this one eight fingers…this one six.'

'That's because it's more useful,' I said. I didn't like the criticism. 'If you've got more fingers you can do more things.'

She pulled a face. 'And where are the eyes?'

'Here,' I pointed to some small blobby ring shapes.

'But shouldn't they be *inside* the head?'

'It's hard,' I said. 'I wanted to leave room for a nose and mouth and I can't fit them all in.'

'Where's Misty?'

'I'm just doing her,' I said crossly. This was hard work. After a laborious effort I'd made a long sausage sort of shape making sure I'd given it some legs.

'But that's five legs,' protested Gam trying hard not to laugh because she could see the effort I was making.

'That one's a tail.'

Later, by the fire, we talked more about the letters and the pictures.

'Have you never seen pictures before?' Gam asked.

'I don't think so,' I said. 'There's a thing like a picture in the Big Hall where they have meetings and store food in the village. It's the head of a stag and I think it's a picture but it might be a real head,' I paused to think and then, 'but there are pictures on the flags, the standards the soldiers have. Yes, I saw the dragon, the Wyvern. And the King's standard, the Fighting Man. So I have seen pictures,' I said triumphantly. 'And I've seen pictures on the ships. They have pictures on the sails and they have flags with pictures.' I told Gam about the Wyvern and what the men had said about it spitting fire from its mouth and its tail.

'It's a legend,' said Gam, 'like an old story. There's always stories about dragons.'

'I haven't seen a dragon I don't think,' I said thoughtfully, 'but I have heard them roaring in the wood at night and I've heard talk of them but I think they might be further north.'

Gam exploded with laughter. 'There aren't dragons, Ash. 'They're just stories.'

I looked at her in disbelief. 'Of course there are dragons,' I said, 'everyone knows that.'

'There are not.'

'There are,' then, 'and there must be because I've seen the Wyvern on the flag.'

'But it's not real,' protested Gam, 'it's a picture.'

'I know,' I said decisively, 'but they must have got the picture from somewhere.'

'Eh?'

'Look,' I pointed at the pictures she'd made, 'that's you and me and Misty. And here we are.'

'So?'

'If the picture is there and we're here and there's a picture of a dragon then there must be dragons. So there.'

'Shall we do something else?' suggested Gam.

In the day we would explore the wood. I showed Gam the good things to eat and what to avoid; how to gather mushrooms, berries and nuts. Together we wove hazel baskets which we used as fish traps where the river ran shallow into the lake. She loved it when the trap was filled with wriggling perch and bream but recoiled when we caught eels. They twisted themselves furiously and made as if to bite us. If you tried to grab them they'd squirm out of your grasp. It was best to throw some dried grass in the trap, let them get caught up in that, grip them by the middle and strike the head off with the *seaxe*. When I first did that Gam turned pale and was sick in the bushes.

I showed her how to track, the different prints left by deer and hog and the footmarks of travellers in the wood. I was amazed that she didn't know how to do any of those things. She showed me how to use the crossbow but we couldn't fire it properly because there was only the one bolt left which I'd retrieved from the dead hog and which we were keeping for emergencies. We tried making bolts with sticks but they weren't heavy enough. We dammed the streams to make pools and lakes where we could paddle and splash.

'What are those marks?' asked Gam, pointing at my arm. I'd stripped my clothes off to wade into the deep water. We were used to each other's body now. That odd modesty from the first day in the hollow had gone. My skin, I'd noticed, was darker than Gam's. She was pale and unblemished whereas I seemed to have marks and scars all over me.

'This, here,' I said pointing at a sort of crescent moon on my calf, 'is where a dog bit me. And this,' pointing to my left arm, 'is from falling out of a tree. And here I burnt myself on one of Till's hot irons. This,' a recent bruise on my chest, 'was from Ern.'

Gam pulled a sympathetic face. 'You've been in the wars, Ash. But these, like rings, amulets,' she pointed to my upper right arm where there were three patterned circles.

'They're marks.'

'What are they for?'

I shrugged, 'Dunno. We all have them. They're our marks. Our people.'

'What, your family? Your tribe?'

'I suppose so. The wise woman does them. She makes the circles on your arm with a sharp stone and some special colour. It hurts like anything and, sometimes, it swells up and pus and stuff comes out. Some people even get a fever. But if you get it done and you don't make a fuss and you don't get a fever that means things are good. It will go well for you.'

'What will?'

'Things. Everything. And, as you grow up, you get more of them done. Different shapes.'

'Why?'

'It's to do with who you are. Some people have lots done. On their arms, chests, backs, even their faces if they're important. Being just a hog….just a boy….without anything because Dad's not a free man I don't get much done. Just these circles. But I'd like to get a bird, here on my shoulder.'

We climbed trees, we painted our faces with red earth and pretended we were soldiers. We had races along the narrow paths, hiding from each other in the bushes and trees then springing out in ambush. We made a game called run and find. One of us would run off and hide; the other waited a bit then followed and had to find them. Or we'd hide from Misty and she had to find us. We practised bird calls, hallooing each other and making secret codes for *danger, follow me, go back, go forward* and *all safe*. The woods were our own, we kept away from the paths where people might be. We were lost in our own world.

In the evenings we would light the fire and eat. We'd tell stories about the pictures on the wall. I told Gam I was sure they were the shapes of shifters but I thought they could be ghosts that rested on the walls in the day and went out of the hall at night to feast on lost travellers when we were asleep. Or, I said, they were the spirits of animals that had died and which now rested on the walls.

'But what about the plants and fruits?' she asked.

'It's their spirits, too,' I said.

'And the strange beasts? The dragons?'

'Their spirits, too.'

'But, I keep telling you, there aren't such things, Ash,' she complained.

Mostly, though, we'd paint on the wall. Gam drew the eagle. It was wonderful and terrible. We decided we needed colours and we tried making them using clay, berries and charcoal and some of the grey iron shale.

9. WULF

I was woken suddenly by a noise: a shout in the night. Was I dreaming? A hand on my arm made me jump with fright. Axeface? Ern? Dad? No, it was Gam. For a moment I'd forgotten Gam, sleeping beside me but now awake and sitting up. She put out a comforting hand.

'Did you hear it Ash?'

'Yes, an animal, probably.'

She put a finger to her lips. 'Listen. It's been going on.'

We waited in the silence. Some gentle snapping of sparks from the low embers of the fire. Then, again, there it was: a shout, a terrible roar, unearthly and not so far away. Misty had lifted her head, ears pricking up. Gam and I looked at each other in the dim light thrown from the fire and snuggled closer together.

'What do you think?' she whispered.

'Dunno.'

It came again, deep, less urgent, more a moan of something in pain.

'You sure it's an animal?'

'No, too deep, I think. More like a human.'

'Could be a bear.'

'There are bears but I don't think it is. Foxes can make a racket but more of a high, ghostly kind of cry.'

'Is it ghosts do you think?' she shuddered.

'No. Till says there are no ghosts.'

'But you said you've seen ghosts.'

'I know,' I said, 'I can't work it out. I believe I've seen ghosts but then I believe Till when he says there's no such thing.'

'Ash, you don't make sense, sometimes.'

We heard it again. But a bit fainter.

'It does sound sort of human. Not Axeface is it with his magic?' Gam asked anxiously.

'Nah,' but I didn't feel too sure of myself.

'What shall we do?'

'Nothing we can do until it's light.'

'Whatever it is won't find us here will it?' she was anxious, too.

'No. But we must get ready, in case.'

I made sure I had my *seaxe*. We had the Norman broadsword and Gam had her knife. She also had the crossbow and the one bolt. We felt well armed but neither of us slept much after that. Time seemed to stand still. We put more wood on the fire. The mysterious animals on the wall began their unending roundabout chase through the painted forest. We heard the cry again but fainter as though further off.

I must have dozed because I woke suddenly from a dream as the first light of dawn filtered through the window of broken wall. Gam was awake, too. We sat listening but outside we heard only the familiar woodland sounds: the early birds calling, the rattle of woodpeckers, the shriek of buzzards, the steady rhythm of the stream, the wind in the trees. It was comfortable by the smouldering fire in the hollow and we weren't usually up and about this early. We went through our breakfast routine: some bread, some bits of cold fish, some warm water brewed with delicious herbs. We went cautiously outside to the stream to wash. In the early light the day seemed normal. We knew we needed to investigate the source of the night-time noise but we were nervous and reluctant to begin, dragging our feet, wasting time talking about it. Should we go together or should one of us stay behind in case? In case of what? What were we afraid of? We went together. These days, more and more, we did everything together.

Armed with the *seaxe*, sword, and crossbow we left the hollow and climbed cautiously up the steep winding path to the top of the hill. Strange, I thought, the first time here there was no path, it had all seemed impenetrable. But now we had made a path by walking. At one time I thought I'd never make my way down the steep descent. I'd clung on for dear life. Now both of us could go up and down quite easily, almost at a run. Our feet were wearing a clear track. We knew the secure footholds, the awkward crumbly bits, and the handholds amongst the roots and branches.

When we got to the top we waited for a moment, lying down in the ferns and peering at the forest floor ahead. Nothing. It was quiet. We made our way carefully to the first of the tracks on the hillside. Nothing out of the ordinary, just the usual woodland sounds of the morning. We walked slowly on feeling more confident with each step and putting the fears of the night behind us – childish imaginings and phantasms - until, suddenly, Misty froze and bristled and we both stopped, crouched and peered carefully ahead. There was no movement but we could see a shape in the bracken just off to one side of the track. A wild boar perhaps. The thought made us fearful. Some cautious creeping steps forward until we could just make it out in a tangle of undergrowth: something big, bigger than a boar, a deer perhaps, a stag possibly with its antlers caught, a bear. We waited, breath held like hunters, then some more slow, gentle steps.

A big man, but an old man was lying in the bracken with his long white hair spread out around his head. A litter of belongings were thrown down: a bag, a battered shield, a rusting soldier's helmet and a great battleaxe lay in a heap beside him. His face was white-bearded, a bit bloated, scarred and blotched but pale. We stood still as stone, waiting for him to move but both with the same thought that, probably, he was dead. We hesitated then approached cautiously, me ahead with the broadsword, Gam behind covering me with the crossbow.

We were stepping together silently when the air was rent open as the man let go a ripping, rattling fart. I heard a suppressed giggle from Gam behind me. The man sighed loudly with relief and sat up but, as he did so, he grasped his leg and stretched his mouth in pain. We were expecting a shout but, instead, staring ahead and without looking at us, he spoke in a deep reverberating voice.

'If you're going to use that sword on me, boy, you better make haste because, unless you do, I'll cleave you from top to bottom with this axe which, unlike that lump of metal you've got trembling there, is properly sharp. And I mean sharp.'

He groaned again before continuing and still without looking at us, 'As for your friend with that silly little crossbow you better tell him to take more care because if he trips he'll send the bolt into the back of your head.' He chuckled to himself but checked as he gasped in pain. 'I've seen one of those mishandled before. Took the top of a man's head off, helmet as well, and pinned it to a tree. A chestnut if I remember. The head was still talking. I heard it say, *Just be careful with that crossbow, mate.*' He roared with laughter at his own story then groaned in pain again and massaged his leg.

I took a step back nervously and do did Gam.

'Which of you is the chief?'

We didn't answer.

'Who's in charge? The squirt with the sword or the milksop with the crossbow? What are your forces? How many of you?'

Gam found a voice, 'Just the two of us,' she said.

'Two, eh? But then I suppose you have reinforcements in the trees. Archers and such. Cavalry, too I should guess.'

'Cavalry?'

'Yes, boy. Cavalry. That's horses.'

'I know what cavalry means and it's just the two of us,' said Gam, 'three with the dog.'

'That dog doesn't count. I've seen bigger weasels. So it's two against one. Hardly fair I think.'

'We're not against,' said Gam. 'And we're only boys. You're big and we're little so it is fair.'

The soldier laughed and snorted. Then he became solemn. 'Lying here,' he said, 'lying here I watched a buzzard circling over those trees and two little birds – jackdaws, I'd say - flew out and saw him off. They flew at the old buzzard who could have crushed each one in his claws. But they chased him and harried him till he'd had enough of it.' He turned to look at us for the first time. 'You don't need to be big to be brave,' he said. 'I think you're like those birds: boys with big brave hearts.'

'And the dog,' said Gam. 'She might be little but she's brave, too.'

'Yes,' laughed the soldier. 'The dog, too.'

'We heard you shouting. We came to help.'

'Shouting?'

'Last night. We heard shouting.'

'Well, you'd shout if you were attacked.'

'Attacked?' said Gam, aghast.

'Set upon by an army of wild men with clubs and axes.'

'An army? They attacked here!' exclaimed Gam in surprise.

The big man opened his mouth and laughed. 'No,' he tapped his head, 'in here. Just my dreams, boy. I have bad dreams: an old soldier's demons. Pain too. A bit of a roar does the pain good; makes it feel a trifle better.'

A pause. We stood nervously, staring, not sure what to do.

'Put your weapons down, lads. You can see an old man, lame like me, isn't any match for two strapping boys.' He looked at me with his eyes, old and watery but full of light, and gave a wink. 'Lay the sword down boy. It's trembling so much it'll fall out of your hand in a moment anyway.'

He was right. The sword was awfully heavy and wavering in my grip.

'And,' speaking to Gam, 'I say again, undo that crossbow. Those things make me nervous. Horrible invention. Wouldn't have anything to do with them.'

We put our weapons down.

'Well don't just stand there. Help a fellow soldier will you. Can you get me a drink? Aaaaargh,' he let out another terrifying bellow, 'It's my leg.'

'Is it broken?' Gam asked.

'I don't think so but thanks for asking. I notice you do all the talking. Has your friend lost his tongue?'

'I can talk,' I said. 'I'll get you some water.'

'Water!' He threw me a leather bottle. 'Fill it if you can with your finest wine, if you have any or, if not, some of that sour beer they serve in these parts.'

I looked at him blankly.

'All right lad, water will do but make sure it's good and clean and fresh.'

I took the bottle to the stream, rinsed it out – it smelt badly of some strong drink - filled it with water and took it back. Gam was sitting next to him, chatting amiably.

The big man snatched the bottle from me and drank thirstily. 'Chance of any food?'

'I could go back and get something,' I said. 'It'll take a while.'

'Quick as you can boy.'

Gam and Misty sat with him while I went back and scrambled down to the hollow for supplies. I made up a basket of stale bread, some cuts of cold fish, cheese and apples. When I returned, Gam had got the man's boot off and was applying a poultice of damp leaves to a purple and swollen ankle.

'It's broken,' she said.

'It was an ambush,' said the man, 'a wicked combination of too much drink, darkness coming on and a tricky tree root.'

He looked at the food gratefully then at Gam. 'Have you a knife, lad?' He made a cutting motion and pointed at his mouth. 'The old teeth, you understand.'

We sniggered and Gam cut the food into tiny pieces, passing the morsels to the man who gummed them contentedly. The bread was hard so we soaked it in water. I'd brought some fire seeds with me and we soon got a fire going and watched him as he ate.

'Where are you from?' asked Gam.

He waved vaguely, 'All over. Lately, the north.'

'Where are you going?'

'To the coast. To fight for my King.'

We looked at each other doubtfully. He seemed well beyond fighting age.

'You boys,' he said loftily, 'have saved the day. I thought last night that this is where I'd die. But you two have come along.' He looked at us quizzically. 'Where did you come from? You must have come from somewhere or did you just fall out of the trees?'

Gam mimicked him by waving her arm vaguely. 'From around here. We live in the woods.'

He roared with laughter, 'Wild wood boys, eh? Runaways, I expect. And your names?'

'I'm Gam. This is Ash. And this, our dog, is Misty.'

'Hmmm,' he was giving our names some thought. 'Misty because, I suppose, she's hard to see. And a mystery, perhaps and,' he chuckled, 'mischief, I expect. Ash is good. Ash is a strong timber and has a strong heart. Ash is good for handles,' he reached out and stroked the haft of his battleaxe. 'My axe handle is ash. But the ash tree bends with the wind.'

He said it quizzically and I asked, 'Is that good?'

'Can be,' he chuckled, 'depends which way the wind is blowing.' Then, more reassuringly, 'It's a good name, Ash, but what in tarnation is Gam?'

'It's a way of saying Guillaume,' said Gam.

'Frenchy,' are you?

Gam nodded.

'I've been there,' he said. 'I know the Frenchy and some of their talk.'

'And what about you?' asked Gam. 'Who are you?'

'Me?' He sat up straight and spoke proudly, 'Me. I'm Wulfnod but they call me Wulf,' and he raised his head, leaned back, opened his mouth and howled like a wolf making us shiver and sending Misty off to hide under a bush.

'That was the noise we heard last night,' said Gam, 'it gave us a scare.'

The old soldier laughed. 'That's what it's meant to do,' he said proudly. 'It's a battle cry. I've seen men throw down their weapons and run for their lives when they've heard it.'

'What are you?' asked Gam.

He looked at us hard, 'I'm the Fighting Man.'

10.TILL

It was obvious we would need help. The man's ankle was broken and we had to find him some shelter. There was no hope of getting him down to the hollow. The best thing, I thought, would be to take him to Till's forge. But we'd need Till's help to get him there.

I left Gam with Misty and set off to find Till. It was strange taking the same track back up towards the village. It seemed a long time since I'd been there and I realised how wrapped up I'd been in my time in the wood with Gam. I realised, too, how used I'd become to our own company and I felt nervous about meeting anyone I knew. I wanted to avoid the village. There was no need to go there because the forge where Till lived and worked was a little way off up by the ridgeway. But I wanted to have a look in our hut which should be safe because it was outside the main part of the village. I wondered if Dad might be there.

It was a shock. The hut had gone; burned to the ground. Nothing was left other than a pile of blackened timber. The livestock had gone, too. Everything picked over. A vengeful act. Ern.

I hurried on towards the forge but approached it cautiously wondering who might be there. But it was only Till hammering in a shower of sparks and smoke, the charcoal furnace glowing and throwing out a welcoming heat. It was dark inside and, against the bright light of day I must have shown as a curious figure because Till, normally calmness itself, looked up startled. 'Who is it? Ash? Is it you?'

'Till.'

'Ash. Look at the state of you, boy.'

'Eh?'

'You're a mess. Where've you been?'

'Keeping out of the way, like I was told to.'

'Yes, but you look….you look wild. You're dirty and, your hair. Come here.'

He took me over to the deep hollowed stone which was his water tank. I lowered my head, looked into the still burnished surface and startled myself because I did look like a wild boy. I thought I'd kept myself clean but I was smeared with mud and clay from my climb. My hair was growing long and tangled, a bird's nest of knots, bits of twigs, seeds and grass. I couldn't suppress a giggle of surprise.

'It's nothing to laugh about,' said Till. 'You can't let yourself go like that. Even wild animals give themselves a wash.'

'I do wash,' I said defensively. 'I wash in the stream.'

Till pulled a face. 'You don't smell too good, young'un. We better get you cleaned up. And you'd better tell me what you've been up to.'

'Not now,' I said. 'We need help. There's a man. He's hurt and we can't move him,' and I told him about the injured soldier.

'We? Who's we?'

'Me and Gam.'

'Gam?'

'He's another…boy. It'll take time to explain.'

'Is he as wild and dirty as you are?'

I laughed, 'Expect so. We're probably each so dirty we don't notice.'

'Bit like hogs, eh?' said Till, 'I know how fond you are of hogs. Seems you're trying to live like one.

Where've you been sleeping? Out of doors? What have you been living on, boy?' He stood back and took a good look at me in the light, 'You've grown a bit, filled out, too. You don't look too bad but I've been worried about you.'

'You don't need to worry about me,' I insisted. 'We just need to help the man in the wood. He can't walk.'

For a moment Till seemed unsure of himself. 'If he's a big man, I can't carry him. Anyway I've got work to do.' He suddenly seemed crestfallen. 'My boy Lang's gone. He's gone off with the army. They stopped by here and put all sorts of ideas in his head. I argued with him but he wouldn't hear me. I reckon he's gone off to join your Dad.'

'At least they'll look out for each other.'

'Reckon so. I hope so. But without him I've more to do here than I can manage. There's only the girl, my Elfin, to help. Lots of boys and men from the village have gone now. I could do with some help and I can't see I've got time to waste with someone in the wood who shouldn't be there anyway.'

'I'll help you here, Till, you know I will. Gam will, too. But come and help us with the man. You're good with injuries. If you can bind him up perhaps we can get him on his feet and walk him back here.'

'I've got too much to do,' Till protested. 'Who is he anyway? Does he have a name?'

'He told us he's a fallen warrior. He's big. Like a giant. And he's got an axe. A huge battleaxe. He goes by the name of Wulf, howls like one, too, and he says he's the fighting man.'

'What?' Till gave a start. 'Where did you hear that name? What did he say?'

'He just said he's the fighting man. Why? What does it mean?'

'The fighting man,' Till repeated the words almost in a whisper. 'Did he say anything else?'

'Lots. He's got lots to say but much of it is nonsense. I think his mind's wandering. He told us he's going to the coast to fight for the King.'

'The King?' Till repeated the words almost reverentially. 'What does he look like?'

I described him as best as I could: the helmet, the sword, the boots, the shield.

'Then, it's all starting,' Till said as though speaking to himself. 'I reckon he's an old *housecarl*. They're tricky people. I better come. I'll bring some things.'

'I've seen what's happened to our house,' I said, as we set off to the wood. 'Was it Ern?'

Till nodded grimly. 'Ern's getting out of hand,' he said, 'and he's ready for a fall. There's more than just your Dad has had enough of him.'

'Any news of Dad?'

'No. Everyone's talking about what happened with him and Ern. How your dad stood up to him. He got you out of a pickle there, young'un. I know your dad wasn't always the best but you've got something to thank him for.'

'Do you know where he's gone?'

'Wherever the army is. Like I say, my boy Lang has gone as well. Your Dad's broken his bond with Ern and, whatever we all think about Ern, that's not a good thing in the eyes of the law. But if he's now a king's soldier, then Ern can't touch him. Or you. But he can do

135

what he likes with your property and you can see what he's done.'

'What do you think I should do?'

'We can't have you running wild. You can't live on your own in the wood. It's not right.'

'I'm all right with Gam. The two of us are all right.'

'I expected you to come up to me,' said Till peevishly. 'You know you can stay with us. You'll need to work to earn your keep and you can sleep by the fire. You'll be dusty but you won't be cold. There's plenty to be done.'

'I will if Gam can come too.'

'I'll have to look him over,' said Till. 'Would you give him a recommendation?'

I didn't know what that meant but I said, yes I would and that he wouldn't go wrong with Gam. And then I couldn't help but blurt it out, 'He can do pictures and writing.'

Till looked at me oddly, 'Can he now? And where did he learn to do that?'

I realised I'd gone too far and said nothing more.

We walked on.

'You certainly know how to nip through these tracks,' said Till. I noticed he was perspiring and a little breathless.

'Till', I said. 'What did you mean when I said about the fighting man. That it's starting?'

For a moment Till said nothing as he panted along behind me. Then, 'I think there's trouble coming Ash and the young'uns like you should have no part of it. You need to keep well out of it.'

'Trouble. The Normans?'

'Reckon so. That William, the Norman duke, wants the throne of England. He wants the crown. That's King Harold's crown. Why he wants it I don't rightly know. I've been to Normandy and, I can tell you, it's a fine country. In fact it's pretty much like this country. The coast is the same, the fields, the woods. They've got the same trees we've got and the same animals although they go by different names over there. And the people are much the same. They dress a bit different to us. They cut their hair short, they keep their faces clean shaved and they speak a language that I can't believe anyone could ever understand. Otherwise, apart from the words, it's all much the sameness. In fact you could say it's the image of what we've got here.'

'Did you like Normandy Till?'

'I didn't like it any more or less than here,' said Till. 'Food's the same. Same air they breathe. Same sun in the sky. Moon and stars like ours. Rains, too, just like here. The only thing I will tell you I didn't like and that was the boat. I was sick. I was sick from almost the moment I stepped aboard and I was sick night and day. We were on that boat for three days but it seemed like three years to me. And it wasn't just me. Everyone was sick. When we arrived, which I thought we'd never do, I just lay down on the shore and I swore I'd never go on the sea again. Even the sailors were sick. They said it was a bad crossing.'

Till paused for breath as he worked himself free of a thick briar which had become entangled with his jerkin. 'Well, of course, we had to come back. We were in Normandy for a year. I was with my father then. I was only a young man. But every day in Normandy, while we were hunting and trading and looking at the way the

137

Normans did their ironwork, I'd be thinking about that return journey across the water. When the time came for us to go back I asked if there wasn't some way we could go round by foot. I said I didn't mind how far it was as long as I could walk on firm ground. But they laughed at me and said the water's the only way. We got to the boats but we had to wait for the wind to be right. And all the time you're waiting, the fear of the sickness is in your mind which makes it worse.'

'And were you sick on the way back?' I asked, laughing.

'It was worse on the way back,' said Till. 'There must be something in the sea doesn't like me because I came back twice.'

'How come?'

Till paused again to draw breath and I couldn't help thinking that if he talked a bit less he'd be able to keep up with me. I wanted us to hurry on but I had to keep stopping for him, pointing out boggy bits where he might trip or slip. He'd have been better off keeping quiet and keeping his eyes on the trail.

'Well,' Till resumed, 'we were halfway across coming back and you could see the coast of England. There it was. I thought I might almost reach out and touch it and I was even sure I could see our village.' He stretched out his long right arm, 'Would you believe it? The wind changed and blew us back to France. To make it worse the sailors got out the oars and made us row. They wanted to get back to England too so they tried to outdo the wind by taking the sail down and getting us to row. Can you imagine, rowing all the way back across the sea to England? Course it was no good. You can't row against the wind. That's like piddling the wrong way in a gale, excuse my French. Upshot was we were blown back to where we started and there I was laying on the beach again but it was the wrong beach. France, not England. We had to wait another week before we got a trip back and with a kindly wind behind us. The sailors said I should have got what they call my sea legs but I hadn't. So I was sick again but at least I was on my way home. And I tell you what, to make it worse, one of the sailors asked my Dad – me being only a young man but he could see I was a tough un – asked him if I'd like to work with him and learn to be a sailor. I said I'd rather drown. No,' he shook his head emphatically, 'you won't get me on the water again.'

We walked on, Till talking, puffing and panting.

'That's what I can't understand. He's got a good country there, has Duke William. Why does he want this one as well? He's better off enjoying what he's got and leaving us to enjoy what we've got.' He stopped and spat on the ground. 'He's like Ern. People like that are never contented with what they've got. They always want a bit more. They have a hide of land, livestock, a hut, a barn and then they want what someone else has got. I don't understand it.'

Another pause and a gasp for air. He wiped the sweat from his face. 'Are we nearly there, lad?'

'Almost,' I said. 'But you think he'll come, William? You think the Normans are coming?'

'I'm sure of it, Ash. I think the only thing that's stopping them is they haven't got the right wind. It's the wind will keep them stuck in France and that's probably God's will. And if we all pray hard enough the wind'll keep them there until the winter. They won't come then.'

We walked on.

'But what do you mean by it's starting?' I asked again.

'That there'll be a fight,' said Till. 'If they've got any sense the Normans'll keep away. But then I don't think they've got good sense. And the sniff of a battle is enough to bring the worst kind of people out. That's what's starting. They're like kites and crows and ravens circling. They sense something is up and people – all sorts of people who, mostly, are afraid of honest work - are beginning to gather, trying to get a piece of something for themselves. Those birdmen who came through. There's suddenly more like them, travellers on the road up to no good. Soldiers or, rather, folks who think they'll be a soldier, looking for a chance, sniffing around like wild dogs looking for plunder. War is a horrible thing, Ash. I've seen bits before – skirmishes – nothing like this and, I tell you, it's a horrible thing. But it attracts the worst kind of scavengers. Like birds circling overhead.'

'And what's the fighting man?'

'The fighting man is the King's own banner. That's the one they tell me you all saw when you were with the *fyrd*. When you saw the king. It's his banner. And the fighting men, well they're the men who gather round the king and protect him. Some of them are the *housecarls* – they usually have a broad sword – and some are the *bearserks*. The *bearserks* just go non-stop into the fight. They drink a special potion and it sends them crazy after a while. But while they're under the spell they think they're unstoppable. They think nothing can hurt them or touch them. They have no fear. There's stories of *bearserks* being wounded near to death but still fighting on not noticing or feeling any pain.'

By now we were close and, ahead of us, we saw Gam, Misty and the old soldier, Wulf. He was sitting up now, quite comfortably, chatting to Gam. I was surprised by Till's behaviour. He seemed shy, deferential, almost fearful. He took off his hat and gave the fallen giant a nod. Wulf nodded back at Till and the eyes of the two big men seemed to lock, each trying to get the measure of the other. Finally, Wulf spoke, 'Good man. I'm grateful to you for coming. I don't like to take a craftsman away from his work. A smith are you?'

Till nodded, 'I hope I can be of help. It's an honour to help a fighting man.'

'You honour an old one,' said the warrior, 'I am not the man I once was.'

'Wounded?' asked Till.

'I could show you scars from wounds I've taken,' said the big man, 'but this,' he gestured at the bruised and swollen leg, 'alas, just carelessness. I lost my way in the wood, in the dark. It wasn't a fighter brought me down, but a tree root. I think too, that drink was at the bottom of it,' he said guiltily. 'This young man,' he gestured at Gam, 'has been most helpful. But the ankle – he nodded at the swollen and bruised leg - is broken. I can't stand.'

'So this is Gam is it?' Till nodded and smiled. 'A strange name.'

'It's what Ash calls me,' said Gam. 'I'm really Guillaume.'

'A knowledgeable young man,' said the old soldier. 'We have been speaking together in the language of France.'

'Have you now?' Till looked at Gam curiously but then gave attention to the swollen foot. He started to empty his bag of treatments: herbs, ointment and strips of leather and linen. 'I need to set this and strap it,' he said. 'It will hurt. Some of this will help,' and he took a stopper from a small horn filled with a thick liquid and passed it to the old man.'

'Wine?' said Wulf hopefully.

'No, nor beer,' said Till with a smile. 'It's a herbal drink from the wise woman. It's not tasty but will ease the pain by making you drowsy but not too drowsy as we need to get you away from here and into some shelter.'

Wulf drank the bitter potion pulling a comic theatrical face while Till busied himself with the ankle, binding moss, then leather strips, then a wooden splint and cloth tightly round it, chatting all the while.

'What brings you here?'

'I am here to defend our land. Our kingdom. I have served the old King Edward and I have been on campaign with young Harold. I was a *housecarl*,' he said proudly. 'I marched next to the King.....aargh!' he roared, 'easy, man, that hurts, aaah..... when he was Harold, Earl Godwinson. I travelled with him to France. I fought with him in Normandy when he was fighting alongside the Duke there, this same William who, they tell me, now claims the English throne. I know the Normans. I know their ways. I can be of service to the King. I think...aargh.....for heaven's sake have a care with that foot....I think a battle can be avoided. Yet, if he is to fight the Duke, he will need help. He will remember me and welcome me because I have done him good service although I am a little older than when he saw me last.'

'You won't be seeing the King with this ankle,' said Till. 'You won't help anyone with this. It's badly broken. You need rest, not travel. If we can get you there

I'll take you to my forge. I can hammer out a brace for your foot, then you'll need to put your backside on a bench and your foot on a stool. By the time it is healed the Normans will have arrived and will have been sent packing by the King's army and, once again, there will be peace in our land. Then I can go back to what I do best: making useful tools for the farmers and workmen and not weapons for farmers boys who think themselves warriors.'

Suddenly the demeanour of the old man seemed to change. Perhaps it was merely Till's painkiller but his face became even whiter and his eyes grew and seemed to bulge in his head. He looked at the three of us, each in turn as though seeing something beyond us.

'It will be terrible,' he said solemnly, 'I tell you, I have seen the Normans. If they are against you they are terrible. They are devils. There are bad times coming, worse than any we have ever known. These men are devils.' Suddenly, he grabbed Gam's hand, 'A battle would be terrible,' he said, 'I have seen the Normans in battle.' He seemed to be speaking to himself as he muttered, softly, 'The grandson of a tanner....,' his voice trailed away into a mutter.

Gam and I looked at Till quizzically.

'It's an insult they throw at William,' he explained. 'The rumour is that his grandfather was a common tanner. When William was on campaign in Normandy he laid siege to a castle and the people in it waved animal hides at him to insult him. But they were sorry for it when he took the castle. He punished them horribly. Nobody laughed at him after that.'

Our journey back to the road and the forge was slow, laborious and painful. We helped Till to cut and fashion a pair of stout crutches but the old soldier needed our support particularly where the path thinned or ran out. We whacked the briars and branches with our sticks to clear a way. I wore the heavy shield on my back the way I had seen them carried by the *housecarls* except that it was so big it kept snagging on the ground and banging and bruising the backs of my legs. I carried his battleaxe on my shoulder but it was a struggle and I was sure it would fall from my grasp. Gam wore the helmet which kept falling over her eyes so she couldn't see and carried his enormous pack. We'd had a struggle to take his things from him. Even though the shield and helmet were rusted, dirty and dented he passed them to us as though they were the greatest treasures. We almost had to force the hefty battleaxe from him.

'Take care with that,' he shouted. 'If it slips from your grasp it will take your leg off.'

I saw a crow looking at us from a branch. It looked astonished and I thought what a sight we must be: two big men, one hollering out with pain, frustration and irritation, tripping on every snag on the trail and leaning against the other who guided him calmly but firmly, speaking to him all the while, gently encouraging his progress. They were followed by two children weighed down with heavy armour and bags and a dog that ran ahead then back, barking, jumping never still, getting in the way and in danger of tripping them up.

We stopped often to wipe away the sweat, to rest, to drink from a stream. Till was right about the medicine. The old soldier was becoming more and more drowsy and more difficult to guide and coax along the twisting

144

woodland paths. 'Is it uphill all the way?' he shouted. 'What kind of land can this be? Is there no level to the place?' he complained. Then, 'Are we not there yet? Where is this place? How far now? Why, man, do you live so far off?'

'Gently, gently,' coaxed the patient, sweating Till. 'Not far now. Almost there,' which I knew was a lie because the trail ahead was a long one.

It was almost dark by the time we reached the forge. Elfin had a fire going. There was food, warm water and a bed for Wulf where, so gratefully, we laid him down. The old man looked up at the roof of the forge where tools, pots, baskets and drying bunches of herbs were hanging. He said a single word, 'Home,' farted loudly and fell asleep.

Home. I knew what he meant. The forge was warm, the fire glowing. There was the smell of cooking and clean straw. Steam rose from the pot of hot water. Hens ran past the door and swallows, feeding themselves up for the change of season, flew in and out of the barn. I looked at Gam and, reluctantly, we turned to go.

'Where are you two off to?' demanded Till.

'We better go back,' I said.

'Where to?'

'The wood I suppose,' I shrugged and, suddenly, I didn't want to go. I wanted to be here where it was warm and dry and bright.

'You'll stay here,' said Till firmly, 'there'll be some food for you and a bed. But you won't be lying around. I've missed my work today, so there'll be plenty for you two to do to help me catch up.'

'What about Ern?' I asked.

'Let me worry about Ern,' said Till.

'What about the birdmen?'

'Gone,' said Till, 'and good riddance to them.'

I looked at Gam and she nodded vigorously.

And so our life at the forge began.

11. NEWS

We were quick to learn and we were soon busy. Till was right. There was a brisk trade at the forge. It was now late summer, there was still warmth in the weather and tools that had been broken and bent in ploughing, cutting, chopping and digging were brought to us to be mended. Edges were sharpened, new handles were fitted, new tools were made. But with the brisk trade there was unease and what our customers wanted most were weapons and these were not to Till's taste. 'I'm not a man for weapons,' was his constant protest, 'It's not my line of work.' But for every plough or spade or billhook we fashioned, we had to make two axes or cudgels for fighting.

My task was the general work: sweeping, lifting and carrying, keeping the workshop clear and the fire going. That meant, most of the time, sneezing with dust.

Ern came by on two occasions and spoke to Till and, each time, Till whistled and gestured to me and I went to the back of the shop busying myself in the shadows and making sure that Misty was well out of the way. Ern must have known I was there but, if he saw me, he made no sign.

It was Gam who took to the work of the forge most readily. She could make pictures, she could write words and knowledge of her talents soon got round. Gam carved names on the handles of spades and weapons; she designed marks and figures which could be burned into wood and stamped on blades. She was skilful in making the figure match the owner's name or personality so that each of our customers came to have their own mark: a bird, a tree, a dog, a horse or a make-believe creature.

'Their *familiars*,' I said. She could decorate metalwork and weave the handles of tools and weapons with coloured leather bands and thin wire. She was soon in demand.

Wulf had slept, snored, farted and complained, swearing dreadfully for two days and, for a while, Till was concerned by his leg which became more and more swollen. The wise woman was a frequent visitor, washing the leg, changing the dressing, administering hot poultices and potions. However, he was, she declared, a tough old bird and, as she predicted, he soon began to recover. Till kept his promise and fashioned an iron brace to keep the foot and broken ankle in place. It was, he confided to us, bigger and more elaborate than it needed to be but it was a device that pleased the old soldier. It made a resounding clunk with every step and he wore it like a weapon, with pride. 'Do you see that?' he'd ask visitors. 'I'm a *destrier*.' Then, pleased to see their puzzled expression, he'd explain: 'It's the Norman warhorse. A terrible creature. It doesn't just run at you with a knight on its back. It can twist and turn; it can bite and kick. The squires put metal studs on its hooves too so that, if it kicks you, it'll take your head off. And he would strike his metal brace on the ground for effect, 'Aaaargh, blast it!' His cry of pain and stream of rude words would bring Till to the door of the forge asking him to behave or he'd have no customers left. But, as we quickly found, Wulf brought us custom and good trade. We found him a seat – a bench by the open doorway of the forge – and here he sat, a warhorse at rest, his leg with the brace raised like a weapon on a stool, and there he held court.

What Wulf liked was news. It was the air he breathed. He attracted stories in the way that a piece of iron, when filed or polished, will drag smaller cuttings and filings towards it where they cling like suckling hogs to a sow. He was, too, like a weathercock in the breeze knowing where the news had blown from and the speed and direction in which it was travelling. He could weigh stories too, testing their veracity, dismissing them sometimes as wild speculation, at other times nodding to the truth. 'That could be so,' he might say, 'but seems a bit far fetched.' At other times, 'Yes, yes, that sounds like it.' I don't know how it happened that people and gossip found their way to him but there didn't seem a moment when he wasn't on his bench by the road, bending his ear to listen and opening his wide mouth to chuckle, curse, bellow, argue and explain. It was argument he liked best. People came to him for an opinion or for information but what they soon got was an argument.

It was from Wulf we first heard about the traitor Tostig who, he explained, was a disloyal brother of King Harold. Tostig, said Wulf, thought he had a claim to the throne but, he said, tapping his temple, he wasn't clever, just jealous of his brother and greedy for land and power. Wulf was the most loyal supporter of the King and rarely uttered Harold's name without the parenthesis *God Bless Him*. He took any slight against the King personally and enemies such as Tostig or William were always bracketed with a curse (*God damn him*) or worse. We soon got used to this way of talking. Tostig, we learned, had invaded the Isle of Wight where, Wulf said, the fool supposed he could set up a camp ready to invade the south coast. But King Harold had marched with a force of 500 men to see him off and this was quickly done. Wulf roared his delight and stamped his foot as he told us, 'Tostig – *may the Devil take him* - made off like the cowardly dog he is. All our good King saw was the rear end of the retreating boats which, they say, were both under sail and being rowed off they were that afraid.'

Wulf accompanied his pronouncements by using a pointed stick we cut for him to draw maps in the dust by the road. In fact the drawing of maps and the showing of which army was where became such a key part of Wulf's explanations that Gam and I made a perimeter of stones to mark out the drawing territory and to stop anyone inadvertently stepping on the map. This had happened once when Wulf in full flow explaining where an invasion force might land and where it would be best repelled, gave a roar as some innocent, slack-mouthed member of his audience stepped too close. 'Zounds, man,' bellowed Wulf, 'you've just crushed a quantity of archers and foot soldiers under your mudded sole. What the devil do you mean by it?' The listener leapt back and, to our giggling amusement, actually lifted his foot and examined the underneath of his sandal expecting to see the squashed militia sticking to it like dog dirt.

Generally, Till was too busy and, anyway, since Lang's departure for the army had no appetite for the talk of war and the long debates and discussions at the entrance to the forge. But he enjoyed the old soldier's company and, as much as the rest of us he was, secretly at least, hungry for news. 'That old boy can talk for the whole of England,' he chuckled while we worked. 'I reckon there's nothing he don't know.' And, sometimes, when the fire was being mischievous, 'We'll just have to get him in here to talk at it. He can make plenty of hot air.'

So, Wulf told us, Tostig had gone, seen off by his brother, Harold. Then we heard from some breathless travellers that the *fyrd* was disbanded and the King was back in Winchester. This news was greeted with dismay by most but not Wulf. 'He couldn't hold em,' he explained. 'He could only hold the *fyrd* for two months. They'll be wanted back on the farms for the harvest. No king wants an army when their hearts aren't in it. You want fighting men with hearts that belong to the cause,' he beat his stout chest, 'not milksops wanting to be at home looking after their crops and animals. And I reckon he knows,' and here he tapped his red and pock-marked nose, 'there'll be no invasion just yet. He has his information. He has eyes and ears everywhere,' and he looked round fiercely and suspiciously at his gaping audience, 'just as William, the treacherous duke, has his informers here I expect,' looking at each one as if to say, *I know just who it is*.

From early morning until late in the day, Gam, Elfin and I would be helping Till in a din of hammering, the heat and dust of charcoal, lending only half an ear to what was taking place with Wulf on the bench outside. But, from time to time, there would be news that would draw us away from our work. And so it was on this day, hard on the heels of the news that the *fyrd* had been disbanded. Wulf shouted Till's name with an urgency which made us leave the heat, hammer and tongs to walk out of the forge and into the bright light of day. Wulf was announcing to a growing crowd, 'There's an invasion. An invasion in the North. The Norsemen.' And here there followed a string of obscene words.

151

'Where?'

'The North. Towards the city of York.'

There was many a blank face in his audience so Wulf, tutting with exasperation at the geographical ignorance surrounding him, drew a crude map marking where we were, 'Here!' he stabbed the dust, in relation to, 'There!' another stab in the dust, 'which is where the North is.'

'Is that far, then?' ventured one poor soul staring in bewilderment at the drawing in the dust.

'Far?' roared Wulf, 'of course it's far. Two hundred miles and a week or two of walking.'

There was first incredulity at this news and then a relieved response. 'Couple of hundred miles away. Well that leaves us safe down here then.'

'Safe?' roared the old soldier, 'If they have York they can march on London. They could take the country the cunning…..' and he released more obscenities that made Till turn on his heel and return to his hammering in exasperation.

'Who is it then, these Norsemen?' asked one of the group squatting by the old man's bench.

'It's that…..' loud hammering from Till…..'Tostig and, he paused dramatically allowing a hush to fall, 'with your Norway man, the king there….Hardrada.'

A shudder went through the crowd with the manner in which he intoned the name, roiling the letters on his tongue. 'Hardrada. He's the hard ruler. He's the worst of them all. Bring them all on but not him boys. Not him. It's in the name. He's the hardest beggar of them all.' He sat disconcertedly looking at the dust and the crude map he'd drawn.

'Have you,' a voice ventured, 'have you served with him…?'

Silence. Then Wulf viciously stabbed the dust with his stick, spoiling the map, 'No….but I've met those who have and there's not one of them with a good word for him. You're as badly off serving with him as against him. The man is a tyrant.'

'First Tostig and now Hardrada,' said someone softly and with a false authority.

'Tostig's a fool,' snapped Wulf, 'but with Hardrada, that's a fiercesome combination.'

'How did Tostig get there seeing he was down here not that long ago?'

'He would have sailed,' said Wulf, 'around the coast,' and he drew a wiggling, unsteady line to indicate the length of Tostig's perilous journey.

A new day brought fresh news. 'The King, intoned Wulf, 'has recalled the *fyrd* and, together with his best housecarls, has gone north to meet the invader.'

There were loud cheers from the group around him but Wulf looked at them slowly and the cheers died in their throats. 'He's gone North,' said Wulf, 'because he had no choice. But,' and he looked over their gaping heads southwards towards the coast, 'he's left the back door open.'

A shudder went through the crowd.

'He'll be back though,' ventured a shaking voice. 'Won't he?'

'Oh, they'll be back,' said Wulf. 'The King, won't let us down.' He looked to the south again, 'I just hope he comes soon.'

Everyone followed his gaze except for Till who had come to the open doorway to listen and who was still looking to the North. 'My lad will have gone with them,' he said softly.

12. STORM

And then, a few days later and without warning, the storm broke. Early morning, not yet light and we were sweeping the floor, coaxing the forge fire, yawning and readying ourselves for breakfast when we heard the dogs barking. Then hogs, cows and goats on the Bodle Street as though being driven, some running off and disappearing into the meadows and woodland. Behind them came villagers, some clutching bundles, most dishevelled, hot with hurrying, some half-dressed. A man with a basket of hens, some carts piled too high with household goods and pulled by nags driven half to death by their frenzied owners who were shouting, 'They're here! They're here! We seen them!' bringing us running to the highway.

We were quickly busy, filling horn cups with water, encouraging these fleeing refugees to stop, rest, eat and talk. They paused to refresh themselves then hurried on urging us to do the same, to move further inland to safety. A man, wide-eyed, shouted desperately at us through a gaping hole of a mouth in a dirty, perspiring, frightened face.

'The sea, full of ships as far as you can look and more than you can count. The devils. They're on the beach and they're running their boats into the marshlands,' he swept his hand across the horizon. 'Hundreds of ships. Ships with great sails and painted, leering dragons on the fronts. More than hundreds. Ships full of soldiers. Armour and shields and weapons. Supplies. Hay, barrels, wood. And horses. They've got horses. Hundreds of horses. Great beasts of ships and dragons on the prow. Full of men and shields and weapons.'

'And horses,' shouted another.

The man turned round venomously, 'I've already told about the horses.'

Till had come quietly to the door, standing half in the shadow, 'Is this something you've seen,' he asked sceptically, 'or are you just telling us what you've been told?'

'I seen 'em,' said the man, 'God's honour. I seen em.'

'We've all seen em,' said another, butting in. 'The sea,' he said in a hushed dramatic voice, 'was covered with ships as far as you could look. More than you could count. That was early yesterday in the morning. Then they were bringing them up on to the beach and the fighters were running straight off, covered in armour and weapons, like they was expecting a battle.'

'They're already moving inland,' said another, 'going along the coast towards Hastings. They're taking stuff as they go along. Grabbing what they can.'

'And burning. What they can't grab they're burning. We're driving the animals, all our stock, into the woods. We'd rather they were lost than stolen by the Normans.'

'It's robbery and probably worse. Robbery and murder.'

'Ash?' Wulf had woken and was limping towards his bench by the door, 'get me my gear, boy. Get me my shield, my helmet and my axe. 'It is come,' he said solemnly, 'and we must put our armour on.'

He turned to the crowd gathering uncertainly and afraid, rubbing the sleep from faces white and drawn with anxiety. 'The King is in the North,' he said. 'We are on our own boys and this is what I feared. Go to your homes and put your armour on. If you don't have armour, your stoutest jerkin. Caps, too. Prepare your weapons.'

The crowd drifted away. The dishevelled travellers on the road argued amongst themselves uncertain whether to move further on or to set up a temporary camp here on the high ground. There was the parting of the ways. Some declared the Normans would be on the road and behind them and it would be safer even further inland. Others that they could go no further. Two or three were carrying older family members on their shoulders. Tired and perspiring they decided this was far enough. Soon a makeshift camp began to grow along the sides of the highway.

Wulf, looking at his armour, muttering to himself, seemed despondent. Till took us aside. 'Perhaps you two could do some work on that.' He pointed to the shield, helmet and axe and for the rest of the morning we were busy. While Wulf sat lost in thought or engaged in conversation with people coming down from the road, we polished the axe and rubbed the rust from his helmet. Gam had already worked secretly in her spare moments and had painted a magnificent eagle on the shield. I fetched the Norman sword which, day after day, I had cleaned, polished and sharpened. Gam had helped me to decorate the hilt with coloured leather strips. With Misty at our side we took the gleaming helmet and weapons and solemnly presented them to the old man. He was touched and almost tearful as he prepared himself for a battle which, in his heart, he knew he could no longer fight. Gam showed him the painted shield and he admired the eagle.

'It's an emblem, for you,' said Gam.

'Why an eagle?' he asked.

'It's the fighting man,' said Gam.

'Who says so?'

'I do,' she said emphatically.

'But I'm the fighting man,' argued Wulf good naturedly.

'That's what you said when we first met you,' said Gam, 'and I still don't really understand what you mean.'

'When I was with the Earl, Harold Godwinson who became our King, *God bless him*,' said Wulf solemnly, 'I did him some service and he looked at me and said to all the company, *This is the man who will be on my own standard which I will have always by my side and which will be named The Fighting Man*. And they had the standard made.'

'I've seen it,' I said. 'I saw it when we were down at Bosham towards Winchester.'

'And what was it like?' asked the old warrior.

'A man with a helmet holding an axe,' I said.

'Like this?' asked Wulf as he raised his axe and pulled a fierce face.

'Yes. And it had colours and metalwork and stones on it too,' I said.

'And it is me,' said Wulf tapping his foot with emphasis, 'I am the fighting man. The King carries me on his standard.'

'Well, I think this is prettier,' said Gam pointing at the eagle and they both laughed.

I offered him the sword. He whistled in appreciation as he held and balanced it, testing the edge carefully with his thumb, peering along the length of the blade to judge its straightness.

'Where did you get this, boy?'

I told him the story of the birdmen.

'It's a magnificent sword,' he said, 'but not for me. I'm not a swordsman. I don't have that skill. I trust to this,' and he patted his axe. The disappointment must have shown on my face, 'It's a sword for when you're a man,' he said, 'but I hope you'll never need to use it. If we can send these devils from our land there'll be no more need for fighting.'

Another day went by and we continued to work at the forge but uneasily, not sure what we should do. Always one of us would be stationed at the highest point on the ridge, keeping an eye on the road. There were more travellers each day, all in the same direction, moving away from the coast. Some moved on; others joined the growing camp. From them we heard more stories of the Normans out on foraging parties, stealing. Mainly they were after food, supplies of grain and livestock. Animals were running free in the wood because people would rather let them go than have them stolen. The Normans, too, were stealing anything – wood, metal, stone, leather - that might be used as weapons against them in a fight. We sat with Wulf wondering what to do. We were a fair way from Hastings. Would the invaders come this far? We felt a little more secure when we were told the Normans were, mostly, marauding up and down the coast, that they were fearful of venturing further inland because of ambush from the local *fyrd*. From our high spot on the ridge at Bodle Street we could see for miles and we saw the smoke from villages where they had set their fires. Further towards the coast there was more smoke and we guessed this must be where the Normans had their camp.

We helped Till to pack up things from the forge. He had precious metals and tools which, he knew, would be taken by the invaders. We took them into the wood. Others from the village were doing the same. Here, in secluded spots, were the *den-holes*, the deep pits that had been dug by our forebears in the olden times of the Viking invasions. This is where we hid our treasures. Some families had their own pits, others with little to hide, shared what space was available. We wrapped the metal and tools in greased cloths and straw, lowered them into the pits and covered the ground with rocks and scrub. Later, Till showed me a secret pit hidden further in the wood, 'away from prying eyes,' where he'd buried his money and precious items, the jewellery, buckles and armbands he liked to make from copper, silver and gold, a bag of metal, ready to be melted down and coins.

'It would be strange,' I said, 'if we lose where this is and someone in years to come digs this up. I wonder what they'll make of it? They'll wonder why we did it.'

All this was hard and sweaty labour. It took us a long day and Wulf watched our efforts with an unconcealed contempt.

'It's just a precaution,' Till had protested. 'If things go wrong the devils will take all this – my iron, my tools. It's taken me years to build this. If I lose my tools then I have nothing.'

'It's a seed,' argued Wulf. 'It's a seed of defeat and it will grow. It will spread like weeds in the barley. It will choke your courage.'

'Should I do nothing?'

'Carry on your business. Show others you are not afraid.'

'I'm not afraid,' said Till angrily, 'I just don't want to lose my things.'

'Your king will protect you,' was all Wulf would say by way of reply.

'It's all right for you,' snapped Till. 'I could lose everything. What have you got to lose?'

I had noticed how, each day, the two big men were becoming more tetchy with each other. I knew it was only because of the anxiety of the times as, generally, the two could be friends and they could be fun. In the exhaustion of that evening, as we sat together, Wulf looked at the muddy, weary Till and said, 'It's like a riddle.'

'What?'

'A riddle,' said the old soldier. 'What is it that we dig out of the earth and shape in the fire? It gives us life and, when we die we take it with us back into the ground to become earth again.' He looked at me.

'Iron,' I said.

'Yes,' Wulf said, 'show me your knife.'

I handed him the *seaxe* and he held it in the glow of the fire. 'Look at that craftsmanship,' he said with an appreciative nod towards Till. 'There's magic in this blade but, one day, it will go back in the earth with you and both of you will become what you once were.'

Till must have seen the look on my face because he ruffled my hair and laughed, 'Don't worry Ash. You've got plenty of time ahead of you yet.'

The group gathering around Wulf got bigger every day. There was discussion, requests for advice. More and more came terrible stories from the coastal villages of what the Normans were doing: stealing and burning.

Many locals and neighbours had packed up their possessions and were heading further inland towards London where they had friends or family; others were just prepared to take their chances in the wood; more and more joined the makeshift camps growing by the side of the highway.

Every day the question was asked. What news of the King?

At last, a great cheer went up. Wulf made the announcement. The King had defeated Tostig and Hardrada, had sent those… loud hammering from Till…. Vikings packing. A great victory. The north was safe.

Till, looking north, moved his lips in prayer for his son. I thought of Dad.

Hard on the heels of this came even better news, the King and his army were on the march again, heading south towards London, gathering more troops from the *fyrd* on the way. We need have no fear. The Normans would soon be driven back to the sea.

Another day of nervous waiting, near panic and indecision as we heard more and more stories of Norman misdeeds along the coast and creeping further and further inland. Each day we were ready to run, then stalled by doubts and we stayed, rooted, unwilling to leave the security of the forge.

In all this time we hadn't seen much of Ern. Now, suddenly, the big man appeared at the forge. He was in a rage, shouting even before he reached us. He had a holding, two hides of land, at Penhurst just a few miles away. The Normans had arrived brazenly with horses and carts. They had taken his livestock: hogs, oxen, geese, hens, cows, all gone. They had taken grain, hay, cloth and beer, every scrap of food. This was alarming. This was close. Ern rounded on the group by the door, 'What shall we do about it?'

'We'll have to fight 'em,' said one, 'I'll not stand by and let them rob me of all I've worked for. I'd rather die fighting than starve.'

'Fight 'em!' Ern was incredulous. 'Have you seen 'em? This is an army. They've got weapons and armour and horses. We can't fight 'em. This is for the King and the thanes.' He rounded on Wulf, 'So where are they? Where's your great English army? You're the ones should be protecting us. Where are they?'

Wulf fidgeted uncomfortably under this blast of criticism. 'They will be here,' he said as confidently as he could. 'The King is the protector of all our land, not just Wessex and this little corner.' He drew a map. 'This is the land. We are but a small corner. At the moment he is travelling from the north.'

'You talk nonsense old man,' said Ern turning viciously on the old soldier, 'you sit there in the sun with your beer and your gossip and you do nothing. You talk about fighting and my guess is you've seen none of it. You do nothing, you know nothing. You're nothing but an old fool.' He spat on the map and kicked the dirt, spoiling it with his foot and looking round at the crowd, 'Don't listen to this old fool. Get out, I say. Get out before they get here.'

He looked at Till and the forge. 'And this,' he said, 'they'll tear all this down,' and he stormed off.

There was muttering and fear in the air. The group of villagers who had been listening to Wulf began to drift away. The old man sat and, for the first time, seemed lost for words, looking into the dust. It was Till who spoke, his voice tense and urgent, 'I've no time for Ern but

163

there's much that's true in what he says.' He gestured at the forge. 'We better bury the rest of the stuff. We can hide the iron. But what about us? Where can we go?'

I looked at Gam and she spoke to Till, 'We know somewhere,' she said and she told him about the Old Place.

'So, that's where you've been staying,' and he surprised us by telling us how he remembered talk of a hidden place when he was a boy. 'My grandfather used to tell us stories about it. Where the Old People must have been, hidden in the woods. I remember we looked for it as children but never found it. We used to think it was just stories.'

Yet, taken as he was by our description of the hollow and the safety it offered in the woods, Till was determined not to leave the forge. 'I'll stay here with Wulf,' was all he would say. He was, though, anxious about Elfin and agreed that she should go with Gam and me so she would know her way if things turned out badly and we had to run for the woods.

It was a long trek. Both Elfin and Gam were nimble but, again, I was aware of how easily and quickly I could move along tracks that seemed hidden to the others. We had packed a little food and bedding in baskets which, although quite light, were awkward and made the journey through the tangled woodland more difficult. We came to the edge of the drop and, although she hesitated for a moment, Elfin quickly followed us as we clambered down the steep path to the stream at the bottom. Again Elfin hesitated nervously as Gam and I wriggled our way into the tunnel but she followed us bravely into the hidden chamber. We got a fire going, had some food and then, proudly, we showed Elfin the dancing shapes on the wall and the pictures that Gam and I had drawn. She marvelled at them and watched in fascination the magic of Gam drawing a third figure next to the two of us. 'There, that's you,' said Gam cocking her head on one side as I'd seen her do when she was the birdboy, and looking at her picture proudly. She slowly made some sharp and curvy shapes.

'Those are letters,' I said knowledgably although they were still a mystery to me.

Gam spelled them out for Elfin: *'A-L-F'.* That's you.'

It was strange, I thought, because it looked just the same as my name by the figure next to it. Same shape and size.

Away from the noise and anxiety of the highway, the three of us sat by the fire and talked about what it would be best to do. Now that we knew the King was on the march we felt more confident but, we agreed, this would be the best place to make a temporary home if things went badly. We knew, though, it would be a refuge for only a few of us. Wulf would not be able to move far from the forge and Till, we knew, would be reluctant to leave his home. We lay on the rugs by the fire, chatting, dawdling, in no hurry to get back. We knew, though, we couldn't stay the night. Till had been worried about us going off alone and would be anxious if we were away until the morning.

'Gam,' I said cautiously as the three of us soaked up the warmth of the fire, listened to the crackle of burning wood and Misty's light snoring, 'Gam, should we tell Elfin….you know…?'

'Tell Elfin what?'

'You know…about you….'

'About me, what?' she was being difficult.

'That you're not…you're not…,' I was interrupted as they both exploded in giggles.

'All right, I'll say it,' I said crossly. I hated being laughed at. 'Gam isn't a boy.'

There was more laughter.

'Put him out of his misery,' said Gam to Elfin still laughing.

'Ash,' said Elfin patiently, 'I know.'

'Eh?'

'I know that Gam is a girl.'

'How?'

'I just know. I've always known ever since I met her.'

'Well, why didn't you say?'

'There was nothing to say,' she retorted. 'I knew Gam was a girl.'

'Does Till…does your Dad know?'

'Of course.'

'Does everybody know?'

'I think so,' said Elfin, then 'except Wulf. It would confuse Wulf like it's confused you,' and they giggled some more.

'And did everybody know that you knew that I didn't know?'

'Eh?' said Gam, laughing.

'Do you see what I mean about it being confusing?' said Elfin.

As we made our slow return, darkness was almost upon us and we could see the burning fires along the ridgeway where refugees were making their camps. But there was no light or fire at the forge and there was no sign of Till or Wulf. We looked, we called. Nothing. We were exhausted and soon fell asleep.

We were woken in the very early morning before it was light. Till was there making the fire and Elfin was up and about helping him. As we had a hasty breakfast, Till told us what had happened. While we were away at the Old Place, Ern and some of his friends had come by. They had plied Wulf with drink and taunted him, accusing him of being too frightened to fight the Normans. They accused him of telling lies, that he'd never been a fighting man or been involved in any of the feats about which he'd boasted. He was, they said, full of hot air, a wind bag better used to make the charcoal in the fire glow than to protect them against the invaders. Wulf had argued with them and Till had left his work to chase them off. But, when they'd gone the old soldier sat despondently lost in thought, muttering to himself. Till tried to cheer him up but emboldened by the drink, Wulf had shouted he would march towards the coast and tackle the Normans himself. Till had argued with him and managed to hide his axe, helmet and shield hoping this would dissuade him. He tried to restrain him but tempers were lost on both sides. Till seemed awkward in the telling and we were aware that the two of them had quarrelled badly. Wulf, swearing terribly had hit out, 'He's got some strength that old boy when he's wound up,' said Till, 'he knocked me down.' Wulf had stumped off, a limping figure moving slowly along Bodle Street and towards Hastings. 'I expected him to calm down and come back,' said Till sheepishly. 'When it got dark I got worried and went to look for him. I was worried he might have fallen but there was no sign of him.'

'We'll go after him,' I said, 'he can't have got far.' But Till was concerned and argued against it. Going south, he said, would be dangerous. He'd gone as far on the track as he'd dared. There was no knowing who might be on the road; there were sure to be Normans scouting in the area. But, I argued, the King was on the way, Wulf would be slow, Gam and I could run fast, could keep to the edges of the track and, if we ran into trouble, could easily slip into the wood where no-one could catch us. Finally and reluctantly, Till agreed providing, he said, we left the crossbow, sword and Misty behind. 'You're both far too small for a fight,' he said. We felt vulnerable without weapons and uneasy without Misty to guide and protect us. We could, though, see the sense in what Till was saying. I was aware, too, that Misty had been limping more and more of late, sometimes dragging her back leg. She was still tired from yesterday's journey. It might only, as Till suggested, be a rheumaticky ache but I knew the real reason was the cruel blow she'd received from Ern in helping me escape.

13. CAPTURE

It was still early and the ridgeway was eerily quiet. Animals – sheep, goats, cows, an ox, even – cropped the grass at the roadside and sidled into the woodland as we approached. We passed baggage, some broken baskets of clothes and pots that had been dropped and left by hurrying refugees. We walked for some time without seeing anyone. Then we met some families hurrying along. They, like us, were anxious for news. They warned us not to go on. The area around the coast, they said, was thick with Normans. Nothing and nobody was safe from them. These frightened people were hurrying further inland and we tried to reassure them. We told them about Till and the forge where they could stop to eat and rest, the camp that was growing in size there and gave them the welcome news that the King and his army were on their way. All would be well again. We asked if they'd seen an old, limping soldier but they shook their heads. They had, though, seen a group of strange travellers heading south with a horse and cart towards Wartling. They were a mystery, they said, in a time of war. Some were wearing costumes for show, they banged drums and blew horns. There were birds, too. Falcons. Gam and I looked at each other and moved on.

We heard the birdmen long before we saw them. The noise was coming from off the highway and down a track towards a farmed clearing in the woods. We could hear the rhythmic beating of the drum, the shrill blast from horns and then, clearly, Axeface's showman's voice. We crept round the edge of a meadow keeping to the fringes of the wood. Here we climbed into an accommodating oak tree and peered cautiously across the clearing.

They were grouped around a tumbledown hut. A cart was there, an old horse nearby cropping the grass and piles of baskets and baggage set out in a circle. Axeface and the birdmen had been reunited with the troupe of tumblers and performers but it was clear that things weren't going well. An argument was taking place, Axeface in the centre of the group speaking quickly and angrily, waving his hands with theatrical flourish. Some of those around him were sitting on logs or piles of skins and clothes; others, dressed in the silly soldier costumes with little shields and straw weapons, were on their feet shouting back. Axeface was trying to organise a mock fight, a charade, the kind of thing I'd seen in Rye but it was going wrong, the performers were protesting. 'What are they doing?' I whispered.

'They're rehearsing,' said Gam.

'What does that mean?'

'They're practising, getting ready to put on a show. We used to do this over and over when I was with them. Scur, your Axeface, is the master and he always wants to get things just right.'

'But they can't do a show here,' I said, 'there's no-one to watch.'

Gam shrugged, 'I don't understand it either. Anyway, something's wrong. Axeface is always arguing but this looks different. Something's up.' Then she nudged me, 'Look.'

She pointed as a figure sat up in the cart the troupe used for carrying their gear. Wulf.

'They've caught him,' said Gam.

For a moment I wouldn't have recognised him. He was a sorry figure, sitting dejected, still with the look of a warrior but, instead of a battleaxe, he was holding the Fool's painted stick with the hog's bladder on the end. Instead of a helmet he wore a ridiculous head-dress made of feathers and leaves which dipped down over his eyes.

'What have they done to him?' I whispered, aghast and angry.

'They've turned him into a fool,' said Gam. 'They'll use him in the show.'

'What can we do?' It made me furious to see the dignified old man humiliated in this way.

'I don't know,' she said, 'but I'm thinking.'

And, while she thought, we continued to watch.

After a while the shouting calmed down. Axeface seemed to have won the argument as he usually did and the show began to unfold much as it had done when I saw it in Rye except the only audience were the lines of trees and shrubbery fringing the meadow and the two of us, the hidden watchers. The tumblers tumbled as before, the jugglers juggled and the swordsman threw his flashing sword high into the air, catching it and twirling it round. Axeface shouted out his showman's patter encouraging the silly soldiers but this time it was different. They were dressed as King Harold's men, Saxons. They wore the same long robes but had masks cleverly made from straw, moss, leaves and clay moulded into fierce faces decorated with feathers and hair for beards and moustaches. They looked both ridiculous and frightening running round and round as I'd seen them in Rye, brandishing bent sticks, bumping into each other and tripping over. And, this time, it was Norman soldiers nobly dressed and with helmets and shields who entered the circle, chasing and kicking, smacking the silly Saxons with their swords until they ended up as a heap of bodies in the centre. A tall man came in wearing a crown and holding a staff but this time it was clear this wasn't King Harold, it was Duke William. While the horns sounded and the drums beat out in triumph the strongman took the shafts of the cart in which Wulf was sitting and pulled it round and round the circle while Axeface pointed and shouted.

'What's he saying?' I whispered to Gam.

'It's horrible,' she said. 'He's saying horrible things about Wulf. He's laughing at the Saxon *housecarls* and saying they're all weak, old men like this. He says they're horse manure, that this is a dung cart.'

As she spoke, Wulf was dumped on to the pile of Saxon soldiers and, had Gam not held my arm, I would have leapt from the tree in anger. 'Wait!' she hissed, 'just watch and wait.'

Axeface was now talking to the group, praising and scolding, giving instructions and making them redo some of the action. Gam chuckled a little as she watched. 'I don't like him,' she said, 'but Axeface certainly knows how to make a good show. He makes them do it over and over again until it's exactly right.'

They all did their dance, much as I'd seen it in Rye, and then the birdmen walked stiffly in holding their falcons.

As the falconry display began, Gam whispered to me urgently, 'I've got an idea,' she said, 'but it's a risk. If it doesn't work out you've still got to trust me.' Then, seeing me hesitate, 'Remember, I trusted you once.'

'If you think we can help Wulf.'

'It's a chance,' she said, 'but if…if it goes wrong and they catch us there's just one thing to remember. No, two things,' she said.

'Go on.'

'Well, you've got to act stupid.'

'Eh?'

'Act like you're, you know,' she tapped her head, 'a bit daft.'

'What?'

'Come on, that shouldn't be so hard,' she said giggling. 'Just be yourself.' We both started laughing and I was worried I'd fall out of the tree.

'And the other thing is,' she went on, 'Wulf is your grandfather.'

'Wulf isn't my grandfather,' I spluttered indignantly.

'So, you're already acting the first part are you?'

'Eh?'

'Look, Stupid, I just mean you have to pretend he's your grandfather. You're a pathetic little boy who has come looking for his sad old grandfather who's wandered off and you've come to take him home.'

'They won't believe that,' I protested.

'I can't think of anything better,' she said. 'Anyway, let's just see if my idea works out.' She was watching the men with the birds. 'I'm going to try to get Ox to come over here.'

'But he won't help, will he?'

'I think he might. He's not a bad man, he doesn't like Axeface and I got him out of trouble once so he owes me a favour.'

'How will you get him to help us?'

173

'If I can get the eagle over here, he'll follow. Watch.'

We waited while the smaller falcons were flown and the eagle was brought forward on the perch with its hood removed. They exercised it back and fore across the meadow and we watched it take some meat from Ox's gloved fist. Then, as it landed, Gam whistled – a high long mournful sound. The bird settled on the perch but looked sharply in our direction. Gam whistled again, another long unearthly note and the eagle lifted itself, hesitated uncertainly for a moment, then took effortlessly to the air and headed towards us. It circled the tree soaring higher until Gam whistled again, long, slow and the bird drifted down, landing on a branch just above us without a sound. I was closer to it than Gam and shrank back from the enormous creature as it stared at me with those penetrating eyes as if I were a morsel of meat. But then it turned its attention to Gam who was making a series of pacifying sounds, muttering, murmuring, whispering and whistling quietly. She climbed past me moving slowly towards the bird until she was able to stretch out her hand and gently stroke the light plumage on its breast.

'Did you know,' she said to me quietly and calmly, 'that the birdmen call her the queen? And they're right. She's the female and much bigger and stronger than her mate, the king.'

'Look,' I didn't want to point and alarm the bird so I gestured with a nod of my head, 'Ox.'

The rehearsal had come to a stop. The troupe of jugglers, tumblers and silly soldiers, Axeface in the middle, stared across the meadow to the tree where we were roosting with the eagle. But Ox, the big falconer, was striding towards us swinging a long leather leash baited with meat to lure the eagle down.

'Can they see us?' I asked.

'No, they've got the sun in their eyes which helps,' she said scrambling towards the trunk. 'Wait here Ash. Keep talking to the bird. We want to keep her in the tree. I'm going to speak to Ox.'

'But what do I say to it?'

'She's a *queen* not an *it*. Treat her with respect but just say anything. The important thing is to keep your voice steady and soft and to stroke her.'

She slithered quickly down through the branches, jumped to the ground and crept cautiously through the bushes trying to attract Ox's attention without being seen by the others. I looked at the eagle who looked inquisitively back at me and hopped closer. I'm good at talking to birds but perhaps this majestic creature thought herself too high and mighty because she didn't seem to hear me. I whispered the names of the birds I had seen in the woods and talked of their strange habits, reaching out at the same time with a cautious hand to stroke the wonderfully soft breast feathers as Gam had done. Stroking, I talked about the tiny birds, the secretive wrens and finches, the birds that creep into the holes of trees, the raucous gossiping magpies and the sweet throated blackbirds. I tried to talk softly without alarming the eagle but, with Gam gone, she seemed more agitated. Below me I could see that, instead of luring his treasured bird, Ox had, himself, now been lured further into the fringe of woodland and was holding an animated conversation with Gam. They were talking in French; Gam was trying to hush him but his voice kept rising and he waved his hands a good deal which agitated the eagle more.

I talked about the crows and ravens, the big birds, the swans and geese that spend so much time on the water. I talked, too, about the summer swoopers, the swallows and screaming swifts which build their nests in the village thatch and which we welcome because they bring the warm weather. When they fly away, low over the lakes and ponds, lower and lower we know the cold weather is returning. Then they dive beneath the water where they sleep until the summer returns.

Below me, the conversation between Gam and Ox was coming to an end and not a moment too soon because Axeface, wondering what had happened to Ox, was looking in our direction and had started to walk across the meadow towards us. The eagle began to shift its feet as if getting ready to fly off. I whispered the name, Ari, and told it bits of the story I remembered so well from Rye. But I knew it was no good. The bird had been captive too long. She reminded me of Dad. There was a fastness about her.

Axeface was getting closer but Gam was back, climbing up towards me, panting from the effort. 'Ox will help us,' she said, 'but we must try to keep the bird here,' and she started to stroke the eagle, clucking her tongue and whispering. My heart was beating with anxiety but Gam seemed calm. 'Watch,' she said.

Below us, Ox suddenly burst from the wood, running towards the startled Axeface and the group of performers. He was shouting in French. I got the gist of it but Gam, delight on her face, repeated his words for me, 'Run, run for your lives! Saxons in the woods! Saxons are coming. Run!' And her plan seemed to work. They took to their heels. Axeface stared at Ox who was playing his part well, running, shouting and waving his arms, then turned and joined the panic of retreat, the whole troupe in a mad dash across the meadow and towards the wood on the far side. Ox ran behind them shouting as though the attack had started. Within moments the camp was clear apart from the scattered props and baggage, the little horse quietly cropping the grass, the broken down hut and Wulf sitting quietly on a log. He seemed to be dozing.

'Quick,' said Gam, 'go and get him. I'll keep a lookout and stay here with the bird. We might need her if things go wrong.'

I scrambled down the tree, out through the fringe of woodland and in to the open meadow. I ran towards Wulf. It seemed quiet. Too quiet. I called his name as I ran towards him and he looked up in shock and surprise as though waking from a dream. 'Ash?'

'Quick,' I said, 'we've come to take you home. Where's your stick?'

He looked round, bewildered. 'I haven't got anything. No stick, no shield, no axe. The smith....,' he looked puzzled.

'Till.'

'Yes, that's him. Tried to stop me. We had a falling out and he hid my axe. If I had my axe these rascals would never have taken me.'

'Never mind that, we're taking you home,' I repeated. But he shook his head.

'I don't want to go back there. They called me an old fool. I'll show them what an old fool can do even without a battleaxe.'

While he talked and complained I'd pulled him on to his feet. 'Come on. You just have to lean on me,' I said.

'Where are we going?'

'Home. Back to the forge, to your seat in the sun where you should be. Till doesn't think you're a fool. He saved your life once. He's a good man. He's like you. He's loyal.'

'I want a strike at the devils,' said Wulf. 'That man with the birds said he'd take me to the coast where they're camped but I need my axe.'

'Come with me,' I said, 'Gam's waiting for us.'

He brightened at the mention of Gam's name but he was finding it hard to stand. He was heavy, leaning with a big strong arm on my shoulder. We must have been an odd sight.

'We need your stick.'

'I lost it when I was taken by these men. And the smith,' he complained, 'put this thing, this iron on my leg. To hobble me.'

'He did it to help you,' I was becoming impatient. 'You'd broken your ankle. Don't you remember? Till is your friend.'

'We could take the cart,' he suggested. 'They brought me here in the cart.'

'No time,' I said as we limped forward but the trees where Gam was waiting seemed far away and, as I'd feared, a few steps later I heard a series of urgent bird calls. Gam was calling our danger signal, the one we'd used in our games near the hollow. I stopped, unsure and, turning, I saw figures emerging cautiously then more boldly from the woods on the far side, an angry Axeface at the front.

What happened next is still a muddle to me and I've often thought about it since. There was something more to Axeface than there seemed to be and it was the same with Gam. They each seemed to work a kind of power and I felt it pushing against me from each side making it hard to see and think clearly.

I remember that Axeface was getting closer. He was sharp and I reckoned he immediately understood what was happening. The others, behind him, were hanging back a bit, unsure, wary in case the Saxons Ox had been shouting about might appear. As he advanced Axeface pulled a short sword from his belt and raised it menacingly. We couldn't run so Wulf and I turned to face him and we stood our ground.

'Don't worry, Ash,' said Wulf calmly. 'We'll do things the Saxon way. We'll make a shield wall.'

'But we haven't got shields,' I said, 'or weapons.'

'Yes we have,' said Wulf, 'there.' He pointed back to where the shields and swords used by the performing Normans had been left on the ground, 'Run. Grab them and let's put our backs against this.' He lurched over to the eagle's perch, a tall cross of stout timber on a small hillock. Nimble on my feet I dashed towards the advancing Axeface and grabbed the two round shields and one of the swords that had been thrown on the ground by the men who had played the part of Norman soldiers. Somehow I dragged and carried them back to Wulf. They were heavy and I still don't know how I managed it. Wulf, later, told me that when you need it in battle or in any difficulty, you can find a superhuman strength. That, he said, was what being a *housecarl* was about. And Wulf, faced with threat, seemed suddenly transformed: no longer a limping, confused old man but a warrior: strong, tall and formidable. Within moments we'd made the shield wall. I crouched behind my round shield protecting Wulf's legs. He stood tall above me, his back to the perch, holding his shield in one hand and brandishing the sword in the other.

Axeface hesitated looking anxiously behind him for support. As he did so, Wulf threw his head back, opened his mouth and let out his powerful, howling battle cry at the same time banging his sword rhythmically on his shield. The noise was a force in itself, I could feel its power and it brought Axeface to a puzzled halt. At the same time there was what seemed an echo behind us: a shrill, yammering shout. We turned our heads and saw Gam running from the tree line where she had been hiding. She was, in reality, a small girl running, shouting and brandishing a stick but, in the low, sharp sunlight, her hair streaming behind her, she looked magnificent: a warrior, waving a magical sword and singing a terrifying battle cry. My heart flew out to her and, like an echo of that feeling, a fast-moving shadow followed then passed above her as the eagle swept over us and straight towards Axeface who ducked and stumbled. The bird circled and flew high responding to Gam's whistle, then sped fast and low again. Axeface dropped the sword, fell to his knees and covered his head with his hands. Gam had joined us now crouching, panting next to me behind the shield and the eagle alighted on the perch behind us joining our defensive group. But the determined Axeface was soon up on his feet again and quickly joined by the other two advancing birdmen and some of the players. Wulf spoke to us calmly, reassuring, just as we had done, earlier, to the bird.

'Keep steady. When he comes at us, grab his legs. Don't be frightened, he's no more than a scarecrow. Grab his legs and he'll go down like sticks and straw. That's all there is to him. He won't hurt you while I've got this sword.'

And it worked. I knew I should have been frightened but I wasn't. I didn't mind what happened. We had the eagle, I was with Wulf and Gam and I loved them both.

There was, though, no attack. Instead, a stand off, the three of us facing Axeface and the growing crowd of performers. We stood proudly, staring boldly at the group surrounding us. Most of them seemed grim and angry and I guessed they felt a bit ashamed of the cowardly way they'd retreated from the phantom soldiers. But some seemed to see the funnier side of it. They looked more friendly and were grinning appreciatively at the sight of our odd, little defensive shield wall. There was a good deal of shouting and insults, mainly from Axeface but Wulf was more than capable of answering back and he sent a volley of abuse and obscenities at the stick-thin, crow-like figure before us. He even challenged Axeface to single combat and scorned his wheedling refusal.

I'd felt the strange pull and push of power between Gam and Axeface and its force now seemed to be with Gam who quietened things down and set about a negotiation. She called out to them. 'You can see how things are. There's far more of you than there are of us but we'll make a good fight of it and there will be bloodshed. Do you want that? And besides,' she said, 'Ox was right. There are soldiers in the wood,' she gestured behind her, 'Saxons there,' and gesturing the other way, 'Normans over there. I should think we've made enough noise for them to hear already and that's not a good idea.'

There were more insults from Axeface but I could also see some nods of agreement from within the group. They were more relaxed, too, some sitting down.

'All we want to do is to go home. I expect you do, too. Back to Normandy,' said Gam, trying to make peace.

'This is Normandy now,' said Axeface triumphantly. 'We are here. The good Duke is here and this is Normandy.'

But his words were drowned by an angry roar from Wulf, 'Not yet! You must overcome us first,' he shouted.

But Axeface simply shrugged. 'There is an army waiting for you,' he said, 'if you want a fight. Your king seems far away.'

There was more by way of bitter and insulting exchange between them before Gam spoke, cutting through their argument.

'The eagle,' she said gesturing at the bird on its perch behind her.

Axeface looked at her sharply, 'What?'

'You can have the eagle but you let the simple boy and his old grandfather free.'

'Grandfather?' spluttered Wulf.

I turned to him and winked, 'Yes, grandfather.'

'What's wrong with your eye, boy?'

'Grandfather, shush.'

'They are nothing to me,' said Axeface. 'We could have left the old man on the road but he made so much fuss. We took him because he swore he was a fighting man for the Saxon traitor Godwinson and he insulted Duke William who is the rightful king. But he is a nuisance and the little sparrow is of no importance.'

'Then let them go free,' said Gam. 'The boy came only to find his grandfather and to take him home. You can have the bird.'

But Axeface simply gestured to Ox who whistled, holding up a gloved hand with a piece of meat. The untethered bird who, it seemed, thought more of her stomach than her loyalty, flew to him and sat on his arm tearing at the food. With his other hand he tied her jesses to his wrist.

'We have the bird now,' said Axeface decisively, 'and we will take you too. You and the bird work well together. Come back to us. Work with us again. I have taught you much. There will be one more show on the coast and then it is your choice, to stay or cross the sea.'

There was something in his voice as he spoke, pacifying rather than confrontational, which made Gam weaken. I could feel her power ebbing now that the eagle had gone. The force, instead, seemed to have returned to Axeface. Whatever power they had seemed to switch with the bird. Gam said nothing but seemed to nod and lower her head in agreement stepping away from us. 'You can go home, Ash,' she said. 'Both of you.'

'No.'

'I'm going with them,' she said firmly. 'You two should leave. That's the bargain.'

'Then I'm coming, too.'

'And me,' said Wulf.

'That's not the idea,' said Gam.

'We don't care,' I said, speaking, I knew, for Wulf. 'If you're going we'll come too. We're not leaving you on your own.'

'But I know what he's planning,' said Gam. 'It's dangerous even for me and I'm a Norman like them.'

'It'll be just as dangerous for us to go,' I said. As I spoke I realised the flaw in our plan. Released, Wulf and I would probably be in more danger. How could we get home? Without the horse and cart the journey would be hard for the lame Wulf even if we stuck to the road. There would be soldiers on the lookout and Wulf wouldn't be able to travel nimbly through the woods or to climb and hide like me. We'd be cut down. It wasn't, though, just the danger. Something inside told me I should stick with Gam. That it was my destiny.

'I stay with you. Wulf?'

The old soldier threw down the sword and shield by way of reply and put his hand on his heart. 'We stay together.'

Axeface was, suddenly, the confident showman again. 'Yes, we stay together,' he announced as though speaking to a crowd. 'We can make a show. Two bird boys and a soldier. We can make our trick with the egg. The golden crown,' he laughed mischievously, 'and this business with the shields. Perhaps we could work that in.'

Gam shook her head in frustration. 'It wasn't meant to be like this, she said.

'Enough,' said Axeface. 'It is agreed. Too much time wasted. Prepare the birds.'

Gam went off with one of the tumblers. I led Wulf over to the cart where he sat and watched and muttered as the show picked up again. The hawks resumed their flight. When Gam came back she was in the bird costume, dancing, hopping and pecking.

When the eagle was brought forward again I felt my heart beating in my chest. The bird was flown back and forth across the meadow, from one perch to another. Axeface made a great show of talk in French and I knew he was describing the bird and its rarity. Gam put the glove on just as she had done when I first saw her in Rye, and the eagle swooped and grabbed the morsel of meat. Of course, I knew what was coming. Axeface was clicking his fingers and gesturing at me. I left Wulf and walked over reluctantly. They put the glove on my hand and I held my arm aloft. But Axeface intervened. 'No,' he said sternly, 'we must make a show. We want laughter. You must pretend to be afraid.'

I remembered what Gam had told me and I acted the part, staring dumbly and blankly at Axeface as though I didn't understand. He came up to me, bent over me pulling a terrified face. 'Like this,' he said severely. I gave a half smile. 'No, no, no,' he shouted. He turned to Gam and spoke to her in French. Gam took the bird hood off and came over to me. She spoke slowly and loudly. 'Ash…you…must…pretend…to…be…frightened,' she pulled a terrified face, 'and you must try to run.' And she ran round and round in small circles. 'It's like a game,' she said as though talking to a small child.

Slowly, painfully slowly, they put me through my paces. I wasn't like Gam. I wasn't an actor. I didn't like the attention. My face grew hot with embarrassment and I couldn't look at the other performers watching me critically. When I acted the part well, letting the glove fall off my hand, pretending to hide behind Gam, running off and being dragged back by one of the tumblers, Axeface muttered his appreciation. At other times he smacked his head with the palm of his hand, shouting in exasperation.

Piece by piece, we established a routine. The eagle was brought into the ring. She was released and flew swiftly back and forth between the perches making low

185

passes just above the ground. Axeface made his speech, gesturing at the bird. The drum began to beat. Gam put the glove on, walking around the circle holding her hand aloft, grasping the piece of meat. The drum stopped. The eagle swooped and took the meat. The drum began to beat again and the horn was blown. Axeface looked round at the troupe and pointed at me. I pretended to hide but Gam and the little fool ran forward and dragged me into the centre of the circle. They gave me the glove and I pretended to run away. Gam and the fool chased me and dragged me back. Axeface gave me the piece of stinking meat. I held up my arm. The drum was banged faster and faster then suddenly stopped. The eagle swooped and I fell on my backside. Axeface shouted at me in a theatrical voice. Gam and the fool pulled me back up on to my feet. This happened three times until I stood still and the meat was taken. The bird flew back on to her perch. The drums and horns began again. The troupe of performers, Axeface too, applauded. I felt quite pleased with myself and Gam showed me how to give a neat bow to the invisible crowd.

'It is well done. It is how we build a show,' said Axeface proudly. 'It is how we make them laugh and shriek.'

But who will laugh? I thought. *Where is our audience?* I was about to speak to Gam, but as if she knew what I was thinking she shook her head meaningfully.

We rehearsed for what was left of the day. Finally, Axeface allowed us to rest. A fire was made and food and drink were produced. But this was poor fare. The group, I realised, were on hard times. We made do with dry, stale bread and a little fruit. I sat next to Gam and

Wulf. The old man, wearied by the day's events, dozed by the fire. Gam and I stared into the flames. I thought of the other places I'd rather be: free in the wood with Misty, in the dark, warm, noisy bustle of Till's forge, in the safe hideaway of the Old Place. And, I thought, all this trouble had started when I had taken that sword.

In the dark, by the glow of the meagre fire, Axeface broke the silence speaking quietly to the melancholy company. 'Tomorrow,' he said, 'we go to see the camp of Duke William.'

Even though the troupe must have known what he was planning, there was a stunned reaction: silence, then muttering. Voices were raised. Questions were asked. An argument began. Mainly they were speaking French so I didn't understand what was said but the sense of unease in this company of showmen was palpable. Axeface responded, sometimes scolding, sometimes soothing, using his honeyed words. Then in English, appealing, using the same word Gam had used: 'Trust. Trust me. These are our kinfolk,' he said, 'their blood is our blood. I know these people,' he continued persuasively, 'they are an army at rest. The men are waiting, they want to do battle but there is no-one here for them to fight. They want distraction. They want entertainment, they will pay well and we will share the wealth.' He paused then said significantly, 'Besides, I have information for the Duke. We will be welcome. You will see. These are our people and we will be safe. We will make a show for the army. We will take our reward then we will take ship for France. We will go home.'

Home.

The word seemed to silence the dissenters. All of us stared into the fire, thinking of home.

'Otherwise,' said Axeface, 'you can go.' He gestured at the darkness beyond the fire. 'Remember you are Normans. The enemy is in the woods. Take your chances if you dare.'

I looked round at this group of weary performers. I could sense their fear, read it in their faces: tired, desperate people.

It was a long and uneasy night. We slept beside the fire and at first, as the snoring around me began, I expected a signal from Gam, another plan, some way of sneaking away into the shelter of the concealing wood. I whispered to her in the dark but she simply shook her head. She was, I could tell, anxious and unsleeping. I could see the hunched silhouettes of Axeface and his birdmen on the opposite side of the fire. I was sure they were unsleeping too, and vigilant.

In the morning, by the first light of day, we saw that some of the company had gone – they'd done what I'd been tempted to do – they'd crept away in the night. We were now a small and pathetic band: Axeface, the two birdmen, Ox and Frog, two or three tumblers, the jugglers, the fool, Wulf, Gam and me. Axeface paced around the smoking remains of the fire. 'Cowards,' he spat. 'Where can they go? They will be taken and, if not, they will starve in the woods. Good riddance to them.'

As we busied ourselves packing up the camp and preparing a meagre breakfast I had a whispered conversation with Gam.

'Gam, we should leave here now.'

She shook her head.

'What? Are you really staying? Are you going with them?'

'We all are,' said Gam.

'To the coast? To where the Norman army is?'

She nodded. 'We have to.'

'Not me, I protested, 'not Wulf. I thought you'd find a way to get us out of this.'

'You'll be able to go,' said Gam uneasily, 'but after the show.'

'But how?' I hissed. 'If we go on any further we'll be worse off than we are now. Axeface will say anything. He's a liar. If he takes us to where the Normans are they won't just let us go again.'

'We have no choice,' she said. 'The two of us could probably escape but we'd have to leave Wulf here and that wouldn't be right.'

'It's all right for you,' I said sulkily, feeling betrayed, 'the Normans are your people. But we're Saxons. They'll kill us.'

'Trust me, Ash. I think it'll be all right.'

'You think?'

She didn't sound convincing and I didn't know what to do. My mind was whirling. I looked across the rough ground of the meadow towards the wood. Should I chance it and run? But what would happen to Wulf and Gam if I did? How far would I get anyway before a bolt from a Norman crossbow or an arrow from a Saxon longbow brought me down? Should I try arguing with Axeface, tell him this was all a stupid mistake, demand that he take us back to the forge in the cart? But, even as I was fretting and thinking, the little cart was being loaded with gear. The ancient horse was backed between the shafts and Wulf was finding a comfortable seat amongst the baggage together with the birds on their perches.

189

The horse stepped out. I walked behind. Gam was at the front with the birdmen. Axeface gave her a drum to beat. I was given a horn to blow.

14. NORMANS

Slowly, reluctantly our ragged little troupe set off. As we reached the ridgeway we could see the early light on the horizon above the coast. We could also see smoke from the fires of the Norman camp we were heading towards. The road itself was empty. The only sound came from our creaking, banging cart wheels, our shuffling feet and the rattle of our pathetic possessions.

When we saw our first Normans they were a surprise because they didn't look like soldiers. They wore leather jerkins and I couldn't see any armour or weapons. They had a horse and cart and they were collecting firewood: logs and brushwood for kindling. Except for their hairstyles and the leather tunics, we would have thought no more of them than that they were farm labourers. They simply stared at us as we approached. One of them shouted something and the others laughed. Axeface shouted back in a friendly manner as though making a joke, trying to appear at ease. We moved on past.

But then we saw more soldiers. They were blocking the road, sitting playing some kind of game: hazard, with dice, I guessed. One of them was sprawled out as though he'd been sleeping. Axeface picked up his drum and began to beat out a cheerful rhythm. At his signal, Gam and some of the others did the same and, together with the tumblers, I began to blow the horn. It was a horrible racket. The soldiers got to their feet, slow and insolent, irritated that they'd been disturbed in the middle of their game. Again they had no armour but wore the same tight leather jerkins. They had weapons, though: short swords, a spear and one had a crossbow. They

191

stood in the road watching us approach. We moved steadily towards them with our cacophony of music and I was waiting for Axeface to slow our march and for us to stop. But, instead, he kept us pacing steadily forward, closer and closer to the group of soldiers until he was about an arm's length away and with a theatrical flourish he brought our progress and music to a dramatic stop.

And it had the effect he was after. The soldiers laughed.

Axeface gave his showman's bow, speaking mellifluously while he gestured proudly at us and then towards the coast. But it didn't impress the soldiers who replied roughly and gestured back up the road. *Good*, I thought, *they're sending us back*. But Axeface didn't give up. He talked more, sometimes putting his hand to his heart and gesturing towards the countryside through which we'd travelled. It didn't seem to impress the soldiers at all until Axeface said a word. It was a name. *Eustace*. He repeated it – *Eustace* - and the demeanour of the soldiers changed. They talked amongst themselves for a bit then they came and looked at the cart, prodding the baggage. I looked anxiously at Wulf who seemed to be dozing. They found some weapons, some knives. They took them away then one gestured for us to move, to go with them, two of them walking ahead and two behind.

I stared angrily at Gam as if to say, 'So this is the mess you've got us into!' but she looked away.

As we walked on we passed more and more soldiers. Some were sitting by the side of the highway, some were carrying wood, baskets of food, some leading animals all of which, I guessed, had been looted from the surrounding villages. Soon we were at the top of the ridge which leads down towards the coast and which gave us our first view of the sea and the Norman encampment. The first thing we noticed was the ships. It was just as the refugees had told us. There were ships, hundreds of ships, pulled up all along the shingle where the land meets the sea. More ships, their sails down, were bobbing on their anchors in the shallows. Further out, even more ships in full sail and heavily laden with goods were moving towards the shore. The stories we'd heard were true. The sea was covered with ships, more than we could count. You could walk from ship to ship, I thought, all the way to France and not get your feet wet.

The sun was higher now and it illuminated the drab huts and wretched farm buildings of Hastings and there, above the settlement, was something extraordinary: a castle. How they'd done it I don't know, but there was a castle on the hill. It had tall wooden walls and a defensive earthwork had been thrown up around it. Flags were flying and we could see the bright helmets of soldiers behind the ramparts. Spread out from the castle like a broad apron was the Norman encampment stretching across the hill as far as we could see. There were soldiers here in their thousands. There were lines of coloured tents, there were fires and neat stacks of stakes and glittering spears. There were soldiers in neat groups. Mock fights were taking place. There were fenced enclosures where horses grazed. Elsewhere horses were being exercised, running in circles, chasing and charging at each other in mock battle. This was a monstrous army and greater than anything I had seen before or have seen since. The sight overwhelmed me. I felt crushed, my knees gave way and I collapsed, dizzy, against the side of the cart. All of us, the whole troupe, Axeface himself, had been stopped in our tracks, astounded by the sight before us.

The soldiers around us saw what was happening and laughed at our incredulity. One of them gestured sweeping an arm across the vision of the invading force in front of us then pointing contemptuously towards the land at our backs – our land – and, smirking, drew a finger across his throat. Then with a harsh word he signalled us onwards. As we walked he spoke again, an order, and Axeface began to beat his drum, turning towards us so that we picked up the tune, trying to skip and make it sound carefree but, no matter how we tried, our nervous drums and wailing horns played out a mournful death march. We made our way down the road, passing more soldiers many of whom began to walk with us, some commenting appreciatively on the hawks and the eagle, especially; others laughing and mocking. My anxiety grew as Wulf, woken from his sleepy reverie in the steadily jolting cart and becoming aware of his surroundings seemed to be spoiling for a fight and, when the soldiers made a derogatory comment or laughed or whistled or catcalled in our direction he started to shout insults back. I stopped blowing my horn and pleaded with him to be quiet but the soldiers themselves just seemed to find the whole thing amusing.

We were now approaching the fringes of the Norman encampment at the base of the hill that rose towards the towering, formidable castle and here, without explanation, we were stopped. The soldiers who had accompanied us on the road walked away as though they'd found something more interesting to do. Axeface, for the first time, seemed unsure of himself. There were soldiers all around us but they each seemed busily caught up with a task – carrying, chopping, digging, mending - and none seemed to give us any attention. It was as though we were of no importance to them. At a signal from Axeface we started forward again only to be halted by a short, sharp, barked shout from a nearby soldier which made it clear we were to go no further. But, again, as we stood there, we were simply ignored.

So we waited: at first, standing expectantly, then sinking down to sit around the cart. We were hungry and thirsty. We found a small supply of bread and some horns of water in the cart but this was soon gone. Once or twice Axeface tried speaking to a nearby soldier, smiling and pleading, but he was ignored as if he was of no consequence. One of our troupe picked up a horn cup and walked forward to look for water but with a sharp whistle and an impatient gesture from a nearby soldier he was sent back to the cart. I tried to catch Gam's attention but she sat with her back to the cart, her hood pulled over her head. I knew that things had gone horribly wrong.

At last, in the afternoon, a soldier approached us, bustling and business-like. Axeface saw him coming and leaped to his feet. The soldier spoke to him quickly, firing questions and giving him hardly space to reply before asking more questions. Axeface was trying to explain. He pointed to our group, he pointed to the birds, he did a little dance, he put his hand on his heart then tapped the side of his nose as though he had secrets to tell and, again, slowly and carefully repeating a name *Eustace* as if it had some significance. The soldier looked at him and, abruptly, turned on his heel and walked away.

Again we waited and, as we waited, we watched. There was much to see. Mostly we saw soldiers going out with empty carts and others arriving laden with food and wood. Some of the carts were pulled by the soldiers themselves; others were bigger, wagons, pulled by horses. Animals, mostly hogs, goats, cows and oxen, stolen from the nearby villages were driven past us and put into pens. Soldiers walked by carrying baskets of hens and ducks, some had geese wriggling under their arms. It was hard to rest as this was a noisy place: loud shouts, the clashing and clattering of weapons, the shriek of iron being sharpened. Weapons were being made and repaired here and I thought of Till and his cosy forge. Loud hammering and the chopping and shouting of builders echoed from within the great castle. The air was full of smells, too: smoke from the fires and the mouth-watering waft of cooking; horse dung, the sweat of men, leather and grease.

Hungry and thirsty, we had, though, fallen into a kind of sleepy reverie, losing any sense of time passing, when we noticed a sudden change in the demeanour of the soldiers nearby. They continued their busy work but, now, even busier, their backs straighter. Some, who had been lying on the grass and chattering jumped to their feet as a small party of soldiers walked rapidly and purposefully towards us. This group stood out from the others. They were more smartly dressed with long cloaks. Amongst them a man in a fine, coloured, embroidered tunic: a nobleman, a knight.

Axeface leapt to his feet and bowed obsequiously, gasping, 'My Lord Eustace,' but the nobleman ignored him and went straight to the cart to look at the birds with the interest of a connoisseur. He was particularly interested in the eagle. He ran a finger over its plumage and lifted its wing with the ease and knowledge of an expert, clucking his tongue so that the hooded creature lifted its head. He was turning to ask Axeface a question when he saw Wulf. And Wulf saw him. There was a roar of mutual recognition and the two of them were suddenly clasping hands, laughing and slapping each other on the back. Those of us watching – our ragged group of troubadours, the Norman soldiers and Axeface, in particular – stood back in astonishment as the two men laughed, chatted and asked each other questions like old friends. They spoke sometimes in French and sometimes in English. They were shouting out the names of former comrades and places they had been together. Suddenly Wulf was calling me to him, 'Ash, Ash,' he said proudly, 'I told you about fighting in France with Harold Godwinson. Here is one of my companions. We fought together. We were in Brittany. We fought Conan. It was a great campaign. We took the keys to the town in Dinant.'

The knight was beaming and keen to confirm the story, 'Your father….grandfather…,' he seemed uncertain and Wulf simply nodded vaguely, '…a great warrior. He looked after me well and taught me much. I was a young man. My first campaign. We were with Godwinson….,' but here he turned and spat on the ground, 'before this terrible betrayal. We were fighting with Guillaume our duke who soon,' he declared, 'will be your king. And he, this good old man, with the strength of an ox, saved some of our soldiers who were snared in the quicksand. They were flailing and sinking with their armour,' he mimed the sinking movements of a drowning man, laughing all the while, 'and he, with the strength of ten, pulled them free.' He turned to Wulf, 'You remember? A great day.'

They laughed some more but suddenly the knight grew serious as though he had said too much, had forgotten himself. He turned to Wulf speaking more formally, 'But what brings you here? Do you wish to join us against the traitor? This is not a fight for you. This is for young men. You have done your service. You deserve to be sitting by the fire with your family and telling them of your deeds.'

Wulf nodded towards Axeface, 'This is the fellow to ask,' he said bitterly. 'We are in thrall to this rogue.'

The knight turned on Axeface, 'What brings you here? This is not the time for jollity, to be selling birds and what right do you have to interfere with the liberty of this honourable old gentleman?'

Axeface, pulling faces and sweating desperately began his honeyed words, 'The old soldier, my lord,' he gestured at Wulf, 'is with Godwinson. We ran into him on the road and I thought it best – he is our enemy – to bring him with us. He is old and feeble, no great threat to be sure but he is with the traitor and could make mischief. He knows the ways of Godwinson's army and is a lodestone for news. He rallies the simple people to rebellion against the Duke. We are merely travellers, my lord, returning to Normandy because of the troubled times. We came here to show the birds, to offer our humble services: some entertainment for this great army. But chiefly, my lord, your name was given to me as one who might make use of the information I have. I travel much in this region and have knowledge of the roads, the people, the ragged English army.' He began speaking rapidly in French his voice rising to a whine and a whisper.

The knight grew impatient, 'Come with me,' he said, 'I will weigh your information and we will decide about this entertainment and what is to be done.' He seemed uncertain. 'This is most irregular. We will soon be in the field, in the fray. Godwinson could attack us at any time although we have men on the road and eyes in the woodland. We will not be caught unprepared.'

He turned back to Wulf, 'I will do what I can for you my old companion. I will send some food and drink. But I think it better that you had not come here. You are not in our colours. You tell me this fellow is a rogue but I will listen to his information and consider if his tongue is straight. These are difficult times for us all. This is our land now and the traitor – your Godwinson - must be punished.' He spoke to the group of soldiers and they marched away with the bobbling Axeface in their midst.

Our attention now turned to Wulf who had stood down from the cart and who had grown in stature basking in our respect and admiration. He began to answer our questions and to tell us of his adventures in France, how he had fought with Eustace who was then just a youngster. Their party had been lost crossing the sands in Brittany and, with some modesty, he explained how he had played his part in rescuing them from the quicksand. He was in full flow when he was interrupted by the welcome arrival of food and drink brought to us by hurrying, rather begrudging men from the field kitchens. There was water, beer, meat, fish, bread and cheese and we flew at the meal like starving beasts and feasted hungrily.

The day was moving towards its end and this was a day, I thought, that was out of balance. We had started out in an early morning that now seemed an age away. We had travelled a long road and then dawdled for long spells here in the camp of the enemy. Now, our meal finished and with the day on the wane, the evening settling and at a time when sleep began to beckon, the pace picked up unnaturally and rapidly. At a signal we were marched further into the heart of the Norman encampment and within the long shadow cast by the towering castle. Here was an arena where the horses had been exercised and where, from a distance, we had seen soldiers practising their manoeuvres: running with lances and swords, parrying blows with their long shields, swerving and ducking. Axeface met us there. Although he looked soiled and sweaty some of his showman's assurance had returned. He gestured at the arena, told us his request to perform had been granted and to make ready for the show.

It was to be a strange performance. The arena was huge and our players were nervous. They had been used to a small village green, playing to groups of families: excited children and wide-eyed country folk. Now, the audience were hardened soldiers far from home and with their minds fixed on the fight to come. It wasn't a big audience, certainly. These were men, off duty, who had drifted in to the arena and who regarded us with a non-committal curiosity and a kind of hostility which shook the confidence which performers, tumblers and jugglers particularly, need. We did our best but we weren't very good. The tumblers rolled and jumped and vaulted; the jugglers threw and caught. There was some light smacking of hands but little interest. We were quickly losing the attention of our audience some of whom began to drift away but the juggling swordsman drew their appreciation. He threw and caught his sword to applause but his act, unexpectedly, brought some of the watching soldiers to their feet keen to show similar skills and, soon, we were surrounded by a group of men throwing and catching their weapons in competition with each other. The air was quickly filled with whistling, swishing and jingling murderous swords.

I sat with Wulf in the cart. The old man had said little but had watched everything and now, as he looked around the ring he clutched my arm, aghast. 'This was my dream, Ash. When you boys found me in the woods. This is what I was dreaming. I remember this. I dreamed I was surrounded by Normans then, when I reached for my axe, it was gone. I couldn't find my axe and they were all pointing and laughing. I dreamt it all. The eagle, too. The bird was in my dream.'

The afternoon light had almost gone. Fires and torches were being lit. The birdmen were preparing the falcons but fretting they wouldn't fly because they were losing the light. Axeface called for the crowd's attention and made his announcements. The first bird, the goshawk, was about to take to the air when, without warning there was a roar as if we were being attacked: raucous shouts, the clattering of weapons striking shields, feet stamping. All around the ring the Norman soldiers were on their feet cheering and bellowing their war songs in unison. I had never heard a sound like it. The noise was like a weapon itself, cutting into me. I shook with fear and noticed that Wulf was visibly pale. For a moment Axeface beamed thinking this was applause for him then, like the rest of us, he watched as a group of knights and noblemen slowly entered the ring. As they sauntered in there was a flurry of activity and a place immediately opposite us was cleared, chairs and benches found and covered in rich cloth, a table set up with platters of food and horns of drink. Bowls of water and cloths were offered by servants so that these new arrivals could rinse and dry their fingers. These noblemen waved at the soldiers acknowledging their shouts and songs then settled themselves, eating, drinking and talking to each other and giving little regard to us. The noise from our audience of soldiers slowly subsided as they sat down again.

An exclamatory whistle burst from Wulf's lips as he stared at the group dumbfounded, 'The Duke,' he whispered to me, 'William.'

And I saw him. It was the Duke William of Normandy surrounded by his knights sitting only a short distance opposite us and who, looking up, seemed to notice us for the first time. I had always thought of him as a giant. My idea, I suppose, was that dukes and kings would be much bigger than other men. In fact he looked ordinary although it was obvious that he was the commander in chief because of the fine glittering cloak he was wearing and the way he managed to be the centre of everyone's attention. All eyes were on him and his eyes looked back. And it was those eyes that were striking. They were deep and dark but, somehow, shining and piercing as though he could see everything. I felt him look at me. And I mean that I didn't just notice his gaze, I felt it. His eyes, like the war songs, seemed to pierce me. Then he looked at Wulf and, as he did so, Eustace, the knight who had been a friend to us earlier leaned over and spoke to him as if explaining who we were. A look of not unfriendly recognition spread over the Duke's face, a kind of curiosity. For an awful moment I thought he was going to beckon us over and I wondered what we would do if Wulf came out with one of his *God damn Duke William* curses, or worse. Luckily the Duke was distracted by the man next to him. This was a huge man with a fine richly embroidered cloak and a smooth, fat face. He was chewing greedily even as he bent to speak to William, laughing as though sharing a private joke.

'Odo,' whispered Wulf to me, 'that's Odo the bishop.' He spat on the ground, 'he calls himself a man of Christ and so he won't carry a sword. Instead he wields a great war club, the cheating, murdering....'

'Shhh.....be quiet,' I hissed in terror, 'They'll hear us.'

'Odo and the Duke himself,' whispered Wulf, to himself. 'If only I had my war axe.'

Axeface was almost beside himself with excitement at the sight of this royal group before him. He went into his showman's patter – speaking in French – addressing the noblemen directly – telling them about the fine qualities of the birds. He gave a signal, the drumming began and Gam danced around in her costume. This caused amusement and, as she ran at the crowd, some of the men shouted and waved their swords at her in mock threat. The falcons were paraded around the ring and flown expertly by Ox and Frog with smatters of polite appreciation from the soldiers. One of the knights patted the table. The hawks were carried to him and examined. One was allowed to perch on the back of his chair and he fed it with small pieces of meat to the amusement of his companions.

Then the great eagle was brought out. There was a question from one of the knights and Axeface and Ox carried the bird on its perch towards the duke. Some time was spent as these hawkers appraised the eagle, keen to show their expertise. Axeface brought the bird back to the centre of the ring and resumed his patter. He spoke rapidly in French but I easily understood that he was explaining that the eagle had come from the high mountains of Byzantium and that he was offering it as a gift to Duke William, the rightful King of England. It would be, he was saying, a symbol of the victory to come. William acknowledged the gift with a nod as if it was no more than expected and I knew he would be a hard man to please.

At a signal, Gam began her dance, hopping higher and faster now as if to acknowledge both the importance of the big bird and the presence of the Duke. The eagle was flown, swooping low across the ground, from one side of the arena to the other. Gam was given the glove and held the meat which the bird snatched neatly from her hand before settling back on its perch. There was some polite applause from the noblemen some of whom banged the table in appreciation. A knight held up a coin and beckoned to Gam. She ran over, took it, bowed, and ran back.

My stomach tightened as I knew it would be my turn for the glove and the egg trick next. The fool was running round the circle with his bladder on a stick. Axeface was preparing to pull me into the centre of the ring. I knew the routine before me: pretending to run, hide, fall on my backside, have the glove snatched from my hand, the golden crown, the egg. I hated the humiliation. I knew these rough soldiers would laugh. I thought of what Wulf had said about his dream and wondered if I, now, was dreaming. How could it happen that a small, frightened boy like me could be standing in the middle of the Norman encampment? I felt my lip trembling and my eyes misting. I hated the thought that I, a Saxon boy, would let the side down by sobbing like an infant in front of these men who were invaders with no right to be here. I dreaded what I knew was coming…..but it didn't happen.

There was a sudden shout of alarm from Axeface as Gam, instead of pulling me from where I was hiding behind the cart, ran fast and hard towards Duke William and his knights. As she ran, she pulled the bird cap from her head and threw herself on her knees at the feet of a nobleman seated in the group almost next to the Duke. The man leapt to his feet in alarm and the others followed. Food and wine went flying as swords were drawn and some of the soldiers rushed forward to protect their leader. The nobleman shouted in anger and surprise at Gam who was now kneeling before him, her head in her hands almost touching the ground. She was speaking rapidly and passionately and, I was sure, she was weeping. Suddenly the knight's voice broke and he was on his knees too, hugging the little bird figure, laughing and crying. He pushed the soldiers away, lifted Gam to her feet and hugged her. Chaos – shouts, alarm – was followed by laughter. The knight, still hugging Gam had turned to talk to the Duke and his colleagues, pointing at the girl in the bird costume, talking rapidly, explaining. Gam was talking too and gesturing at me and Wulf.

Our show was suddenly over. The noblemen, laughing and talking, clapping each other on the shoulders, stood up. The knight, a strong, powerful figure lifted Gam easily holding her high, higher then hoisting her on to his shoulder laughing and chatting to her fondly as, together with the others, he strolled away. Our audience of soldiers drifted off too and we were left stranded once again. There we were in the empty arena in the heart of the huge Norman encampment and beneath the high wooden walls of the Hastings Castle.

Axeface stood alone in the centre of it all. He spoke into the air but was speaking to himself, 'I think that went rather well,' he said.

15. ESCAPE

Once again we sat by the cart and waited but this time not for long. A soldier, young, brisk and officious strode across the arena. Axeface leapt to his feet expectantly but the soldier pointed to Wulf and me and indicated that we should follow him. We wove our way slowly, Wulf limping painfully, through the encampment now dark as night descended, to a place where a small open tent had been set next to a bright burning fire. There were fine rugs and a low table with food, drink and bowls of water for washing. There was wine for Wulf and beer for me. The young soldier indicated that we should sit. 'My lord,' he said, 'sends his thanks and good wishes for your kind services. My lady speaks well of you and tells us you have been wronged by the man with the birds. He will be punished. My lord asks you please to eat, drink and take your rest. In the morning you will return to your home.'

So, I sat with old Wulf who, strangely, I was beginning to think really was my grandfather. We stared at the fires around us aware that the bustle of the day was continuing unabated into the night. The sounds of building work continued from the castle. There was the constant movement of men, weapons and goods, carts groaning and creaking back and forth, the neighing of horses, the shouts from sentries at regular intervals. Occasionally, there would be a roar of men shouting and cheering together.

'Hear that, Ash,' said Wulf, 'I don't like him but that man, that Duke, is a good chief. You hear the shouts. He isn't sleeping. He's walking in the night, going from group to group, talking to his men, making them bold of heart.'

Having drunk heavily from the bowl of wine we had been offered, Wulf was soon asleep. For me it was a long and restless night. I thought about how clumsily things worked out. Why was it all such a mess? When I thought and dreamed about what I wanted to do it was all so orderly. The same when I worked with Till. I knew where to put the tools and the order in which to heat and beat and reheat and bend. One thing happened and then another, as things should be. Here, though, I was in a muddle, stuck, wondering how things had gone wrong and how they would work themselves out. I knew that something remarkable had happened but I didn't understand what it was. It was my guess that Gam had been reunited with her father, or an uncle perhaps or brother. But had she planned it this way and, if so, why had she said nothing to me?

Thinking about these things I fell asleep at last only to be awoken in the early hours of the morning by a roar of alarm which rang and echoed throughout the camp. I heard the call to arms. Drums, horns, shouted orders the sounds of men running, armour being clapped on, the clash and flash of weapons. Then, as quickly as it came the noise and alarm subsided. Soldiers walked slowly back to their camps talking quietly and settled themselves calmly down again. I must have slept again because when I awoke, it was a cold dawn and Gam was standing over me, looking down. She looked different: more grown up and, suddenly, no longer a boy.

'I didn't want to wake you.'

'You didn't. I couldn't sleep much. It's strange being here. All the noise. It was quieter in the Old Place.'

She laughed, 'I'll never forget it. I've never felt so safe as I did there.'

I sat up and she sat down beside me. She looked at the sleeping, snoring Wulf and smiled affectionately. Then she was suddenly serious as she handed me a tiny silver ring.

'I brought you this. A vervel from the eagle. I've just released the birds. They deserve to be free. I took away their hoods and jesses. I worry, though, they are not used to freedom so they might not fly away. They flew up there, to the castle. They might just come back. These, the vervels, I took from the eagle. We can have one each.'

She showed me the tiny silver ring then threaded it on a leather lace and put it round my neck. 'See, I've got the other one,' she bared her neck to show me. 'We have one each. A pair.'

She took my hand and we sat quietly for a moment looking out over the Norman camp. There was a thick creeping mist in the woods and hollows. We were high above it but the tent and ground were wet. Soldiers appeared in and out of the mist which was made heavier and thicker by the morning fires. We could smell cooking and the loud noises of the day went on, the building of the castle, but more muffled now.

Together we looked out across the lower ground before us, across the woodland. Somewhere out there Till would be starting his day at the forge. Misty would be chasing the hens and whining for her breakfast. Out there, buried deep in the mist and the woods were the shapes in the Old Place. Would they be moving and dancing even though we weren't there?

'But didn't Axeface give the eagle to...to...William, the Duke?'

'Yes. But the Duke will have forgotten and will be too busy to notice or care. All they do is talk war. The birds should be free. You and Wulf, too. You can leave this morning,' she said carelessly, 'someone will come to take you both out of the camp.'

'I don't think Wulf can walk all the way home. He's lame. That iron on his leg.'

'You can have the cart and the little horse.'

'What about Axeface?'

'Scur? He stays here. He will be punished.'

'They won't…will they…?'

'Kill him? Why not? He deserves it.'

'But I don't think…'

She laughed, 'No. They won't kill him. Perhaps a whipping and the release of his birds is punishment enough. Also he has friends and some influence here. He has given them information. He will be sent back to France.'

'You too?'

'Yes, I leave today. Soon. They say it isn't safe here and they tell me the wind is right.'

'I'll miss you, Gam.'

'Don't say that Ash,' she began to cry, 'I've never had a friend like you. I've never had such fun and adventure.'

'Do you have to leave?'

'Yes. I'm told I must because of the battle and because I am not a boy. I must go home.'

'Must there be a battle?'

'I hope not,' she said. 'If they can talk. If they can settle things. But these men,' she gestured at the field around her, 'their blood is up. And, it's stupid, their blood on each side is much the same.'

'I wish we weren't different,' I said.

'How?'

'Well, I wish we were the same but we're different. Norman, Saxon. A girl, a boy. And different stations, too. You're of noble birth. I'm not even a freeman.'

She took my hand, 'We're the same, Ash. We both want to be what we want to be. These men, they scold me and say I'm headstrong. I think they're right. But I'm like you. You didn't want to be what they said you had to be, a hogboy, and I didn't want to behave the way they wanted me to behave, like a lady. So, we're much the same.'

'I don't care what happens now. I won't ever be a hogboy.'

'And I won't ever be a proper lady.' She looked at me hard. 'We mustn't be like captive birds, afraid to be free.'

'Will you come back?'

'Yes. I'll be back.'

'Or I'll come and find you in France, in Fecamp.'

'Yes, I'd like that,' she said.

'Whatever happens with this,' I gestured at the army encamped around me.

'I hope we can stop it,' she said, 'it shouldn't happen.' She pointed at the sleeping figure of Wulf. 'He has fought with the Duke….and so has Godwinson. They're all north men really.'

There was silence between us then the sleeping Wulf farted loudly and we both laughed.

'I must go,' she said, standing. 'The ships leave early. Come here Ash.'

I stood and we hugged. Suddenly she seemed much bigger than me.

'I wish....,' I began to say but she pressed a finger to my lips and shushed me.

'Goodbye my friend but only for now.'

I couldn't speak. The tears ran down my face. Then Wulf farted again, muttered, began to stir and Gam was gone into the mist.

Around me the camp grew busier. I was becoming used to the shouts and cries, the strange language more and more of which I found I could understand. Soldiers walked past our little tent without a glance, always on the move and busy. I began to envy them their busy-ness. I wasn't good at sitting and doing nothing.

A man appeared with water, some bread and fruit. Wulf and I had a slow breakfast by the morning fire which took some of the damp chill from our bones. The old soldier was observant and talkative, commenting on the preparations for war he could see around him. He was impressed by the organisation of the Norman army, their vigilance and readiness. 'How long have they been here?' was his constant refrain, 'A few days and look,' he gestured at the castle, 'they've built that already.' But I gave the old man's chatter little attention. My body felt empty and aching. Gam had gone and it was as though my heart, my hopes had gone with her. She had helped me find my voice and, without her, my tongue felt dry and wooden.

Eustace, the knight who had been on campaign with Wulf, appeared suddenly out of the mist and sat by our fire, a soldier with him. He was friendly but there was a stiffness in his manner, an awkwardness.

'How are you my old friend?' he asked. 'How did you sleep in this nest of hornets? Have you been stung?'

Wulf laughed, 'I slept well,' he said, 'thanks to the quality of your good wine.'

'Were you disturbed by the alarm?' asked Eustace. 'We thought we were under attack but it was only a nervous sentry. He thought he saw movement in the woods and roused the camp thinking the English were attacking. But it was only a....what do you say....a family...a herd of hogs.'

Wulf looked at me and laughed, 'they were probably your hogs Ash.'

'Ah, yes. Your grandson is much talked about here, the hogboy who has been friends with the lady of the Duke of Mortain. She chose a strange companion.'

I said nothing and let my mouth fall open. I remembered Gam's advice to play a part but this, showing my surprise, was all too easy.

'The lord is pleased with you young man. His lady speaks highly of your care for her.' He saw my tears. 'Dry your eyes. She is above your station. And think yourselves fortunate. Both of you. You have seen our great encampment and yet we are releasing you back to our enemies.' He became serious, 'What can you tell me my old companion of Godwinson? We know he has been to the north and defeated both Tostig and Hadrada. That is a great feat.'

'He is a fearsome fighter as you well know,' said Wulf proudly.

'But he will have been hurt in that battle,' said Eustace. 'He will have lost many of his best men.'

'Perhaps,' said Wulf, 'but there are stout hearts throughout England who will throng to him if they know their land is under attack.'

'He is now in London,' said Eustace. 'He has made a splendid march. To travel to the north, to fight, and now return to the south, that is something to admire but it will have tired him.'

'He has long legs,' said Wulf.

'We do not wish this fight,' Eustace continued. 'We have sent envoys to London to sue for peace. Godwinson has only to acknowledge our Duke's right to the throne and there will be no war.'

I was afraid this would start one of Wulf's abusive tirades against the Normans but he merely grunted.

'If you have any influence,' said Eustace, 'I would urge you to use it. Godwinson, or his brother Leofwyne, will remember you from your campaigns. And you have seen all this,' he waved at the huge Norman encampment. 'We know he will have his spies but they tend to be little men, too ready to tell him what he wants to hear. He will listen to you when you tell him of our preparations, our great castle. As you can see we are not here to turn our backs and flee. Our master, Guillaume, is here to take what is rightfully his. And this has been agreed, too, by the Church. We campaign under the papal banner and that has brought some fearsome fighters to our cause from other lands. If Godwinson surrenders what he has stolen there will be a place for him still at court.' A pause while Eustace scrutinised the old man's face.

'What do you want from me?' asked Wulf.

'You are a warrior,' said Eustace, 'straight and true. We want only that you tell Godwinson what you have seen of our readiness for war, of our belief in our cause which is God's cause, too, and that we are ready to parley. There will have been much bloodshed in the north. We do not wish to add to your woes.' He clapped an arm round Wulf's shoulders. 'Goodbye old man. I hope we meet again soon when all this is done.' He towsled my hair, 'And good fortune go with you little hogboy. Dry your eyes and do not grieve. You can talk to your hogs and tell them of the wonders you have seen here this day.'

He laughed and walked quickly away. The soldier who had accompanied him motioned us to follow and we made our way through the camp. I think he deliberately chose a winding route to impress on us even further the enormity and strength of this invading force. We passed piles of weapons, stores of food, workshops, hundreds of men mock fighting and preparing themselves for war. There were horses in penned off areas. They looked different from anything I'd seen before: small but stocky, tough and alert. Wulf gave me a nudge, 'The *destriers*,' he whispered, 'the warhorses.'

The cart, now empty, and the boney little nag were waiting for us. Two soldiers stood beside it. They motioned us to climb in. One of the soldiers led the horse, the other walked behind. We slowly made our way out of the camp, the soldiers guarding the highway looking at us curiously and shifting reluctantly out of our way. As we reached the border of the camp we looked back up the hill to the castle and the glittering array of soldiers, the bustle of activity, then it was gone as we descended into the mist which still lay in the hollows around us. We passed the last line of sentries and I expected the soldiers who were with us to leave but they walked on with us. I had my head down, disconsolate, but looked up as I heard Wulf whispering to me above the creak of the cart.

'Ash,' he leaned forward conspiratorially, 'Ash. I don't trust these fellows. I don't like the look of them. I think they're up to no good. Keep an eye out and, when I give you the signal, I want you to jump down and run.'

I started to protest but he hissed at me, 'Just do as I say. It's best for us both. Watch me, then when I shout, run. Run for the wood. Go like the wind.' He looked hard at me again and he wore a different, determined, warrior face and I shivered seeing for a moment not an old man but the war mask expression he would have worn as a young *housecarl*. 'Ash. You will do this. Do you understand? You will do this.'

He gave me no choice. I nodded.

16. ALONE

We came to a bend in the track. I looked at the soldiers walking with us and, intuitively, agreed with Wulf. There was something about them which made me feel uneasy. They were hesitant, looking anxiously around and I remembered what the old soldier had said time and time again: *never trust a Norman*.

The cart creaked on for another mile or so to a spot where the track narrowed and the woodland fell away from us on either side towards marshy ground. Without warning, Wulf gave a cry of alarm, jumped from the slow moving cart and doubled-over, holding his stomach and gesturing at the bushes. He limped hastily to the side of the road, pulling at his tunic as if needing to relieve himself urgently.

'My guts,' he shouted, 'my guts are on fire.'

The soldiers looked at each other uneasily. They didn't want to let him walk free. They moved towards him and I saw his arms flail out, grabbing them by their necks, dashing their heads together and shouting, 'Ash! Now! Go!'

As I leapt from the cart a knife, thrown with force and precision, banged into the woodwork where I had been sitting. I ran to the side of the track and dived into the woodland. Something – a knife, an arrow? – screamed overhead as I ran and scrambled down the bank panting, tripping, picking myself up, running, slipping further and further down. Behind me I heard shouts. I thought I heard Wulf's howling, bellowing cry but I didn't pause until I reached the misty, scrubby edgelands of the marsh and could run no further. I threw myself into a gap between some bushes, getting horribly scratched as

I did so, and lay on my back trying to catch my breath. For a moment I could hear nothing above my own panting gasps and the sound of my blood pounding in my ears. As, slowly, I grew calm I listened. Nothing. I could hear no sound of pursuit. Still I waited to be sure, peeping out and watching the woodland through which I'd earlier run. After a while I crept from the bushes and made my way cautiously along the fringes of the wood which were still covered in a cloak of that concealing mist which superstitious villagers call *moorgrim*. I was alert, listening out for any alarm from the birds but all was quiet. I moved instinctively north in the direction of home. I knew it would be a long journey and I had no food or fire or knife. I shivered in the mist trying to push away the stories I'd heard of the creature that lived in the bottomless lake and which conjured up the *moorgrim* so that it could rise to the surface, thirsty for the blood of lost travellers. All I had was the silver *vervel* which, from time to time, I touched like a talisman.

I had walked some time, the sun was higher and burning the mist away when I heard the quick repeated rhythm of a startled bird telling me there was danger and I sensed movement ahead of me. I scrambled quickly up a tall beech tree and waited. A group of four Norman soldiers walked below me along the track. They were, I guessed, scouts on the lookout for the opposing army and now on their way back to the camp in Hastings. I watched them pass so close I could hear them breathing and could smell their rank sweat. They were careless and noisy in their movements, talking casually and less alert than they should be. I waited a good time before leaving the tree and pushing on. I found some nuts and berries to eat and water from a clear spring which refreshed me. I was determined not to be caught and trod carefully, sensing the danger around me. And the day had progressed only a little further when I heard another warning from the birds. A jay screeched and, again, I took to a tree and waited. Nobody appeared and there was no sound of disturbance but the bird screeched its warning again and I froze on my branch, waited and waited.

As if from nowhere, two men crept through the wood moving swiftly but carefully and silently. They seemed to step in unison – quick steps, a stop, a pause, steps again - very different from the Norman soldiers I'd seen earlier. These were tall, lean men of the woods, expert trackers and hunters who knew how to travel secretly. I couldn't have done it better myself. These, I could see, were English, distinctively dressed with loose woollen tunics instead of tight leather jerkins; they had long hair and beards. The King's scouts, I guessed, looking for the opposing army. They were, I reckoned, trailing the careless Norman scouts I had seen earlier and who, I thought, were unlikely to make it back to their camp in Hastings. I was tempted to show myself to these trackers, explain about Wulf and to tell them of my adventures. They might give me food and see me safely home. But the jay, reading my thoughts, spoke to me and said it would be wise to stay where I was.

Seeing these men made me even more cautious and, for the rest of the day, I adopted a similar pattern: creeping forward, hiding, waiting, listening like a hunted animal. I knew, now, that there were soldiers in the wood, scouting and spying. Some might be doing just what I had done, waiting and watching in the bushes and trees. I trod carefully, alert, listening to the birds, looking for movement, sniffing the wind like a nervous roe deer. I had escaped the Norman camp. All I wanted now was to find my way home. Once, when the wood seemed suddenly sinister and strangely quiet, I lost my nerve, threw myself into an old sawpit and covered myself with leaves and branches. I lay there waiting, my heart pounding and expecting to hear footsteps or horse hooves, until I was sure this was a fear of my own making. I dragged myself back onto the track, shook off the worst of the dead leaves and dust and forced myself to move on. My feet, though, took me not to the village and the forge but into the lower part of the country, the valley near the marsh which leads to the lake and to the hollow. As I moved into more familiar territory I walked more quickly and easily. Already, though, the day was giving up its light and the Old Place seemed, perhaps because Gam had spoken of it so affectionately, the destination that was more and more in my mind.

The air thickened above the marsh as the evening mist descended and with it came a damp chill. I needed food and warmth but neither was uppermost in my mind; all I could think of was Gam and all I could feel was the aching loss. Yet luck turns like a wheel. Sometimes I think someone is turning the wheel for us, for good or ill, and sometimes I think it is, as Till says, a wheel we can learn to turn ourselves. I caught a whiff of smoke in the mist and followed the scent. I realised I was moving slightly away from the direction of the hollow towards the charcoal pits. It was the area in which Gam had once been lost and where she had been frightened by the sooty, charcoal boys. I approached warily but saw little activity other than some thin wisps of black smoke from one of the pits. I hid and watched. A man was there sitting on a log by the pit in the misty, smoky dusk. Occasionally he hauled himself up to poke the pit. I watched and waited. I could have simply walked over to him and spoken to him but my nerves were on edge. I was feeling sharp and wary. At last his head fell forward as he dozed. I crept from the shelter of the trees, made my way to the far side of the smouldering fire, rooted quietly around until, with burned fingers, I managed to snatch a smouldering brand of charcoal. I had what I wanted and ran, crashing through the undergrowth with the man's surprised cry in my ears.

It was dusk as I approached the hollow: that time when the light, reluctant to give itself up to the dark, distorts and shifts the shape of things making them into night-time creatures. The twisted roots of hornbeam trees exposed on the banks looked like the stretching claws of monsters. Single trees took on the form of sinister figures waiting to ambush me in the dark. The *moorgrim* mist was forming again, more dangerous in the night than in the morning. I couldn't stop frightening myself by thinking of the stories told by the *gleemen* about *Grendel*, the monster that hid in the lake. I began to jump at every shape and sound. I almost missed the bank and the faint track going down to the hollow. The path which Gam and I had made was already becoming overgrown and unfamiliar and I missed my footing so that I slipped, fell and scrambled down clumsily as I had done the very first time, bruising and scratching myself. I sat for a moment catching my breath. I longed to hear Misty's bark or a friendly laughing shout from Gam but there was nothing. Only the night sounds: the rustle of small animals, the cry of late birds, the rushing of the cascading stream, the groaning of trees chattering and plotting as they rubbed their limbs together in the wind like grasping hands.

I clambered through the rocks and into the dark and cold security of the Old Place. I fumbled around with my hands in the fireplace and found some tinder, blew on my pieces of charcoal and watched as the first tiny flames began to illuminate the grate. There was a small store of good dry wood and soon I had a decent fire going and hunched myself over it. Only as I grew warm did I allow myself to turn and look round the room. In the light of the fire I could see part of the untidy scattered bedding we'd left, our collection of sticks and strange shaped rocks. The painted figures on the wall began their dance, the dogs and animals in their unending chase, the fruits on the vine forever ripe and there, also, I saw the shapes that Gam had drawn, the letters of her name and mine and Elfin's, her pictures of the three of us, Misty, and my own clumsy attempts to make marks, stiff and lifeless, on the wall.

The most terrible sense of loneliness and misery descended on me like the mist outside. I thought of Till at the forge. I thought of Misty, her warm eager excitement, the smell and touch of her fur. I turned angrily on myself, my hog-headed stupidity, for coming here and not going straight home. I thought about Wulf. What had he done to the soldiers? What had happened after I'd turned my back on him and run? Would they have killed him? Who had thrown the knife? Had I been a coward? Should I have stayed and stood my ground? I thought of the great Norman army I had seen at Hastings. Duke William himself. The wonder of it. I thought of the English with Harold marching south and what would happen when the two huge armies met. Surely, they would make peace. I put my hands together and said a prayer for peace. Mostly, though, I thought of Gam and prayed for her, my heart aching with grief now that she had gone. I still didn't understand what had happened. Why did that man call her the *lady* of the lord? What did that mean: daughter, sister? My thoughts went back to it again and again and my mind recoiled from what it might mean. But why had she said nothing? Why hadn't she explained or warned me? Gam, no more my companion but a noble young lady in a ship on the great sea. I hoped she was safe. I wondered again and again about her life before I met her, why she might have left her home in Fecamp and what would become of her now.

I thought these things while sitting in a little circle of warmth and light with darkness all around me. There might have been bits of food in the place if I'd rooted around but I was too miserable to move. I wrapped myself in the rough bedding trying not to think of the hunger gnawing in my stomach. I thought of the food Wulf and I had eaten in the Norman camp. It had been strangely flavoured and different from anything I was used to eating. I decided I liked it and, thinking of it now, my mouth filled with saliva.

And thinking these things, I slept. I slept heavily because I hadn't slept properly for two nights. I slept and I dreamed. I dreamed the hall where I was sleeping was suddenly crowded with soldiers. They were like the soldiers I had seen in the Norman camp. They were sitting all around where I was sleeping, laughing and shouting and chatting and eating. These though were neither Norman nor English. They were soldiers from the old times. I knew, in my dream, these were the Old People and I also knew that I wasn't dreaming. They were there in the hollow with me. I didn't mind them and I wasn't afraid of them and they didn't mind me. When, in my dream – but I wasn't dreaming - they saw me open my eyes to look at them they smiled and winked and nodded as though they shared my secret and I knew they would keep me safe. And so I fell into a deeper sleep.

17. SAXONS

The next morning I drank from the stream, foraged for some berries and hurried up through the wood to the forge. I was so hungry I made no attempt to walk quietly or hide. It was a long haul and by the time I had climbed up as far as Freckly Lane I was lightheaded with hunger and dizzy from my excursions. Nothing there seemed to have changed. I could see smoke coming from the forge, I heard the barking of an excited dog, I heard Wulf's booming voice, 'Zounds, it's the boy!' and I collapsed into Till's strong arms. I began to blurt out questions and to try to tell him what I'd seen but he shushed me and carried me into the sun where Wulf was standing and laughing. He put me on the bench outside the forge and Wulf sat down beside me talking and trying to stop Misty from leaping up and licking my face. They gave me something warm and sweet to drink, and some bread which I dipped into a bowl of milk. Slowly I revived and listened to Wulf who, chuckling, kept repeating, 'Ash, my boy, Ash. The things we've seen, eh?'

'What happened to your face?' I looked up at him. One side of his face was bruised and inflamed. An eye swollen and half closed.

'Normans,' he declared triumphantly, 'but they'll be nursing sorer heads than mine, don't you worry.'

He told me what had happened when I leapt from the cart. 'I knew something was wrong. Always put yourself in your enemy's boots. It's the first rule of strategy, Ash. Remember that. I reckoned those two Normans weren't keen on taking us much further. I listened to them and knew they had orders to take us a good way up the road. And I knew they didn't like it.

They knew we were the enemy and they couldn't understand why we were being set free even though they had their orders to do it. And they knew it was dangerous work. The *fyrd* would be out and they were afraid of ambush. They could have just abandoned us, let us get on, of course, but better and safer for them if...' and he drew his finger across his throat, 'if they could be rid of us and didn't have to answer any awkward questions when they got back. I guessed they were up to mischief. That's why I wanted you to take off.'

'But they might have killed you.'

'Not without a fight,' he said, 'I had surprise on my side and I was pretty sure I could see them off. They took to their heels quick enough. I had a thump at one of them. He managed to get a thump back at me, though.' He pointed to a bruised and blackened eye, 'If only I'd had my axe,' he lamented. 'He knocked me over, but not before I got this,' and he showed me his trophy. A Norman helmet. 'We'll hang it from that beam,' he said. 'And this,' he handed me a sharp, heavy, short-bladed knife. 'This is what one of them threw at you. He was good with it. Lucky you jumped when you did. I pulled this out of the side of the cart. You can keep it.'

'How did you get home?'

'I hollered out for you, to see if I could fetch you back but you'd gone. Then I came back in the cart. Hadn't gone far when I ran in to some lads from our *fyrd*.'

I told him about my journey through the wood and the soldiers, the English scouts, I'd seen.

'That's the great thing,' shouted Wulf. 'The army is on the march. Harold is on his way. Our lads who stopped me told me they had orders to secure the road to stop the Normans marauding further. They're pinching them in, see. And they're scouting, too, for an assembly point. The main army is on its way from London. They were knocked about in the north and, they tell me, lost many of their best warriors in the fight with Tostig and Hadrada. But the word has gone out and men are coming from all over the land to join the fray,' and he raised his fists and bayed like a wolf with joy. 'Mark you,' he went on, 'I had a job to convince those boys of the *fyrd* of my story: that we'd been in the Norman camp and that the devils had let us go. For a while they took me for a spy. A spy! Me!' he spat in the dust.

He sat back on the bench as Till walked out to join us. 'What a thing we've seen, eh?' said Wulf again and again. 'The wonder of it. I was telling Till. You wouldn't believe it. The weaponry they've got.'

I said nothing but guessed the two men had put their differences behind them; they seemed friends again. Till, standing, put a foot on the bench where we were sitting and spoke gravely, 'People are born at different times, Ash,' he said. 'Someone's chosen this time for us to be born and, I think, we'll not see the like of these times again. Things are happening quickly. Soldiers have been coming through. There's talk of an assembly at the old *hoar apple tree* on the road to Hastings. I'm loyal to the king and I'm sure he'll drive the devils out. But war is a terrible and unpredictable thing and we must be ready in case it goes badly and we need to run.'

With the warmth of the sun on me and my stomach full, I began to feel more cheerful. Now there was work to do giving me little time to brood on my loss of Gam. I would need to make the Old Place ready – to take food, tools and supplies there. The road and the tracks in the wood were becoming busy now. The vanguard of the army, soldiers mainly from the fyrd, were heading towards the coast and the word was out for the agreed assembly point. All the talk now was of the King. Harold and his army were on the road from London. Everyone had the same cheerful confidence that the invaders would soon be swept away and peace would return. Having seen the Norman encampment, the formidable force being prepared there, I had my doubts but kept them to myself. Suddenly I was needed and useful. Life had a purpose. The bustle and busy-ness was like nothing I'd been used to. Much of my short life up to that time had been solitary: sitting in our hut of an evening listening to the drips of water off the thatch, wandering in the wood, fishing by the lake, cutting back the woodland growth from the fringes of the meadows. Now I was on the go from dawn to dusk. Here were soldiers in the wood who needed guidance, travellers asking directions and asking questions. I was there to tell and guide them and I felt myself growing.

Then, hurrying towards the hollow, a bundle of supplies on my back I was brought up suddenly by a reminder of Gam. Misty, ahead of me, began barking at a tree. It brought back a memory and I quite expected to look up and to see a birdboy. But it wasn't a birdboy: it was a bird. The eagle, our eagle, dead and hanging upside down, caught in the branches of an oak. It had been harried and driven to its death, I guessed, by the marauding crows. Now, an untidy tangle, it was almost indistinguishable from the leaves of the oak wearing their autumn colours which, like the bird's feathers were burnished brown and red, the rich yellow of old gold. Dead, the bird looked smaller than I remembered. Its eyes had gone, taken by the wicked crows and they'd fed, too, on its soft underbelly of flesh. Flies were buzzing around it. Alive, the bird had been a fascination and terror to me and, even dead, its power – otherness – still made itself felt. I sat for a while staring up at it, almost willing it back into its flight in the sky. Then I climbed the tree and released it gently from the oak limbs. I wanted to carry it down in my arms but it stank badly and I let the carcass fall heavily to the woodland floor. Before I buried it, I plucked the great and beautifully painted feathers from its wings and, with my *seaxe*, I made a mark on the tree thinking that, one day I would return to dig the bird up. The flesh would be gone and I could take its skull and keep that with me. I stood for a moment by its little grave and said a prayer to the gods of the sky, marvelling that this stiff, stinking creature was once the queen of the air, had frightened me so much, had played such a part in my life and had brought me together with Gam. That evening, at the forge, I worked by rush light into the night making a hat with the eagle feathers, stitching them to a band of leather so they stood up thick and tall. When it was done, I put it on and looked at myself proudly in the mirror surface of the water tank. I wondered if it might make me a shape-shifter so that I could fly away to France and find Gam. At least I might terrify the Normans, I thought.

During this busy time while Till, Elfin and I worked, directing soldiers, reassuring those fleeing the coast, hiding our possessions, taking tools and supplies to the hollow, Wulf was becoming more and more agitated. He was convinced a fight could be avoided, that the Normans could be starved out and with winter coming on would take to their ships and return to France. He was determined to speak to the King, to tell him about the Norman encampment and to give advice. He interrogated everyone who came through, asking about the King's progress on the road south. The army, he was assured, was on its way and, indeed, very soon the first of the *housecarls* began to appear. They were very different from the soldiers of the *fyrd*. These were big men on horseback with armour and stout shields of decorated lime wood which hung from their shoulders. They carried their huge battleaxes and rode with a confident swagger. Wulf, standing by the side of the highway, greeted them with a roar of delight. Many looked at him – an old man dressed ready for battle together with a small boy wearing a hat of tall eagle feathers - with a kind of bewildered amusement but some of them recognised him and returned his greetings with the respect due to a warrior. He introduced me as his grandson and one of these big men, saying I was no bigger than a little bird, picked me up and threw me into the air. I was caught by another who whirled me round and threw me to another then another in a circle until I was set back down in the dust next to Wulf, breathless, laughing with them and dizzy.

Some paused in their march long enough to sit and drink briefly with Wulf and to talk. These were quiet, subdued conversations from which we learned that the bulk of the army would soon be here and that they were buoyed by their great victory in the north. Wulf drank in the accounts he was given of the battle as greedily as he gulped his wine. Tostig and Hardrada had made a fierce fight of it but the English had fought mightily. The truth was, however, that Harold's forces were depleted. Many of the bravest *housecarls* had been lost in the fight and

Wulf heard some of the names of his former companions, now fallen, with dismay, holding his old head in grief. The King we were told, was gathering forces as he moved south but many of the men of the *fyrd* were reluctant to fight at this time of year. Many felt they had given enough already to this tortuous campaign: first one end of the country then the other. Worse, there was sickness in the army. The journeys had been hard, the weather bad and the food poor. Many of the men were ill and many were deserting. There was gossip, too, about treasure which had been taken from Hardrada's coffers and which, many felt, should have been shared after the battle in the north. The King had decreed that no wealth would be divided until the Normans had been driven out yet many doubted if they would ever see their fair share and this made some reluctant to fight further.

It was mid-morning when we heard the main army approach: mounted forces in the vanguard, men on foot, walking at a steady rhythmical pace, others running ahead in their haste. The King, we were told, was in the following group. Villagers and those who had been chased from their homes by the Normans were rushing to the highway hoping to see the King, to wave, to cheer, to encourage and some to petition, to beg for his help. Much to our annoyance we saw and heard Ern who had made a reappearance and was making a nuisance of himself, shouting to any who might hear how the Normans had robbed him of all he had and begging for retribution.

Wulf, hoping for an audience with the King, had dressed himself in his finest clothes. He wore a clean green robe bound by a yellow sash, dark leggings and leather boots. His gleaming and painted shield was slung over his back in the manner of a travelling soldier and he proudly carried his glittering, sharpened war axe. As the main section of the army approached he tried to get the attention of the first noblemen he saw. But they were in a hurry, keen to catch up with the outriders and were tired of being polite to the petitioners who crowded them on all sides calling out their woes and worries, desperate to tell the King about their suffering at the hands of the Norman invaders. They pushed past us, their eyes on the horizon ahead, a snaking line of men, horses, and carts piled high with weapons and supplies.

We were shoved to the fringe of the track by the press of traffic, Wulf's fine garments soon splattered with the mud thrown up by the passing hooves and carts. There was still no sign of the King until, at last, a pause in the procession, a gap, a wait before a distinctive group came towards us. Two or three riders at the front, some standard bearers then a group of sturdy, mounted housecarls with – we could see it clearly – the King's own banner of *The Fighting Man*. It was the same banner I had seen earlier in the year near Bosham but I looked at it now with new and wide eyes. Was that really the shape, a picture, of Wulf himself that advanced and moved so proudly in the wind? Here, again, I saw the King, riding, surrounded by noblemen: a group of towering men. That was what I noticed: how big they were. King Harold on his horse was like a giant. Wulf pointed excitedly at the flag and gave me a knowing look as if to say, *There. I told you.* I wondered if the King would acknowledge him but the press of housecarls around him was too dense. Wulf, instead, gave his attention to two finely dressed figures with long fair hair and moustaches. 'It's the brothers,' he shouted, 'the King's brothers. That's Leofwyne and Gyrth. Then he was amongst them bellowing and pushing his way towards the King. 'Leof! Leof!' he called.

The soldiers walking beside the royal group turned angrily on Wulf, pushing him back towards the roadside but he stood his ground. A soldier shoved him with his shield and, with a sudden show of strength, Wulf pushed back, knocking the man off balance and, at the same time, bellowing like a bull: 'Leof! Leof! for God's sake man, hear me.'

As he shouted he was surrounded by guards who wrestled him to the ground. But the royal party had stopped, Leofwyne had dismounted and now walked over to the old man. The guards were dismissed, Leofwyne helped Wulf to his feet and the two embraced as the rest of the royal party moved on.

'My old companion,' said Leofwyne. 'What brings you here? You are too old for this campaign. And who is this in such a fine hat?' He pointed at me.

'My grandson, Ash,' said Wulf proudly.

Leofwyne smiled, 'You are brave to interrupt our journey,' he said. 'It is a pleasure to see you old man but we are on a forced march. The invader awaits. I cannot linger.'

'But I need to tell you. I've been there,' said Wulf, pointing down the track. 'I've been there – the two of us – we've seen their encampment.'

Leofwyne looked at us with disbelief, 'But how?'

'You must listen,' said Wulf. 'I will be brief,' he motioned Leofwyne to sit with him by the side of the road while a soldier stood by, impatiently, holding his horse by the bridle.

Wulf quickly told our story. He talked about the Norman camp, the building of the castle, the vast number of armed men, their determination. Leofwyne was a little dismissive. 'But much of this we know,' he said. 'We have eyes near the coast and on the road. What you say, being in the devils' camp and then allowed free, surprises me. But what you tell of their forces simply confirms much of what we have heard from our spies.'

Wulf told him what Eustace had said, the opportunity for parley, but Leofwyne dismissed it with a wave of his hand, 'We have heard his messengers,' he said, 'they would sue for peace but only on their terms.' He gestured in the direction the King had taken, 'He, my brother, is to rule by the grace of God. He would not hear of peace with this disloyal upstart.'

'Then, if you must fight, there is no need for haste,' cautioned Wulf. 'You have the road and the country behind you. He has only the sea. You can hold him there and starve him out. You would be wise to wait, hold counsel, let your reinforcements arrive.'

Leofwyne shook his head, 'Harold is hurt,' he said, 'he took a wound in the north and it has not healed. And there is a sickness amongst us. We need to act soon before there is more and we cannot hold the *fyrd* for longer.'

Wulf shook his head and began a counter argument but was interrupted by the soldier, 'My lord, we will miss our march.'

Leofwyne sprang to his feet, 'Thank you for your counsel, my old friend. I must be on my way.'

Wulf grasped his hands, 'Do not be hasty in this fight,' he begged. 'Believe me, they are strong. You will need to wait and gather all your forces.'

Leofwyne nodded in the direction the King had taken, 'He will not wait,' he said, 'he is on fire with our great victory in the north. He believes fortune is with him and would have it done again. But I will give him your counsel.'

He took the bridle from the waiting soldier, mounted easily, gave a kick of his heel and rode away. I watched him open-mouthed. He looked magnificent, invincible.

We watched him go then sat by the side of the track as the last of the seemingly unending traffic of men and carts passed by. Others, waiting and watching, who had seen our conversation with the King's brother looked at us with renewed respect. But Wulf hung his head despairingly, 'He wouldn't listen,' he said weakly.

'No,' I protested, 'he did. I watched him. He was taking in every word. He said he would speak to the King.'

'Harold Godwinson is stubborn,' said Wulf, 'and William knows that. He is playing into their hands. The Normans have their spies and will know the King has taken a wound. They will know there is sickness in our force, that the men are tired and some are disgruntled. You and I, Ash,' he continued, 'we have seen a great thing. We have seen the Norman preparations. We have seen how well organised they are. And William is burning the villages. He's pillaging the land and sending families running. He does this not just to feed his army and because of his wickedness. He knows of Harold's pride. This is Harold's domain. It was his before he became king, it is the part of the land he loves and he feels responsible for the people here like a father to his children. William knows, if the villagers here are attacked, Harold will rush headlong to the defence. He should wait, gather his forces and hold the highway. Let

William feel the pinch of hunger and the cold wind of winter on the coast. Let him be the one to act rashly.' He was disappointed and inconsolable but I persuaded him to stand and helped him as we returned to the forge walking against the tail end of the tide of advancing soldiers and followers. This was the weaker end, fools and gawpers and chancers following on, Ern at their centre, still shouting abuse about the Normans, complaining of their hurts and losses and encouraging the army into the fight.

'And these fools,' said Wulf bitterly, 'are doing William's work for him. They will work the King into a passion with their complaints and persuade him to attack before he is ready.'

'But we saw the flag,' I said proudly. 'We saw your flag.'

But Wulf seemed suddenly older. He walked slowly, hanging his head in sorrow.

The highway was now quiet but, as we approached Freckly Lane and the forge, we could clearly hear raised voices. An argument. Two men loomed out of the shadows behind the open doorway of the forge. It was Dad with Till's son, Lang. They seemed bigger and had a swagger about them. They were soldiers now.

'Ash! Look at you. Look how you're growing,' Dad clapped me on the shoulder.

Lang gave me a playful punch, laughing at my hat. 'That's a fine cap young'un.'

Both he and Lang acknowledged Wulf politely but there was an awkwardness in the air. Till was keeping back.

'We can't stay,' said Lang, 'we're with the King and we're here to chase those Norman devils off.' He guffawed confidently.

'They've marched from the north,' said Till nodding proudly at his son. 'They've been both ways, up and down the length of the land.'

'Were you there at the battle?' asked Wulf.

Dad nodded, 'It was a hard one,' he said, 'a great victory. To be honest, though, it was pretty much all over by the time we got there and then we were marched off down here again.'

There was an awkward pause.

'They want weapons,' said Till abruptly.

'And he won't give them to us,' said Lang.

'You've got weapons,' said Till.

'These things,' said Lang contemptuously. He showed us a short sword. 'We got these from the Danes after York, but the northern fyrd were there first and got the rich pickings. These are for farmers' boys not soldiers. I reckon Dad's got better stuff than this hidden away.'

'Haven't,' said Till shaking his head unconvincingly.

'What weapons are you after?' asked Wulf.

'Well that battleaxe of yours would make a start,' said Dad with a nervous laugh. 'Don't suppose you'll be using it.'

Wulf thrust it at him, 'You can have it,' he said, 'but can you wield it? You don't just wave one of these about. It takes training.'

'I'm a woodman,' said Dad, 'there's not much I don't know about using an axe.'

'For chopping wood, yes,' argued Wulf, 'but not in battle. There's not many Normans will stand still like a tree while you chop at them.'

'If you'll let me have it, I'll use it well,' said Dad but Lang intervened.

'Perhaps I should have it,' he said. 'You're the woodman but I'm the ironman.' He touched the blade and then the handle. 'Iron or wood, what do you reckon?'

'Let the woodman have it,' said Wulf, then he offered his shield and helmet, 'these are yours too,' he said. Then, 'Ash, fetch me down that Norman helmet. We'll see you protected boys,' and, as I returned with the helmet, 'Ash, what about that broadsword of yours?'

Dad gave me a hard look as Till turned bitterly on the old man, 'I'll have no more of this here.'

'But they'll need good weapons,' protested Wulf.

'And if they have them,' countered Till,' they'll be put in the front line of the fighting. That's certain death.'

'Well, what do you want?' his son shouted back. 'Would you have us at the back with the land boys with their bill hooks and sticks and stones?'

'I wouldn't want you at the front,' said Till stubbornly. He paused, his voice trembling, 'I don't want to lose my son. And this lad,' he pointed at me, 'won't want to lose a father.'

'Who's talking of losing?' shouted Lang angrily. 'There'll be no losing. If we're properly equipped and with a lot of us shouting and holding up our weapons those old Norman boys will take fright and run.'

'That's right,' added Dad, 'that's what it was like up north. There's more shouting goes on than fighting. The King's men, the fighting men, they're the ones that are in the fray. Most of us are just banging our shields and hollering.'

'You don't need a weapon to do that,' argued Till. He turned to Dad, 'What you get up to is your business but, if you want my advice, there's work to be done here at home, in the village and the wood. Children and elders to be looked after.' Then he turned to his son, 'I don't want harsh words. I'd rather you stay and work with me: ironwork not fighting. There's plenty of others will do the fighting. Together, we've got a nice tidy corner here.'

'And not fight for our land!' shouted Lang. 'What kind of men stand by and watch the land invaded by a bunch of Frenchies and do nothing? There'll be rich pickings too, won't there?' he turned to Dad for confirmation. 'There's stuff taken from the Danes in York and there'll be more from William when we've sent him packing. Weapons, armour, metalwork, we deserve some of that.'

'You've done your bit,' argued Till. 'There's no reason to do more. But, if you must go with the army I don't want you in the front is all I'm saying.'

There was silence. A stand off. Father and son, both of a height, standing toe to toe like two armies facing each other.

'We have to make haste,' said Dad tersely, 'or we'll miss the fun. We'll have to run as it is to catch up.' He looked at Wulf. 'Can I have these old man? I know you've used them well and honourably and I'll do my best to do good work with them.' He put Wulf's helmet on his head but it was too big and covered his eyes. He held it awkwardly. 'This'll need some padding out,' he said. 'I can pack it with moss.' He took the shield, weighed it and manoeuvred it appreciatively before slinging it over his back in the fashion of the *housecarls*. Then he lifted the broadaxe. He balanced it in his hand and whistled in appreciation.

'She has seen long service,' said Wulf. 'Look after her well and she will sing for you.'

Dad grinned awkwardly, 'I'll bring her back for you, don't you worry.' He motioned to Lang that they should go.

Till's son, holding the Norman helmet, looked bitterly at his father. Suddenly he withdrew the short sword from his belt and flung it down. 'That thing's no good. If I can't have a true weapon, I'll have none at all. Thank you father,' he said bitterly, 'for sending me naked into the battle.'

They ran off.

Till, ashen in the face, retired to the back of his forge and pretended to tinker with the fire while Wulf and I stood awkwardly wondering what to do. Wulf moved towards him, started to speak, thought better of it, and walked back to the doorway staring at the highway, empty now, in the direction the soldiers had taken.

After a short while, Till was suddenly standing next to us, his face and voice expressionless. 'Ash,' he said, 'where's this Norman sword of yours?'

18. SWORD

It was in the last part of the afternoon that I set off from the forge with the sword, tightly bound in cloth, strapped across my back. In my bag I had some strips of leather which, Till had instructed, Dad and Lang should use to bind their arms and legs for protection. There were also thicker leather bands which, I was to tell them, should be wound around their heads to make the helmets fit snugly. I tried to leave Misty at home but the little dog seemed ready for adventure and followed me even though she wasn't running so well.

I jogged steadily, following Dad and Lang, in the direction of the army. I always prided myself on my speed but now I was weighed down and slowed by the heavy sword which thumped my back with each step. But I soon caught the tail end of the army and began to weave my way through the untidy ranks. I began to see, too, evidence of what we had learned from the *housecarls*. Many of these men were tired and footsore, walking badly, slowly, some limping. There were stragglers who seemed to have no appetite for the journey or the fight and others who were unwell and who sat glumly by the side of the highway. As Misty and I ran in and out and between the sweating, stinking soldiers I kept a sharp eye open for Dad and Lang. But I couldn't find them. Most of these men were preoccupied with the journey, their eyes fixed on the monotony of the track in front of them. Some seemed more startled then amused by the sight of a small boy with a hat of tall feathers running, looking this way and that, peering into faces, a dog at his heels.

As the highway descended towards the coast where the sea comes up at Brede the army was held up by the wide river crossing. This was marshy country and the track was poor and muddy. There was no bridge over the river, just a shallow area for fording. There was a good deal of muddle and confusion, the troops at the front waiting to cross shouting angrily back at the others who were pressing forward. This seemed a likely place to catch Dad and Lang but it was growing dark and hard to see. There was no sign of them in the melee of figures making the crossing. I left the road, followed the river upstream a short way and picked my way across easily. I then came back to the highway on the opposite bank and watched as the men, horses and carts pulled themselves free of the ford and struggled up the hill. I marvelled at the strength and determination of these men as they pushed forward weighed down with weapons and hauling supplies, shouting encouragement to each other. Again, I searched for a glimpse of a familiar face and, after waiting, I pushed on.

I was now at Whatlington and not far, I knew, from the assembly point of the *hoar apple tree*. This, I also knew, had been a meeting place since time out of mind: a high vantage point with views across to the sea and the junction between the roads from Dover and Canterbury in the east and from Hastings towards Lewes and north to London. Wulf had told me this was a well-chosen spot to make a stand. The track rose up through meadow and woodland to the high ground of the hill known as Caldbec because of the cold streams which ran down its side forming marshland below: a difficult position for an invader to attack. Here Harold's forces were making their huge, sprawling camp. The hill and the surrounding countryside seemed filled with soldiers. There were fires blazing with men sitting around them, their fierce faces reddened by the heat, smoke rising from the wood, steam rising from their damp clothes mingled with the smell of cooking. Many men were stretched out on the wet ground, resting or sleeping. The racket was deafening: shouts, drums beating, horns blowing, axes chopping wood and the hammer blows of stakes being driven into the ground as fortifications. It was, though, unlike the Norman encampment, disorderly and confused. There were men wandering from fire to fire, calling out the names of companions they'd lost sight of in the dark or on the journey. Many of them, I realised, were drinking and seemed the worse for it, swaying perilously close to the fires, tripping over the legs of sleepers, being pushed and shouted at. Women were there too, selling food and drink, shouting and laughing.

My task seemed impossible. I wandered from group to group, staring into faces, my ears bruised with rude comments about my diminutive size and my hat of feathers. There were fierce dogs barking and snarling who sprang out at Misty so I lifted her and put her under my arm. Mostly, though, I listened. I listened to voices alert for our local dialect. Many of the voices I heard were hard to understand and I guessed these were men from the northern *fyrd* or some of what Gam and Wulf had called the Anybodies: soldiers from other countries who would fight for money. Dad and Lang, I thought, would be with our Southern *fyrd* and it might be easier to hear them than to spot them.

As I walked, I climbed the hill and the more I climbed the more crowded it became. Near the very top the encampment seemed more orderly. The *Wyvern* standards, red and gold, were flying and in the circle behind a ring of armed sentries I could see tents illuminated by the fires where, I guessed, the King, his brothers and noblemen would be. I wondered if they were resting after their journey but supposed it more likely they would be awake, holding counsel and discussing what they should do. There were groups of men, too, standing on the summit of the hill and looking across to the coast, about six miles away. I squeezed between them, pushed to the front and followed their gaze. There, in the distance, almost within reach it seemed, were the fires of the Norman encampment. The soldiers around me had their eyes fixed on them and were muttering to each other darkly.

I walked slowly back down the hill wondering what I should do, trying to think where in this vast crowd Dad and Lang might be. I looked for somewhere to sit although I was afraid that if I did sit down, I'd fall asleep. I wandered back towards the base of the hill and here some of the soldiers had hastily built makeshift shelters from branches cut from the woodland. Some of these were no neater than the untidy nests crows throw together. But it gave me an idea. I threaded my way through the shelters until I saw a group that were altogether better made: neater, stouter, sturdy against wind and rain: the work of skilled woodmen. As I made my way towards them Misty began barking. Even from a distance she could hear a sound that had not yet reached my ears but then, when I did, it made my blood beat and brought tears to my eyes. The thin, reedy, high music of Lang's little flute. He was playing that melody, simple, repetitive, like something pulling in my chest and which I'd heard so often as he sat outside the forge of an evening. I paused, listening, moved further forward in the dark and saw a hand reaching to take a skewer of meat from a fire. A brand sparked and there was a shout, a curse and then a laugh as Misty jumped from my arms and rushed forward. Dad. I knew the voice.

'Ash!' Dad and Lang leapt to their feet, their faces glowing with delight. I explained my mission, unwrapped the heavy burden from my back and offered the sword to Lang. He and Dad looked at it with wonder. They asked me how I'd come by it and I told them the story of Axeface and the birdmen. They roared with laughter. They gave me hot food and there was plenty to drink, beer mainly which must have loosened my tongue because then I told them everything. It all spilled out: meeting Gam, the Old Place, meeting Wulf and our adventure in the Norman encampment. It was this they were most interested in and, as I talked, pausing to chew and to drink, I realised that Lang and Dad were not my only listeners. A larger group had gathered around us, some asking me to repeat something I'd just said or to explain what I'd seen in more detail. Having an audience appealed to my vanity and I became careless, possibly exaggerating some of the things I'd seen. Axeface was suddenly in my head and I remembered and copied the cadences of his showman's voice, emphasising words, speaking softly then loudly, putting in a pause for the drama of the thing, shaping my hands in the air, playing my audience like an eel on a line. I talked about the Norman soldiers juggling with their broadswords. I described the Norman camp, the ships, the castle, the weapons, the horses which, I explained, were *destriers*, specially bred to kick and bite. I talked about the way the army seemed organised, drawn up into groups, practising and training. The picture I was painting became more and more exaggerated. Where I had seen groups of 50 soldiers in mock fights I now made it 500; the number of ships and horses grew every time I described them as did the size and strength of the Norman knights and, as I talked about it over and over again, the wooden castle became broader and taller in height. Impregnable. My description drew whistles of surprise, some hurried whispered words and faces looking drawn and grey with anxiety.

None of them, at first, would believe that I'd seen the actual Duke, William, his brother Odo and the knights. They made me describe them again and again and, with each run at it, I made William's face meaner, his eyes more piercing, his knights with their hawks more noble and Odo a terrifying giant of a figure. I told them what Wulf had said about Odo's war club. They made me swear on the sword that I was telling the truth. Dad said, 'I tell you, my boy doesn't tell lies,' just as he'd said it when we were sitting around the fire with Axeface but, this time, he gave me an old-fashioned look, 'I don't know what's happened to you, Ash. You never used to say a word. You've found your tongue now, though. I can't shut you up.'

There was great admiration for the Norman broadsword. Lang was delighted. He felt the balance in his hand, tested the quality of the metal by tasting it with his tongue and gingerly felt the razor-sharp edge with his thumb. 'This, Ash,' he declared, 'is as good a sword as you'll find anywhere within these two armies.' He held it close to the fire and described how the blade had been forged. 'Heated, different metals, wrapped and beaten,' he repeated, 'heated, wrapped and beaten. Over and over, polished and polished again and sharpened again. A smith has worked on this for a good time. A charm has been beaten into it.' He waved the blade gently back and fore. 'Hear that,' he chuckled, 'she sings for me.'

The weapon was carefully passed from hand to hand and some tried to barter with Lang to buy it from him but he took it back and held it tightly next to him. I was beginning to explain again about what I'd seen around the castle at Hastings when tiredness and the effects of the beer hit me like a blow to the head.

'I reckon you've said enough for one night,' said Dad and he pushed me gently back on to a makeshift bed inside the shelter. As the darkness of sleep fell over me I was lulled deeper by the reedy, melancholy sound of Lang's flute and I heard one of the men saying darkly and quietly, 'If the boy speaks true, seems like those Frenchies are ready for us.'

I would have slept for days but it was only a few hours before I was woken at first light by noise and confusion. The fires were being kicked out. Men were on their feet, scrambling to put on whatever armour they had, shouting to each other to make haste and to form up. The rudimentary shelters were knocked over in a general rush towards the top of the hill. Dad and Lang were together, helping each other by binding the leather straps around their arms. I looked at them through a blur of sleep and an aching head. 'They're coming,' shouted Lang. 'They're on the march. This is it.'

I got to my feet feeling sick and unsteady. The noise made my head pound. Orders were being shouted. Men were cheering and that repetitive, awful chant had begun, '*Out! Out!*' There was, too, that ululating, wailing throat noise, the sound I'd heard from the crowd watching the birdmen in Rye and which made me shudder.

'Ash!' Dad shook me by the shoulders, shouting above the noise and confusion. 'Ash, you go home now. Go back to Till.' He looked at me hard, 'Ash, are you listening boy? No tricks, no wandering about in the wood. I want you to go straight back.'

I nodded sleepily.

'You promise?'

I nodded again but he wouldn't let me go. 'No, I want to hear you say it.'

'I promise.'

He knelt down and put his arms round me. 'I haven't been a good Dad for you, have I son?'

Stupidly, I nodded my head as though agreeing.

'After this,' he said hesitantly, 'after this it will be better.'

Lang came over and pulled him up. He lifted the sword and swung it above his head making it whistle in the wind. 'My thanks again for this, Ash,' he said, 'she'll do some work for the King today.' Then he reached into his bag and took out the little flute. 'Give this to Dad to look after until I get back.'

They were gone and I didn't see them again.

I walked away from the hill into the woods where I was sick. Perhaps it was because of the food and drink I'd been given. Perhaps it was excitement, anxiety or, perhaps, it was the sickness from which so many of the men were suffering. I sat for a while, Misty at my side, listening to the drums, horns and cheers coming from the hill as the light crept up from the east. Feeling a little better I climbed a huge old oak tree. The leaves were browning and dropping so I had a clear view to the coast where the sky was bright with the sunrise. At first I could see nothing other than smoke from the Norman fires but then I saw a glint and flash on the horizon then more and more and moving. The light was catching burnished metal: the Norman army on the march.

I kept my promise to Dad and retraced my steps along the high road, back towards the forge. At first the track was empty but then I met groups of armed men, the reinforcements, hurrying along. Each time my repeated answer to their questions was simply, 'It's started,' and, each time, they looked at each other in alarm and hurried on. Then a bigger group approached me. Some armed soldiers walking and, behind them at a slow pace, some horses, carts and mounted riders. I stood well back as they approached and saw the riders were, mainly, ladies. They were muffled up in cloaks with furs across their laps. They looked pale and one, the beautiful lady in the middle of the group, looked directly at me and smiled. As I walked on I wondered what she made of me: a small, dirty, pale boy with a funny headdress of feathers gawping at the side of the highway.

I reached the forge and told Wulf and Till what I had seen: the sprawling Saxon army, the noise and movement and chaos of the battle about to begin, the Normans on the march, the reinforcements I'd met on the road. When I described the ladies, Wulf was incredulous, 'Did you bow, boy?'

'Eh?'

'Bow. That would have been the Queen you saw. *Queen Edith*, the King's wife. She'll be going to watch over things and to pray for victory.'

Wulf found it hard to believe that the fight was, against his counsel, about to begin. He sat on his bench, disappointed, muttering to himself, 'He'd be better holding back, waiting on the edge of the wood. He doesn't need to fight yet.'

Till said nothing, his face still set in a look of anger and loss. I gave him Lang's little flute and he turned away from me with a gasp. I stumbled to a quiet corner, wrapped myself in a warm woollen blanket and fell fast asleep.

19. BATTLE

I was woken in the late afternoon by shouts from the road: Wulf and some travellers in excited conversation. 'They reckon it's all over,' shouted Wulf, 'they've got William on the run.' And, soon, more news. 'They say William's dead. Well, good riddance to him.'

Till came forward to the doorway, cautiously listening. 'Is that it then?' he asked.

Wulf shook his head sceptically, 'Don't know,' he said. 'You never know the truth of these things. Trouble is, the person who told us this heard it from someone else who heard from another person who might have seen it and might not. You never can tell.'

The way time goes is a strange thing. By our reckoning it was taking a good half a day for news of the battle to get through to us. It was unsettling to know that, even as we were getting reports of the first action of the day, the battle would probably be already over.

For a while it was horribly quiet. Most of the movement on the highway was made up of soldiers, the reinforcements, still making their way towards the coast and eager to be in on the fight. It wasn't until the evening that more travellers came through up from the coast with more stories. Again, with that mysterious ability for attraction, Wulf had gathered a crowd round his bench. He was the focus of the news. It seemed to be passed through him, with everyone anxious to hear his view.

'William's hard at it,' a breathless, dusty traveller told him stopping to drink deep from the bowl of beer he was offered. 'Our boys are atop of the hill standing firm and William and his horses are at them time and again.'

'We heard he was dead,' said Wulf indignantly.

'No,' the man shook his head. 'There was a time he was toppled from his horse and they thought he was dead but he wasn't. He got back on his horse and he raised his helmet up to show his face and called out *Here I am boys and with God's help I'll win this fight.*'

Wulf gave a whistle of surprise, 'Whose side are you on?' he asked.

'Ours, of course,' said the man, 'I'm just telling what I've seen.'

'You telling me you saw this?' asked Wulf.

'Not exactly but I heard it from someone who swore he did see it.'

'Well, we were told the Normans were on the run,' insisted Wulf, 'and the man who told me swore he'd seen it himself.'

'Ah,' said the other knowledgably, 'that happened early. They did run off down the hill but I reckon that was a lure to get our boys to chase after them. Well we didn't fall for that.'

'A mock retreat,' intoned Wulf, 'that's an old trick.'

Soon another man described the start of the battle assuring us he'd watched it from a high vantage point. How, at first light the Normans had arrived and had taken up their positions at Telham Hill while Harold's forces formed their defensive shield wall on top of the opposite hill, Caldbec. Difficult, wet, marshy ground between them. Here Wulf nodded his approval. There had been a long stand off and some parlying with messengers riding back and forth. There had been talk of a single combat between the Duke and the King to settle things but this was dismissed and the rumour was that this was because Harold had taken a wound at York. The drums had started, said the man, and even from far back where he was watching the air was filled with the deafening shouts of derision from each side and the chilling battle songs and cries. This went on for some time until one of the Norman knights had ridden hard towards the English line, throwing his sword into the air and catching it as he rode up and down before the English, singing battle songs and taunting them. I looked at Wulf and knew we were both thinking of the show, the sword juggler and the Normans throwing their swords into the air. Then, the man told us, this one Norman knight had ridden hard and bravely into the English ranks, hacking with his sword and doing much damage until he was cut down. It was like a signal and, with a roar, the battle began.

This fellow was a natural storyteller, as good as Wulf, and he had us in thrall. I looked at those listening, taking it in, some with their mouths slack and gaping. The Norman archers had used their longbows to fire waves of arrows, the air black like flocks of starlings.

'Longbows?' queried someone critically, 'I thought those old Normans had crossbows.'

'They've got both,' said Wulf knowledgably, pleased to interrupt the storyteller who seemed to be taking over his role. 'They use the long bows to fire arrows in the air. They come down like hail in a storm and our lads put their shields up to protect themselves – but then that leaves the shield wall open for attack.'

But his rival narrator was keen for attention and wanted to press on. The Normans, he told us, had sent attack after attack at the English shield wall but with little effect. The strong English defence pushed them back hard each time. 'I reckon the King just wants them to tire themselves out,' he said.

'The shield wall,' Wulf nodded his approval and looked at me repeating, 'can't beat a shield wall, Ash. Eh?'

While this was going on I noticed Till. He would venture to the doorway to listen, drawn like a moth to a flame, then as if what he had heard was too painful, pulled himself back quickly into the dark shadows of the forge.

It grew dark. We lit a brazier in the doorway and sat round it. The fire was for warmth but also to attract travellers on the road. Like hungry spiders waiting for flies we were anxious to attract anyone who might have news. And it came too quickly. The travellers who passed now were in a hurry, keen to get away. *It goes badly*, was the urgent message we heard more and more. Then some soldiers, tired and dusty, jogged by making no secret of their retreat. 'Deserters!' spat Wulf with contempt. The English ranks had been broken, we heard. After their repeated attacks the Normans seemed suddenly in retreat and many of the English left the advantage of the hill and ran after them only to be caught by others, cavalry mainly, waiting on their flanks. But still the fight went on. 'But, oh no,' said Wulf, 'we don't give up that easily.'

Then, in the darkest part of the night came sudden, darker news. The King's brothers, Leofwyne and Gyrth were dead. Wulf's face was ashen. How could this be? They had the *housecarls* to protect them, the fighting men. It was the horses, we were told. Once the shield wall had gone the Norman cavalry were in amongst the English ranks and causing havoc. The horses, we were told, those *destriers*, wore metal studs on their hooves and had been trained to kick out. They were a terror to the defending soldiers. Till was called and consulted. Had he heard of these weapons on horses' hooves? He shook his head in disgust, 'Who would make such terrible things?' he asked.

Mark you, we were told, the English infantry had found a way of dealing with the horses by dashing in amongst them, dodging the awful flying hooves, and grabbing a horse by its leather girth and pulling both horse and rider to the ground. The men around Wulf nodded their approval of this courageous tactic.

Then the darkest news of all. The road was noisy now with men running. They no longer looked like soldiers. They were dirty and dishevelled. Some were wounded and bleeding. We gave them water, crusts of food, did what we could. But their cry was the same: *the King is dead*. Harold had fallen. At first we refused to believe it but we heard it over and over and soon knew it to be the truth. I remembered the men we had seen near Bosham at the beginning of the year walking so gaily with the King's army. How many of them were alive now? How different these running, retreating soldiers looked. How many would be returning to their homesteads? Where was Dad?

In the early hours a group of *housecarls* came by. I recognised some as those who had, just yesterday, laughed so confidently and thrown me into the air. These men were now exhausted and welcomed the brief respite of warmth, food and drink. Wulf questioned them gently. They were in shock and they answered as if simply speaking to themselves, staring into the flames. They talked of the bravery of the English forces but their hopelessness against the horses and lances of the Normans once the shield wall had been broken. 'He knew what he was doing,' said one bitterly of William. 'It's a coward's way. They turned and ran and the fools chased after them sensing victory. The fools.'

'And the King?' asked Wulf quietly.

'An eagle,' said one, 'an eagle harried and worried and brought down by crows.'

Wulf looked at me across the light of the fire. 'I told you, Ash. I dreamed of this,' he said.

Slowly, with the warmth and food the soldiers began to rally a little. 'But it's not over,' said one. 'We'll regroup. We'll fight again.'

Wulf looked sceptical, 'Where will you go now?'

'To London,' said the man. 'All the talk is of the *Aethling*, the young *Prince, Edgar*. Let the *Witan* decide. If not, we take to the woods.'

20. THE FIGHTING MAN

When the men had gone Wulf and I sat by the fire dozing, waking and worrying. I looked round for Till but there was no sign of him. A little before dawn there was more noise on the road. Another group, running. They wouldn't stop but one man, a *housecarl*, strode towards us carrying something. A tall bundle.

'Is this a safe house?' he asked.

We nodded.

'And you are loyal to the King?'

Wulf thumped his chest.

'Then take this, hide it and keep it until we fight again,' said the man.

He handed us a banner on a pole. We unfurled it in the light of the fire. *The Fighting Man.*

In the light of day, drawn with tiredness, we knew we must decide what to do. Defeat was in the air. People were running, hiding the last of their possessions, fearful of the Normans who would be abroad and marauding. There had been no news of Lang or Dad. Till's face was lined and grey. I talked to Elfin and we agreed we should take Till to the Old Place and hide. Wulf refused to join us, 'It's too far and I'm too old to go back into those woods,' he protested. 'I'll take my chance here.'

Till also wanted to stay at the forge. He had, he said, no fear of the Normans and his hope was that Lang would soon return from the fight. He spent hour after hour watching the track. He was also uneasy about the banner. 'I don't won't that thing here,' he declared. To him it was a symbol not of resistance but defeat. It was linked, too, in his mind with Lang. Only after much cajoling would he agree to accompany us. Wulf spoke to him directly. 'These Normans will be terrible,' he said. 'You must avoid them. Go with the children, hide and wait. When you come back the devils will have passed through, your son will have returned and all will be well again.'

'And you?' asked Till.

'They will have no interest in an old man like me. Anyway, I speak their language and many of them will know me.'

And so the three of us set out back through the wood carrying some baskets of food and with the heavy, cumbersome standard wrapped in cloth like a long thin corpse. It was a slow and difficult journey mainly because Till found the going so hard. He kept stopping, wondering aloud if he should return to the forge, 'My boy should be back by now,' he kept saying. From time to time we passed soldiers in the wood. They were dirty, blooded, dishevelled, hurrying and anxious, keen to get away. To each of them Till asked the same question: a tall man, Lang, a swordsman, his son? But they shook their heads in reply and hurried on.

Finally we made the steep descent to the Old Place. It was the most difficult part. Elfin and I left the standard and our supplies at the top of the bank and gently coaxed the anxious Till down the awkward, precipitous path. It was odd to see terror on the face of this big, normally unshakable figure. We sat him by the stream while we went back and forth to collect our supplies. Elfin and I crawled through the narrow entrance. I lit a fire and got some rush lights going. Elfin called out to her father but he didn't appear and we found him outside still sitting by the stream and muttering to himself. 'I can't go in there,' he protested, 'it's too narrow. I hate small spaces like that.'

We had to encourage him, coax him through the passageway like a nervous child and, sure enough, once inside he relaxed and looked up, around and at the dancing shapes in wonderment.

When we sat down by the fire to eat Till began to talk more about the stories he'd been told about this secret place when he was a child. His grandfather had described a hall under the earth in the woods with wondrous pictures where he and his friends would hide away for days. They used to say it was the lair of dragons and trolls, that there was treasure to be found which no-one would dare steal. 'We often looked for it as children,' chuckled Till, 'but we never found it.'

He talked about the old times, before us. The hall had been made, he guessed, before the Vikings and when the Old People were here. They were the people who made the iron and laid the roads.

We were pleased that he seemed easier in his mind as the three of us settled by the fire to sleep. Both he and Elfin, tired from anxiety and their journey through the wood, were soon sleeping heavily but I lay awake looking at the dancing figures in the firelight, thinking of Gam, missing her dreadfully, wondering if I would ever see her again, imagining where she was sleeping now and if she ever thought of me. When, at last, I did sleep it wasn't for long because Till was soon sitting up and shouting. He was in the grip of a terrible nightmare from which it was hard to release him. When Elfin and I did manage to wake and calm him he seemed lost, seemed hardly to know us. We spoke to him gently, gave him water to drink and he settled back into a fitful sleep.

The next day he was only a little better. Elfin and I went outside to wash, to gather fruit, nuts and fresh water. Once or twice we heard shouts in the wood and the crashing of, what we guessed, were retreating soldiers trying to find their way through the trees. When we crawled back into the underground chamber Till was sitting by the fire staring in horror at the furled flag which I'd stood in a dark corner of the room. 'Who is it?' he asked pointing a trembling finger at the standard.

'Where?'

'There,' quavered Till, 'that tall thin man.'

'It's only a flag, Father,' said Elfin, 'it was the King's flag.'

'Why has it come here?'

'We brought it here,' she said, 'don't you remember? Ash carried it here when we came yesterday.'

'I don't like it,' said Till, trembling like a frightened child, 'I don't like the way it looks at me.'

Again we managed to calm him. We sang some merry songs and encouraged Misty to snuggle up to him. But that night he was worse. The nightmares returned and Elfin begged me to hide the flag, which I did, covering it with branches and ivy.

Another restless day, a worse night and, on the third morning, Elfin and I agreed we would have to risk the danger and take her father home to the forge or he would be seriously ill. The wood seemed quieter but we didn't know what enemies might be searching and hiding as we tried to make our way warily back towards Bodle Street. It was difficult. Till complained a good deal and had to be guided as he seemed determined to trip on every snag and to take every opportunity to lose his way. He was too noisy to be safe and it made us anxious.

Towards the end of the journey, however, as the surroundings grew more familiar, so he became calmer. We reached the top of Freckly Lane and it was as if nothing had changed. The forge was quiet, Wulf was still on his bench; it was as though we had never been away. There had been no sign of the Normans, he told us. He'd expected to see them on the road to London but William, he'd been told, had marched on to Dover and, he'd heard, the town had been taken. 'They didn't even put up a fight,' said Wulf contemptuously, 'opened the gates and let them in.'

But, he'd heard, there was to be a new king, Edgar, the young prince. 'I reckon he's no bigger and not much older than you Ash,' he said, 'and if he's half as brave and half the man you are then we'll be all right.'

Each day we waited for news. Each day we kept a watch on Bodle Street expecting the Normans and we were ready to run. But nothing happened.

The weeks passed. The air was full of rumour. We were sure, though, that this couldn't be the end. Occasionally some of our soldiers came by, mainly big, wild-eyed hard men who told us that a new English force was gathering. With a new king and able men in the land there would, they assured us, be another battle. But still we heard nothing then, as the year drew towards a close, came the news that London had fallen, that the young Edgar had capitulated and that the *Witan* had asked Duke William to be our new king.

He was, we were told, crowned in the new church in London on Christmas Day. There was no celebration for us. The winter had come in like a wild dog and these were lean times. Slowly we got back to work in the forge and I found myself taking on the jobs that Lang had once done. We were better off than most in the area. Since the battle there were few tools to hand. Every bit of weaponry and metalwork, we were told, had been scavenged from the battlefield. Iron was in short supply. We dug up what we had buried and we were soon busy making and mending which, in turn, earned us a little food and drink. It was meagre fare but far better than was had by most around us. There were constant stories of honest folk being forced from their homes, of hardship, famine, starvation even. Mainly we ate fish. Eels mostly. Even though we were hungry, Till, Elfin and I soon grew tired of the same diet. But not Wulf. He dined on dish after dish of boiled eels with relish.

'It is,' Wulf would mumble as he gummed his eel stew, 'the great blessing of being where we are if you take my meaning. The crops and hogs might fail but you've always got the lake and the eels.'

I thought often of the strange food, highly flavoured with spice, I'd eaten in the Norman camp and my stomach gurgled hungrily.

Till was calmer now with fewer nightmares but had become more and more withdrawn into himself. He wasn't alone in his grief. There were others, too, wanting news of sons, fathers, brothers who had not made the return from Hastings. Till, like them, had attempted the journey there time after time in the hope that Lang had been taken alive and was a prisoner in what were rumoured to be the dreadful dungeons of that great castle or, perhaps, he was merely injured and was lying up in a safe hut nearby. Each time, though, Till and the other seekers had encountered Norman soldiers guarding the approach to the coast and had been chased back. The English dead had been left to rot on the battlefield as a warning to us all and the word was that it was forbidden to visit the place. There was, though, a crumb of comfort. Many of the defeated soldiers, we were told, took ship after the battle. They were travelling to other lands where they could sell their services to other kings and armies and find adventure in hot climes. Day after day, Till stared out towards the coast and the sea, wondering and hoping.

The cold winter dragged, each day a hardship. The water in the wooden butts was thick with ice, the iron we worked with froze and stuck to the skin if touched. The daylight was thin and pinched, the nights long and unforgivingly black. Sometimes we heard strange shouts and cries from the woodland. It was the *green men*, we were told, the rebels who were hiding in the woodland, who would never bow to Norman masters and who were keeping the fight alive. Sometimes I thought Till had something to do with them.

Wulf, Elfin and I tried to keep well and cheerful and to draw Till back from the dark place in which he seemed to be living. One evening he handed me Lang's little flute. 'You might as well have this,' is all he said and I guessed he had given up hope for his son. I was afraid to play it but took the little bone instrument to the woods with me and practised. At first it made only a squeaky, wheezy noise which startled Misty. But I improved. Then, one morning, sitting outside the forge I tried a little tune. Wulf, wrapped in warm furs, looked up quizzically and irritably as if it pained his ears. I hesitated, wondering what Till might do. I played on and he made no objection. I played more each day and, each time, it seemed to brighten his mood. I never did, though, master the strange and mournful melody I had heard Lang play so often.

The coming of the Normans was a terrible thing. But fortune is fickle because now, in this time of trouble, her wheel turned and she chose to favour me.

On a spring morning a rider came, unexpectedly, clattering up to the forge. He was a Norman, dressed in leather and with a sword. He asked for water and some feed for his horse. He asked my name, he pointed at Wulf, 'and his' and I told him, and pointing at Till, 'his' and I told him and he rode away. A few days later a group of Norman riders arrived. 'Devils,' Wulf shouted a warning and Till spat angrily as he moved out of the light into the back of the forge. The group stopped on the other side of the yard as one man dismounted and walked towards us. I knew him immediately. Axeface! I reached for my seaxe and put my back to the wall of the hut. Wulf was on his feet, a threatening, defensive, shieldwall look on his face. But Axeface held up his hands in a pacifying gesture. He made his theatrical bow and smiled ingratiatingly at each of us. 'Master Ash,' he said, and to Wulf, 'you, my old friend, the soldier.'

He was smartly dressed and had a swagger about him but I knew, immediately, his power had gone. There was something uneasy about his manner and yet I no longer had any fear of him.

'We are your masters now,' he said as if beginning one of his showman's recitations. He paused as if expecting perhaps applause, perhaps an argument, then continued, 'I serve our new lord who has charge of these lands, the Duke of Eu.' He pronounced the name *Oh*, his mouth making a perfectly round shape which made us splutter and snigger. He pretended to ignore us. 'I,' he paused for dramatic effect, 'I am the servant of Osborn, his steward. I come to tell you that all is well. There has been enough fighting. There will be no more fighting. These lands are prosperous and we will prosper together.' He looked at us warily as though expecting a response but we simply stared at him in astonishment. 'The forge must continue its work,' he announced as though speaking to a huge audience and not three startled figures and a dog, 'to make good tools so that the forest can be maintained, the land ploughed, the crops harvested and the horses and oxen shod.' Again a pause to which, again, we responded with astonished silence.

He seemed to have finished his speech but continued to stand awkwardly. He seemed uncertain of himself. I thought I saw one of the soldiers in the group behind him smirking. Suddenly, woodenly, he knelt before me. I pressed myself hard against the wall in a defensive move.

'Master Ash,' he said, 'I have done you a wrong and it has troubled my mind. I gave you once, you will remember, a golden crown,' he laughed uneasily. 'It was a silly trick played to entertain fools and now I ask your forgiveness.' He took off his cap, put his hand in his pocket and, carefully, produced a large goose egg. He handed it to me. 'Now you, Master Ash,' may return the insult. 'I ask….beg…you to give me a golden crown.' He recited the words as if he'd learned them by heart.

I could see the soldiers laughing. Wulf's face was a picture. Even Till had emerged from the shadows to watch. I looked at the egg in my hand, I looked at the eggshell fragility of the balding, trembling skull bowed before me. 'This is Gam's doing,' I thought, 'Gam is behind this.' I threw the egg across the yard where it smashed untidily spilling its yellow yolk. Misty ran after it and gobbled it up shell and all, licking the ground all around hungrily. 'Is there nothing she won't eat?' I thought in disgust.

Axeface, visibly relieved, stood up. For a moment I was going to say nothing but my conscience pinched. I looked at him and confessed, 'It was me. The sword. I took the sword and it was me shouting to mislead you into the marsh when you were lost in the wood.'

For a moment his face clouded with anger and I saw the cruel Axeface I remembered from the show but then it lit up with a kind of relief. 'I knew it,' he exclaimed triumphantly, 'the little Sparrow who misled us. I always knew it was you.' He laughed and offered me his hand. 'Then we are quits,' he said.

I took his hand and, uneasily, returned his smile.

'And we are friends, perhaps, too,' he added before he quickly turned, mounted his horse and rode away.

When the group of Normans was out of sight, Wulf exploded. 'Well,' he roared, 'I've seen some things but nothing ever in my life like that.' He stared at me in bewilderment. 'Why didn't you do it, lad? Why didn't you hit him with the egg? A golden crown? It would have been a bloody crown if I'd had my axe!'

Ash paused and sat back on his seat. He looked at the little boy drawing in the dirt with his stick. 'All that was a long time ago,' he said. Then, as if answering a question,

And Gam? Yes, I saw her again. It was a year later in the spring. She arrived one day without warning. A group of Normans on their horses and, almost hidden amongst them, Gam. She had grown. You wouldn't mistake her for a boy anymore. She looked like a lady even though she was dressed in that fancy leather gear the Normans favour. But then she jumped down from her little horse just as she'd jumped down from the tree that day. She hugged me and she hugged Wulf. We looked for Till but he'd vanished as he usually did if he knew there were Normans about.

Gam told me she was on her way to Canterbury. She told me she was making a story of it all and that she was making pictures. The pictures would be put on to a linen cloth and would tell of the things that had happened. 'I'll put us in Ash,' she said, 'and Misty, and the pictures from the Old Place.' She said she'd like to go back to the hollow to see our pictures there but she was forbidden because of what the Normans called the *silvatici* in the wood: the *green men* who were still fighting, who ambushed the Normans making them wary of venturing far from the highway.

'If you want to go, Gam, we could,' I assured her, 'it's safer now. It wasn't for some time but then a law was made, the *murdrum*. If the *green men* do any wrong to the new masters the people in the local area must pay a fine. It's a forfeit. They pay in gold or they lose a life. It's a cruel law but these are cruel times. People are tired of difficulty and fighting. It's stopped the trouble.'

'Wait,' said Gam. She walked back to the group of riders she had arrived with and spoke to them for some time. For a while there was quite an argument but this was Gam and I knew she'd win. The group rode off. 'I've told them to come back for me tomorrow,' she said, laughing.

She left the little horse in the care of Wulf and the two of us set off again for the hollow, Misty running as well as she could behind us. We were nimble, fast and light-hearted. It was wonderful to be re-united. We shouted and sang as we walked. We did our bird calls, dodged behind trees to hide and jump out on each other. We came to the place where we'd found Wulf and talked about the old soldier who was like a grandfather to us both. At last we scrambled down the steep incline and crawled into the Old Place. We soon had a fire going and I laid out the food and drink we'd brought with us.

'Let me show you this.' I brought the huge Fighting Man standard from the corner where I'd hidden it. We unfurled it and looked at it in wonder. 'Is it Wulf do you think or just one of his stories?'

Gam shrugged. 'I don't know and it doesn't matter now. It's so beautiful but terrible.'

She was right. The standard was a wonderful thing, elaborately stitched. The eyes of the fighting man were precious jewels that flashed in the firelight. The axe he was holding was stitched with gold and silver thread. There was a decorative border around the flag, a coil of dragons breathing red and golden fire. That was the beauty. But the awfulness was that the cloth had been slashed and torn. It was stained with what we knew must be the blood of the dead king.

'This,' said Gam in a whisper, 'must be kept secret. This is something my people still fear. Your people would rally to this. There would be more fighting.'

I wasn't sure what to say. I found myself, like Gam, whispering in the presence of the flag. 'There's always talk of fighting back but I don't know how it would be done or where to begin. And your people, the soldiers, are everywhere.' Then, more decisively, I said, 'Anyway I don't want to fight you, Gam. There's been enough fighting. The flag should stay here.'

'In Normandy,' said Gam, 'they say the standard, this, *The Fighting Man*, was sent back to the Holy Father, the Pope as proof of William's victory.'

'But it's here,' I said.

'Yes, and it should stay here. Our secret.'

'I wonder what happened,' I said, 'after the battle. What happened to...to the King? There's so many rumours: that he was buried secretly near his palace or perhaps overlooking the sea. Some say he wasn't killed at all but is hiding and gathering fresh forces.'

'I can tell you what happened,' said Gam. 'I know you hate us...the Normans...but we do some things honourably. Harold and his brothers were sent off in the old Viking way. Their bodies were put on boats, three boats from our fleet with dragons on the prow. The boats were set alight and sent out to sea on the outgoing tide.'

'How do you know?'

'My father told me.'

'I'll tell Wulf,' I said. 'It will please him.'

I told her about Axeface and the egg. 'I think that was your doing, Gam,' I said.

She laughed, 'No,' she said, 'I heard about it though. It would have been my father. He is in Fecamp but he has a long arm.'

'Axeface says we're friends now,' I said sheepishly.

'It's shape-shifting, Ash,' she laughed, 'he's a different man since the battle.'

'I still wouldn't trust him.' I said.

269

For the rest of the day Gam drew. She had a sort of box and in it were what she told me were pieces of vellum, thin skin on which she made pictures and patterns. These, she said, were some of the pictures she would put in her story. She showed me her drawings of the birds, the beasts, the fantastical creatures and dragons, the strange fruit.

That night we lay together by the fire in the dark and talked just as we had before. I told her about being here with Till and Elfin and of the smith's terror in the night. We talked about the time we were in the Norman camp. She confessed she had been very afraid. 'I asked you to trust me, Ash, but I couldn't be sure that things would work out. My lord, the knight Mortain, might not have been there. It could all have gone wrong. I couldn't see very well through the bird mask and it was only when they offered me the coin in the show and I ran up to them that I was sure it was him.'

'You didn't tell me everything about yourself,' I scolded her. 'I guessed you weren't a servant but I didn't know you were a...a lady.'

'I was afraid you would have nothing to do with me if I told you,' she confessed.

'So, is he....is the man....that knight...is he....?'

'My husband? Not yet but it is intended he should be,' she said.

'But...but you're just a girl.'

'It's a betrothal,' she explained, 'an arrangement. It's more an alliance, something that happens between our families. He is the Lord Mortain and, because of who I am, it is expected that I will be married to him.'

'Expected....so you're not yet?'

270

'Married? No, and now I don't think I will be. He took a hurt in the battle, the wound is ugly and will not heal and they think he will die.'

My heart leapt but, 'I'm sorry,' I said.

'No you're not,' said Gam, 'and nor am I. I don't mean I want him to die,' she said hastily, 'but I don't want to marry. I told you, I won't ever be a lady. Can you imagine me as a lady?'

'No,' I shook my head and laughed. 'And that's why you ran away with the birdmen and pretended to be Guil…Gui…a boy.'

'It is hard to be a girl where I am in Fecamp,' she sulked. 'But then it's hard everywhere. I couldn't be a girl with the birdmen. The holy fathers who don't like the talk of shape-shifting also don't allow girls to be in those shows.'

I tried to listen to her as she talked on but everything she said seemed strange and far away. My thoughts were whirling just as my head had whirled when I first met her in the wood and she knocked me down. I was aware, too, of her close, warm presence next to me in the dark and her story was, to me, a labyrinth, a stitched together tapestry of dancing shapes and scenes. A young girl, an aristocratic family, Fecamp, the expectation of marriage, learning to be a lady. As she spoke the life she described seemed remote and yet familiar. Hiding alone: me in wood; she in stone. Scolded, sent away, long cold corridors like hollow lanes, secret staircases, holes in the walls opening to an unknown world outside, mysterious noises, doors slamming, shouts, footsteps, echoes, whispered conversations which stopped as she approached. She learned to sit quietly while the adults talked and learned

271

not to listen, to keep her head bowed, to sit neatly at a table without eating and not to stare. A father: 'Sometimes he was kind and then, I don't know why, he would be angry. His moods were as unpredictable as the weather and 1 had to be careful. Now he is old and quiet, disappointed and unhappy.' A mother: 'I was told different things but I think she came from Canterbury. I don't remember her but, if she is still alive, I want to find her.'

'What will you say to her?' I asked.

'I'll scold her for making me a girl,' laughed Gam. 'Though,' she then corrected herself, 'I like being a girl but I'd ask her why she didn't look after me herself and why I couldn't do the sort of things...well, the sort of things you could do.'

'Hogs? Looking after hogs?'

'There's worse things. I just mean being able to do what you want to do. The things I couldn't. The stuff we did in the wood: running, shouting, chasing, climbing, hunting.' She paused, 'I've always found it hard to do what I'm told I *have* to do. And there was a lot of that: *having* to do things this way and not that way; like *this*, not like *that*, all the time.' She chuckled, 'I had already upset my father. There was another man, before this one, before Mortain, they expected me to marry. He was very rich and very thin, very old and with blotchy damp skin. I only met him once. I was taken into a room and had to sit in a chair while he came to look at me and he was so nervous when he saw me that he farted.'

'Like Wulf,' I said.

'Not as loud as Wulf,' she laughed. 'No one farts like Wulf. This man farted sort of quietly and apologetically but everyone standing there pretended nothing had happened. Except me. I got the giggles and my father was angry and I was sent out of the chamber in disgrace.'

'And I suppose he wouldn't marry you because of that, because you laughed at him?'

'No,' she said indignantly, 'I refused to have him. There was a lot of fuss and it upset my father but he knew I wouldn't give in and the man went away. Good riddance to him. He left me a present: the little horse which I love and which I've kept. I'd rather have a horse than a husband. When Mortain dies I shan't have to marry anyone. Anyway, they say there is a shortage of men in France since the battle. My father gets cross. He says he doesn't know what to do with me. If I were a boy I could do the things I want. I want to be free like the eagle should have been free. I want to make paintings and tell stories. *Odo,* the Duke, I mean the King's half brother, is an important man now, the Bishop of Bayeux and he wants the story of the great conquest. He's an odious man but he has money and influence so it will be done and I have the chance to be part of it.'

'And that will take you to Canterbury.'

'Yes, and I might find my mother. It's one of the reasons why I went with the birdmen. I watched them when they came to Fecamp. They came to the castle grounds and I spied from a window. I heard them say they were travelling to England, that they would go to Winchester and Canterbury. When it grew dark I dressed as a boy and followed them. Scur…Axeface, was suspicious, I think, and didn't want me but then he found I could write and draw. And he could see I liked the birds. Always, I used to watch the birds and I liked the eagle. He could see that I could work with the eagle.' She

273

laughed again. 'The story he told in Rye, Ari and the eagle, that was my story. I used to hear it over and over again when I was growing up. From one of the servants. And I told it to Axeface.'

'Will you tell all this to your mother, if you find her?'

'Yes,' she said. 'I sort of do now, anyway. In my head. Do you, with your mother? Even though…even though she's not here?'

'Yes,' I said.

'Do you remember her at all?'

'I think so,' I said. 'I think I remember her voice.'

'What would you say to her if you saw her?'

'I think I will see her,' I said. 'I expect to see her when I'm dead. I'll say I'm sorry.'

'Sorry?' Gam seemed shocked. 'Why? You've got nothing to be sorry about, Ash.'

But I had and it poured out of me. I told her what was on my mind: how guilty I felt about Dad, not saying goodbye properly, about the sword and Lang. 'If I hadn't taken the sword and if Lang hadn't taken it into battle he'd still be alive. Now I've got a place at the forge. Till treats me like his son. But if Lang were still alive I wouldn't have a place there and I'd be a hogboy or worse.'

'It's the *wyrd,* our fate,' said Gam. 'You didn't do anything wrong. You just followed your path. I think it's all written like the pictures – the animals on the wall here. The story is already there, what will happen and what we'll do, then someone – something - just holds up a light and we move and dance. But the pattern is already there.'

'If it's already there we wouldn't need to do anything,' I argued. 'What would be the point of trying....trying to be free like me getting away from the hogs and you with the marriage and the birdmen?'

'I think the trying is written into the pattern, too,' she said. 'If it's in the pattern, in our nature to try, like with you and me, then we have no choice but to do it. When we were facing Axeface and you and Wulf said you'd stay with me it was the *wyrd*, your destiny but it was also in your nature to make yourself do it. '

'So what's ahead?'

'How do we know?' she gestured at the pictures, 'just as they don't know. For you, I guess, you'll be *handfasted* with Elfin one day. There will be strong children who will work the forge.'

I felt myself blush, my face hot in the dark, 'And what about you?'

'I don't know. It's hard to see. My father says there is no place in the family for a spinster, an unmarried woman who sits and spins the wool, which is why, if I don't marry Mortain, he will send me to live with the holy women. They live in a retreat, a castle which they fortify to keep the world away. But that's not for me. I will, though, work with them to make the pictures and to tell the story of it all.'

'Us?' I said cautiously. 'What about us, Gam?'

She reached across and took my hand in the dark. 'I know you think about it. Us. I do, too. But it couldn't be. Not in these times. The differences, my betrothal, the – what you call stations. Your people wouldn't allow it; nor would mine. I heard terrible stories of the battle. People won't forgive easily.'

'It's the same here,' I said, 'and it goes on. Your people have stolen our land. How can they do that? What right do they have? They do terrible things. We hear stories of people being killed or their crops and animals taken, their huts burned which is the same. They starve and die. Not soldiers. These aren't people who were in the fight, they are simple villagers. These things are wrong and there is hatred. It can't be forgiven and I can't see it ending.'

Gam said nothing for a while. Then, 'They are my people and I have heard some of this. I don't understand it or why there is still so much anger and hatred. It is, I think, greed and power. They are my people, Ash, but it's not me. Not me.'

'I know. But why is it like this? Why is it a puzzle and will it always be the same?' I listened to the fire crackling. 'I wish we could stay here,' I said. 'We could be like the *green men*.'

'We could,' she replied. 'But they would find us and you can imagine how we would be punished. We can't, you know that. I have to go back to Fecamp, for Mortain and my father who grows old and who I must help. I'm sorry.'

She was quiet for a long time and I think she was crying.

Later she said, 'Here. Take this.' She put something in my hand. It was a ring. 'I've thought about this,' she said. 'I shall always want to see you and I shall try to come again. But in case I don't you must come and see me in Fecamp. There is a castle there. Show the ring at the gate and they will let you in.'

We slept little that night. We talked about our adventures, our fears and plans. I told her my worries about Till and how he seemed withdrawn from the world and about Lang and Dad who, I thought, must be dead.

'Perhaps they will come back,' she said, 'strong and weather beaten from the sun and wind of their travels and with treasure and stories of their adventures.'

'And with falcons on their arms,' I added.

The next day we washed in the stream and made a breakfast. Then we walked slowly and reluctantly back through the wood towards Freckly Lane. We passed the place where we had first met in the wood. I told her about the eagle and I showed her where it was buried. I told her about the hat I had made from the feathers. 'Like Axeface's…Crow's…story in Rye,' she laughed.

Back at the forge Gam chatted happily to Wulf and Elfin and she managed to encourage Till to speak and smile. She showed him the pictures she had been making and he showed her the tool he had fashioned with her design – the eagle – which we stamped on everything we made in the forge. It was our mark. He had also made her some metal charms and had fixed them on the reins of her little horse. Misty ran around in excited circles and chased the hens to show off. It was as though there had been no battle, no conflict, as though there was no difference in rank or station. Then the group of riders appeared and Gam mounted her little horse and rode away with them.

21. FECAMP

Ash paused. 'And that was the last I saw of Gam,' he said.

Time passed and Till and I worked together like father and son. I found myself picking up the jobs Lang had done. But I was uneasy. Since the Normans became the new masters things had been hard for us all but we were better off than most. Osborn, the steward, and Axeface, his servant, bothered a lot of the people in the area. They demanded *geld*, heavy payment for the land that wasn't theirs in the first place. And they stopped us using the woods. The woods had belonged to us all, for timber, for hunting, for the hogs to graze since time began. Then, with the Normans, it all stopped. The woods, we were told, belonged to King William. Yet, at the forge, we seemed to be pretty much free of it all. Osborn and Axeface kept away. Nobody came to force payments out of us. It was, I knew, Gam's doing. And there was some dark talk that we were favoured by the Normans, some whispering about Wulf and me in the Norman camp before the battle, some rumours about Gam. I knew, too, that there are eyes and ears in the trees and in the corners of huts and I suspected someone had seen and heard when Axeface had visited and called me *friend*. No-one dared say it to our face, of course and, perhaps, I was imagining it a bit. But it bothered me. I talked to old Wulf. I reminded him that, when we first met he'd told me that the ash tree bends in the wind and I'd been thinking I'd bent with the wrong wind, the one that blew from Normandy, and I should have stood up against it. He said that was nonsense, that I was a good boy and a brave one. But he was always telling me of his adventures, his stories gave me an appetite and I decided to try some travel myself. I said goodbye to Till and Elfin and promised to come back.

I had a little money saved and set off for France to find Gam. It would, I knew, be a difficult journey. The Normans were everywhere and travellers were treated with suspicion. But I had seen more and more traders from foreign parts coming and going on Bodle Street and knew that it was possible. I prepared carefully making sure to dress in clean clothes and having my long hair cut and my moustache trimmed. I also took a piece of fancy metalwork in my bag. It was a present I had made for Gam and, if stopped, I could explain I was delivering it to the Lady in Fecamp.

Crossing the sea was worse than Till had told me. I was horribly sick and then, as we approached the French coast a storm – a squall the sailors call it – blew up and turned us over. I was washed up on the beach and when I came back to life everything had been taken. I was left with just my clothes. The ring Gam gave me had gone and my finger had gone with it – I suppose that was the only way they could take it off. The piece of fancy metalwork from my bag and the silver vervel which had been on a leather lace round my neck - gone too. I suppose I was lucky they didn't cut my throat. I was told the sea had washed everything away but I don't believe that. I think the Norman sailors took everything. It was my own stupidity. They had asked me about my trade and I'd been boastful and shown them the fancy metalwork. They lusted for it and knew they could take it because I was English and they wouldn't be punished. I was just pleased to be alive even though I was stuck on

279

the French shore without money, possessions, friends or language. I'd even lost Lang's flute. I had to remind myself I was Ash and ash is strong. I had a hard time at first. I'd lost blood and I was weak. I went inland a bit and wound up at a blacksmith's forge. He saw what I could do even with a bad hand and without his language. He took me on but he squeezed every bit of labour out of me. I was working mainly for my keep. Mark you, they're skilful craftsmen over there and I learned a thing or two that's come in handy. After a year I had earned enough and I pushed on to Fecamp. All the time with the blacksmith I'd done my best to learn that strange language and, with his help, I prepared a little speech in French for when I reached Gam's home. 'Good-day my good man. My name is Master Ash and I have travelled from England to see the good lady Guianette. She gave me a ring to show you but I lost it in the sea. Please tell her I am here.'

I said this speech over and over. I spoke it aloud as I walked along. I shouted it at the trees and the birds and the clouds, I whispered it as I fell asleep in a tree hollow or under a hedge.

When I arrived in Fecamp I easily found the castle. You couldn't miss it: a huge, grey damp building made of stone towering over the miserable wood and thatched huts that made up this busy town. I was excited at the thought of seeing Gam again. I found somewhere to stay and tried to tidy myself up a little. A woman cut my hair and shaved my chin and I managed to barter for some fresh clothes but the next morning, as I set out for the castle, it began to rain and I was soon wet through and must have looked a mess. There was a long, straight and trim track leading to the castle. People were working on either side tending the land and they stopped their work to look at me strangely and coldly as I went by. As I walked I kept repeating the speech I'd prepared but, as I approached the gate, I found myself growing increasingly anxious and nervous. Two men were lounging by the gate sheltering from the rain under a dripping canopy. They didn't have uniforms or weapons; I wasn't sure if they were guards or just local people. They stood one on either side of the open gate which led into a courtyard. They were talking to each other and seemed to take no notice of me so I kept walking as if to go straight past them but, as I neared the threshold, one stuck out his muddy leg and fired a question which I didn't understand. He repeated it, loudly and in an insulting tone and his companion laughed open-mouthed and rudely. I took a breath and prepared to deliver my speech but my tongue had turned to wood and all that came out was, 'Gam, Gam.' The men guffawed and one asked the question again, speaking loudly and quickly, deliberately I think knowing that I didn't understand. I tried to speak again but, as I opened my mouth to speak, the other man let out a bleating parody of 'Gaaaam, Gaaaaam,' laughing and making his voice quaver to sound like a goat. Then they both shouted something at me and I turned away and walked quickly back down the track with the bleating 'Gaaaam, Gaaaam,' being called out derisorily behind me.

I went back the next day but the same two men were there and began their shouts even before I got close and I lost my nerve, turned and walked away. Later that day I approached the castle through the woodland on the far side. There in a meadow a boy was flying a falcon. I stood under the cover of the trees watching him. The bird flew back and forth and chased the *creance* the boy was swinging above his head. He looked about the same size and age as Gam but it wasn't her. There was a little horse nearby which might have been the one she rode to the forge and of which she was so fond. I left the woodside and began to walk across the meadow towards the boy but, from nowhere, a rider appeared and began galloping towards me waving his arms. I retreated into the wood.

The woman in whose hut I was lodging was kind to me, spoke some English, and understood much of what I said. I told her about Gam, the lost ring and *vervel* and, a little reluctantly, she agreed to help me. So, the following day she accompanied me up the long track to the castle. She was a good woman but as we got closer to the two lounging guards I noticed she was becoming more nervous. The men were more polite to her and listened while she told them about me. One of the men just shrugged, however, and answered in an off-hand way.

'He says the family are not here. They are away,' she said.

'Ask him when they'll be back.'

The man just shrugged. 'He doesn't know,' said the woman.

'Can he tell me where they've gone?'

The man replied irritably and the woman explained, 'He says it's not your business to know about this family and his neither. He says his job is to look after the door and to keep out the riff raff and not to know where the lord and his family have gone or when they'll be back.'

'Could he take a message for me?'

This time the man answered angrily, waving his hands and the other man joined in, repeating much that had been said.

'What did he say?' I asked.

'It doesn't matter.'

'No, please tell me.'

'He was just being rude.'

'But what did he say? I must know.'

The woman sighed and spoke to me gently. 'He asked if you were from England. He said his brother was in the fight there and did not return. He says the English are murderers. They are devils and not welcome here. I am sorry,' she added.

'Tell him' I said, 'tell him that's what we say in England about the Normans. Tell him I lost a friend and I lost a father in that battle.'

She spoke to the men again but they just shrugged.

'It is war,' said the woman, 'it is all men and all wrong.'

We walked back down the track with the men shouting insults at our backs.

The next day I went down to the harbour. I had to wait for three days but then, using the last of my money, I found a ship to bring me back to England. They put me down on the Isle of Wight. The people there still talked of the time when Tostig had arrived with his ships and had then been chased away by the King. They talked about it as though they had won a great victory and they seemed, I thought, to be living in the past. I walked across the island and then managed to get a free ride on a ship for the short trip to Bosham. The place was full of Normans who rode and walked around arrogantly making it clear that they were the masters now. A man told me the town was always full of soldiers because it had once been the old king's stronghold. There was a rumour that the dead king had been secretly buried in the church there and they feared an uprising.

Then I walked home. It was hard going and I had to beg for food and drink. But I was pleased to be back on the ground I knew and, at night, I slept deeply and easily in the woods.

Elfin was happy to see me. Till was worse, the shell of the man he once was and the forge was in a muddle. But Wulf, bent and whiskery, was still on his bench. He looked at me hard and said, 'You've got the grieving sickness, Ash. The love sickness. There's only one cure for that and it's work. There's work to be done here.'

The years went by. One day I was at the forge and a man rode up on a horse. A Norman. Well dressed. I liked his face: something familiar about the look of him and I wondered if he was the boy, now grown, who I'd seen flying the hawk in Fecamp. He didn't say anything just put his hand out and gave me this and rode away.

Ash tapped the leather lace round his neck.

It was the other silver vervel from the eagle to replace the one I'd lost. I guessed it meant that Gam had flown.

Wulf flew not long after that but he left me an understanding of what it is to be a fighting man. You don't have to be in a pitched battle; you just have to find the courage to face your fears. Wulf had told us he wanted to be sent off in the Viking way like his King, Harold. It wasn't easy and I had a disagreement with Till who said it would be too much work. But I'd grown since I'd been away, I was more the master now and I told him it must be done. Elfin looked for a cloth with a motif but

I had a better idea and I went back to the hollow for the last time and carried and dragged the King's standard back up to the forge. Again, Till was difficult. Like a lot of the smiths he had a lust for metal and things that shine and he said we should take the precious stones and wire that were sown into the flag as they could make us rich but I refused arguing they would bring only misery and misfortune. We wrapped Wulf in *The Fighting Man*, put him in the little cart, the one from the show, and took him slowly down to the lake. It was hard going because the tracks are poor and the cart was heavy with old Wulf, some long planks of wood and metalwork that we'd shaped to represent a helmet, shield and axe. Till and I worked all day to make a raft with the wood. We tried to make it look as much like a boat as possible and Elfin helped us with the sail and cut and wove some willow wands to make them look like a dragon on the prow. And that's where we laid Wulf. We heaped the raft with dry shavings and scrub, waited until it was dark, set it alight and sent it out on the lake. We sat and watched it burn late into the night until, suddenly, the fire was gone. We slept on the shore and, in the morning, found ourselves in that thick *moorgrim* mist. It was cold and we lit a fire and told stories and sung merry songs to keep cheerful until, slowly, the sun burned the mist away. The lake was calm and there was nothing left of Wulf's ship, just the flat surface of the lake. He kept us waiting a long time but, at last, a white bird with a long neck rose from the water. It didn't take to the air easily but paddled along on its webbed feet, flexing its wings making them beat noisily before it flew, low at first then higher until it was gone. Together we said a prayer for the good old man and Till, who had found him so much trouble at times, prayed the hardest.

Till soon flew too but he left me the forge and he left me Elfin and, like Gam had said, we had strong children – that's them hammering away there - and, when I fly, they'll have this place.

Misty flew too but she left me puppies.

He laughed at a mischievous dog chasing the hens.

Our shapes shift but it goes on.

The Old Place? It must still be there. I haven't been back. I don't know why. I often think of it: the fire, the birds and animals and flowers on the wall, Gam's pictures, my pictures, our names written as words. They must still be there. But I guess it's all overgrown now. I don't think I'd be able to find it again. I don't think I'd know how. Perhaps someone else will. Children.

Ash looked down at the shape the boy was making with the stick. An eagle. He looked at it and chuckled. The word Ari flew suddenly into his head. The Fighting Man. It goes on. He sighed and leaned back on his bench.

The Normans. Oh, they were bad and bad for many people. But then they weren't all bad and there were bad times for many of us before they came. I don't know.

There was a noise in the tree and the boy with the stick turned to look. Two birds, ring doves, squabbling and beating their wings. One flew off and the other followed. The boy turned back. Ash was still.

Glossary and Notes

These short notes and glossary offer just a brief explanation of and commentary on some of the historical terms and features of the period covered in the novel. I hope they provide clarity, stimulate interest and encourage wider reading and investigation.

Athelstan
King Athelstan reigned from 927 to 939.

Battleaxe
This fearful weapon would have been used by the *housecarls*. The two handed axe would be used to shatter shields and even bring down horses. An axe head, the only authenticated relic from the battlefield, can be seen in the Battle Museum of Local History.

Bayeux Tapestry
The tapestry, which was completed about 20 years after the Battle of Hastings, tells the story of the Norman Conquest from about 1064 until the death of Harold and the end of the battle. The detailed depiction of events in the main body of the tapestry is remarkable. However, I have always been fascinated by the scenes and fantastical figures in the upper and lower margins and I like to think that Gam contributed to these, taking ideas from the paintings on the wall in the Roman bath house.

Berserk
Till is concerned that Wulf might be a berserk. He probably has in mind the feared Viking warriors also known as berserkers, baresarks (because, believing

themselves invincible, they didn't wear armour) or bearsarks (because they wore animal skins). These were ferocious fighters who were reputed to fight on even when injured possibly fuelled by a magical potion drunk before the battle.

Bird Migration
Talking to the eagle, Ash explains that birds which appear only in the summer like the swallow and swift dive to the bottom of lakes where they live during the winter. This was a popular belief before bird migration was studied and understood.

Churl
A common freeman. A peasant.

Creance
The long, light cord the falconer uses when training a bird and to prevent it from flying away.

Den-hole
These, more commonly known as Dene-holes or Dane-holes (den is the Anglo-Saxon word for hole or valley), are found mainly in the South of England. There is some disagreement about their purpose. Possibly they are ancient chalk or flint mines. There is, however, a popular belief that they were used as hiding places at the time of the Viking raids.

Edgar the Aetheling (prince)
Edgar should, many believe, have succeeded to the throne after Edward's death in 1066 as he was the closest blood relative. However, aged 14, he was considered too

young to defend the kingdom and Harold Godwinson was chosen as King by the Witan instead. After Harold's death at the Battle of Hastings the Witan chose Edgar to be the new king but he surrendered to William in December 1066 before he could be crowned.

The Fighting Man
This was Harold Godwinson's personal standard. There are no pictures of the standard and it doesn't appear in the Bayeux Tapestry. The general belief is that the banner was richly embroidered with gold and silver thread and jewels to depict a warrior with an axe. What is interesting is that, reputedly, after the battle it was sent by William to the Pope by way of thanks for his support and evidence of his victory. Perhaps, even now, it is concealed somewhere in the vaults of the Vatican. It would be wonderful to see it again. At the time the standard would have been a powerful symbol of and focus for rebellion against the rule of the Normans.

Freeman
The term is self-explanatory: someone – a churl, thane, earl – who was not a slave.

Fyrd
The fyrd was the part-time army made up of peasants and professional soldiers upon whom the king and his earls could call to defend the land in times of need.

Geld
This was the tax that had to be paid to the Normans for each hide of land owned.

Gleeman

A travelling poet and minstrel who would recite and sing stories, usually in verse form, often accompanied by a stringed instrument, the lyre.

Green Men

It is believed that, after the battle, many of the defeated English soldiers became resistance fighters, living and hiding in the woods (the Normans called them silvatici) and ambushing and disrupting the invaders. Their activities give rise to legends and are probably the basis for the story of Robin Hood. The green man is a pagan symbol often found in stone and wood carvings in churches and is also a pub sign.

Grendel

The monster from the famous epic poem Beowulf. It is likely that the story of Beowulf would be familiar to the Anglo-Saxons. Children like Ash would have heard recitations or versions of the tale, probably from a *gleeman* and while sitting by the fireside. Grendel emerges from the lake to feast on human flesh but is defeated by the heroic Beowulf.

Halley's Comet

The comet features in the Bayeux Tapestry. The comet appeared in April 1066, was visible for about 10 days and was considered an omen of change.

Handfast

Handfasting is an ancient form of marriage established long before the Anglo-Saxons and pre-dating Christian marriage. During the ceremony the hands of the bride and groom are tied together with cloth or cord. Even today we still refer to marriage as 'tying the knot'. When we shake hands to make a contract or agreement we are practising a form of handfasting.

Hares
Ash hunts hares. At the time there were no rabbits in the country. These were introduced by the Normans.

Harold
Harold Godwinson was the Earl of Wessex (which covered most of southern England) and was crowned as Harold II on 6th January 1066 following the death of King Edward (the Confessor) on the previous day.

Hazard
A gambling game with dice.

Hide
A measure of land sufficient to support a family.

Hoar Apple Tree
This was the assembly point for King Harold's army on the eve of the battle on 13th October 1066. The old hoar (meaning white) tree was an established meeting point strategically placed where the road from the coast at Hastings met the road to London following the ridgeway. The site of this meeting place is still there on Caldbec Hill in Battle and offers a good and atmospheric view of the surrounding countryside.

Housecarls
The housecarls, or huscarls, were the household men, strong fighters and bodyguards to the king and his earls. Wulf would have been one of these fighting men.

Jesses
Strips of leather attached to the hawk's legs.

Mews
The birdhouse where the hawks are kept.

Moorgrim
Particularly during the autumn mornings and evenings the valleys near the south coast are filled with mist. Finding his way home Ash thinks about the moorgrim, the mysterious mist associated with stories he would have heard of such lake-dwelling monsters as Grendel who is defeated by Beowulf in the ancient epic story.

Murdrum
There was no peace after the Battle of Hastings. William's army still met resistance and the Witan had declared Edgar as the new king. William laid waste to the land in the south until the Witan capitulated and his coronation in London. He continued to fight, persecute and massacre cruelly, particularly in the north until he had established Norman rule. Throughout this time, however, he faced continuing resistance from local people and soldiers hiding in the woods whom the Normans called *silvatici*. To counteract this the Normans introduced the law of *murdrum* which levied a huge fine on the community if a Norman were to be killed and the murderer not brought to justice.

Odo

Odo, Duke William's half-brother, was appointed as Bishop of Bayeux and, after the battle, as Earl of Kent. It is believed that he is responsible for commissioning the Bayeux Tapestry. As a man of the church he was forbidden to use a sword in battle but is depicted in the tapestry wielding a fearsome club.

Queen Edith

Queen Edith, whom Ash sees on the eve of the battle was King Harold's wife. But which one? It's confusing as Harold had two wives. Edith the Fair (or Edith Swan-neck) is the one I think Ash saw and she was Harold's hand-fasted bride. They had been together for many years and had five or six children. However, soon after taking the throne in January 1066 Harold had an 'official' marriage to another Edith: Edith of Mercia. He probably did this for political reasons and to ensure stability in his kingdom.

Roman Bath House

This is a fanciful part of the story. I wanted somewhere for the children to hide and I liked the idea of a sense of earlier history. I've based the idea on the ruins of the Roman bath house at Beauport near Hastings where the Roman officers would rest and refresh themselves. Archaeologists have suggested that, after the Romans left Britain and the bath house was abandoned it was occupied for a period by 'squatters' – and I thought of the children finding a refuge there. I liked, too, the idea that Gam might copy some of the pictures with which the Romans decorated their walls and incorporate them within the marginal designs of the Bayeux Tapestry.

Seaxe
A long all-purpose knife which, as the *scramasax* gave the Saxons their name.

Shaman
Axeface is a showman but he might also have been a *shaman*, practising magic and foretelling the future. My guess is that in remote regions of the country the ordinary people would still cling to pagan beliefs.

Strigil
This was a hooked metal scraper which Romans used for bathing. They would coat their skin in olive oil then scrape off the dirt with the strigil. I think I'd prefer a flannel.

Thane
A freeman close to the nobility and with military obligations to the king. A thane would be expected to own at least 5 hides of land.

Tostig and Hardrada
Tostig was Harold's brother and, following King Edward's death, he conspired with Duke William in Normandy to overthrow Harold. He attempted to invade England in May 1066 when his fleet landed on the Isle of Wight. However, he swiftly retreated and sailed to Norway where he persuaded the fierce King Harald Hardrada to join him in an invasion. They attacked in the North of England and were victorious in taking the City of York at the hard fought Battle of Fulford. Tostig and Hardrada were celebrating their victory and were taken by surprise by Harold's rapid march from the South of

England. Both Tostig and Hardrada were killed when Harold fought them at the Battle of Stamford Bridge on 25th September.

Vervels
The rings (sometimes made of silver) attached to the hawk's legs and inscribed with the owner's name, mark or coat of arms.

Wergild
Literally the 'man-price' – what a person was worth and the amount of money that would need to be paid in compensation for death or injury.

William
William the Conqueror was the son of the unmarried Robert, Duke of Normandy. He claimed that King Edward, to whom he was only distantly related, had promised the throne of England to him and that Harold had sworn his agreement to this. Harold's oath to William is a key feature of the Bayeux Tapestry. It was believed by the Normans that, in taking the throne, Harold had broken his oath and had committed perjury. This could explain the depiction of his death from an arrow in the eye as blinding was the cruel punishment for perjury at the time.

Witan
The council of nobles (the wise men) who elected and advised the king; a forerunner of our modern day parliament.

Wyrd
Fate, fortune and destiny.

Wyvern
The wyvern flag was the symbol both for England and Wessex. The wyvern has a dragon's head but only two legs and a coiled, serpent-like body with a tail ending in a sharp point or, possibly, a second, fire-spitting mouth. In the Bayeux Tapestry the wyvern looks more like a 3D wind-sock than a conventional flag. Harold probably had two wyvern standards: one gold (possibly white) for England and one red for Wales.